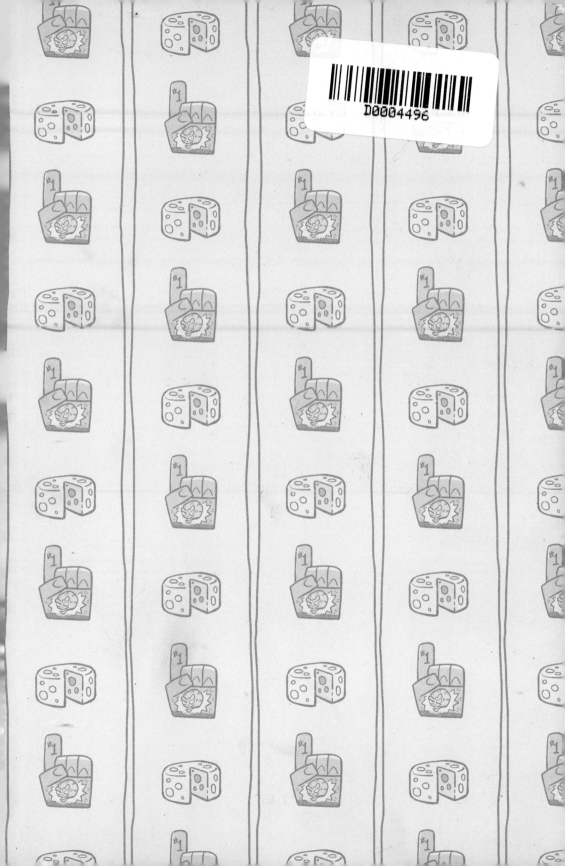

PLANTS VS. ZOMBIES

DREAM A LITTLE SCHEME

Written by PAUL TOBIN
Art by CHRISTIANNE GILLENARDO-GOUDREAU
Colors by HEATHER BRECKEL
Letters by STEVE DUTRO
Cover by CHRISTIANNE GILLENARDO-GOUDREAU

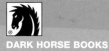

DARK HORSE BOOKS

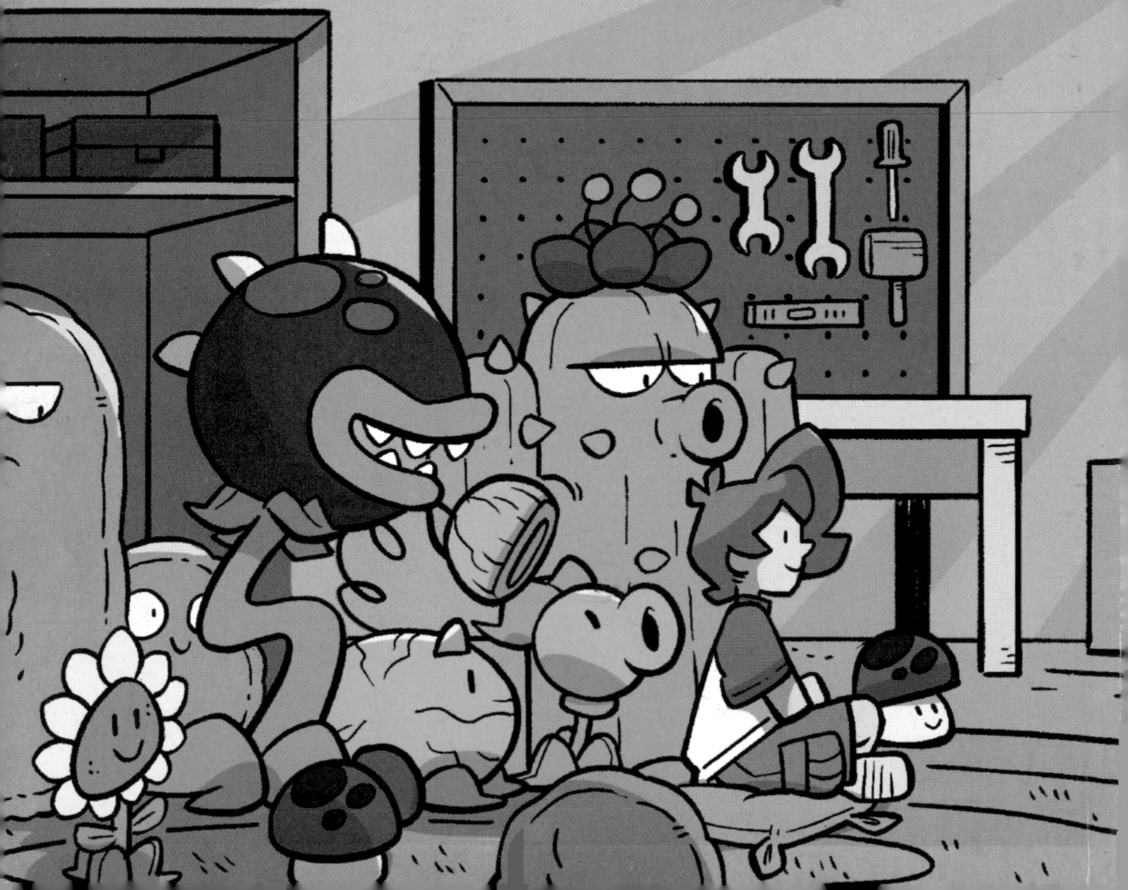

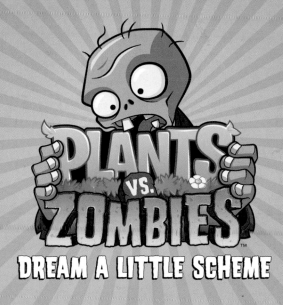

PLANTS VS. ZOMBIES™

DREAM A LITTLE SCHEME

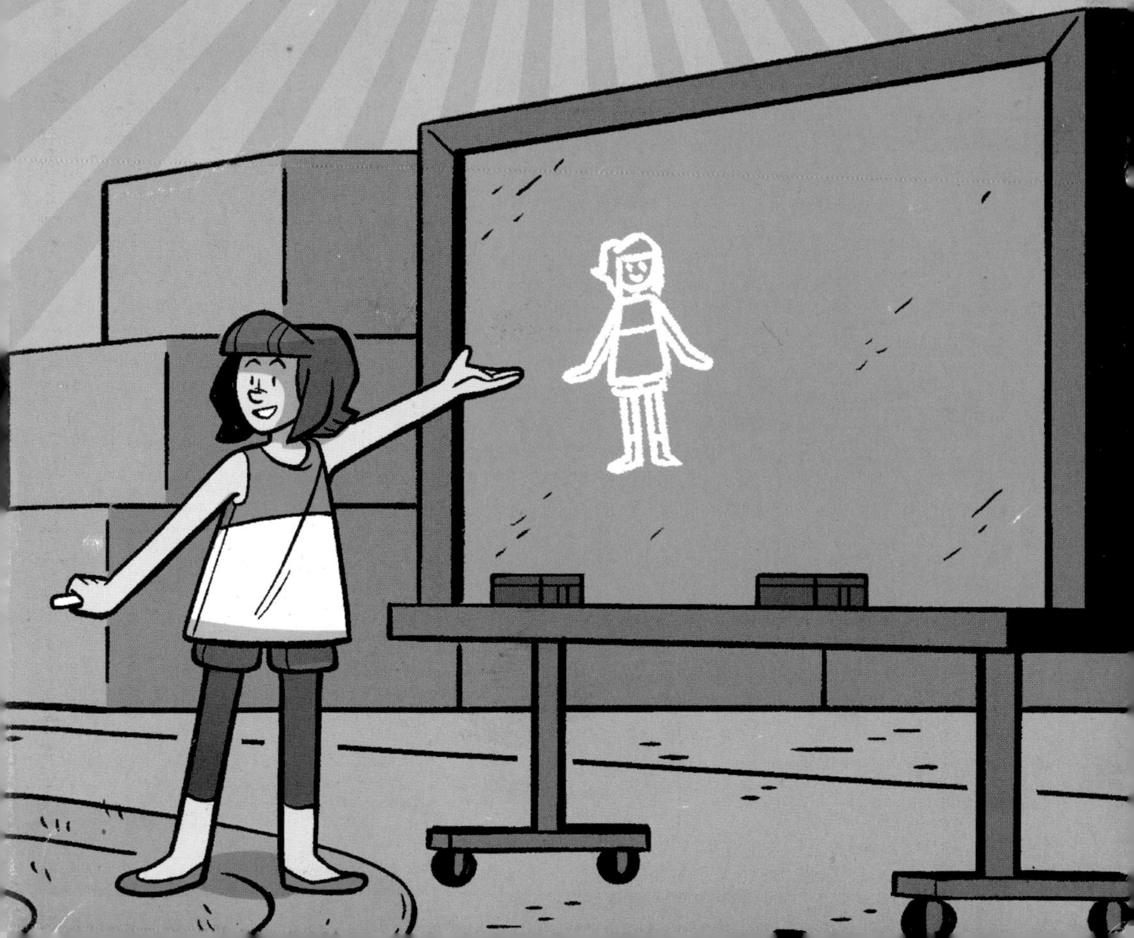

President and Publisher **MIKE RICHARDSON**
Senior Editor **PHILIP R. SIMON**
Associate Editor **JUDY KHUU**
Assistant Editor **ROSE WEITZ**
Designer **BRENNAN THOME**
Digital Art Technician **ALLYSON HALLER**

Special thanks to Kristen Star, Joshua Franks, Nina Dobner, and everyone at PopCap Games and EA Games.

First Edition: November 2021
Ebook ISBN 978-1-50672-095-1
Hardcover ISBN 978-1-50672-092-0

10 9 8 7 6 5 4 3 2 1
Printed in China

DarkHorse.com
PopCap.com

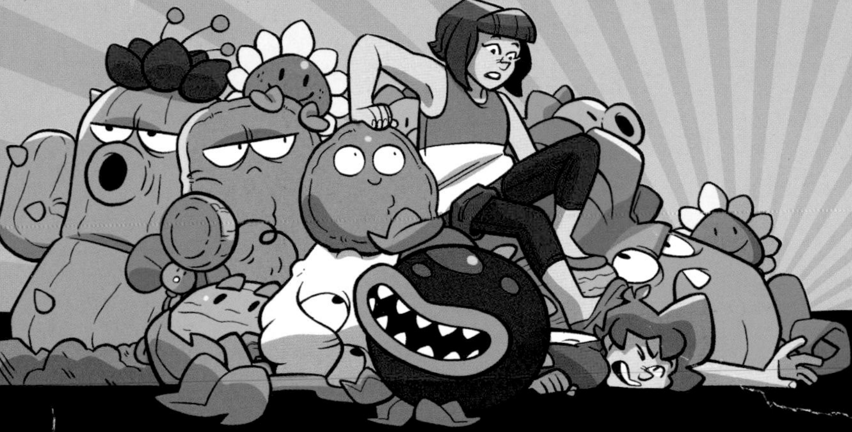

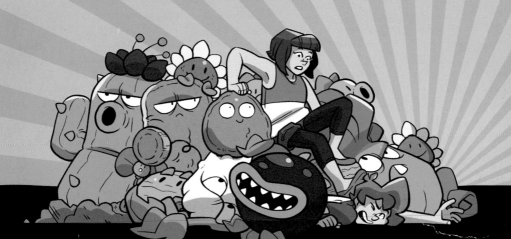

No plants were harmed in the making of this graphic novel. However, many zombies kept having weird dreams after this adventure.

PLANTS vs. ZOMBIES: DREAM A LITTLE SCHEME | Published by Dark Horse Books, a division of Dark Horse Comics LLC. 10956 SE Main Street, Milwaukie, OR 97222 | To find a comics shop in your area, visit comicshoplocator.com |

Library of Congress Cataloging-in-Publication Data

Names: Tobin, Paul, 1965- writer. | Gillenardo-Goudreau, Christianne, artist. | Breckel, Heather, colourist. | Dutro, Steve, letterer.
Title: Dream a little scheme / writer, Paul Tobin ; artist, Christianne Gillenardo-Goudreau ; colors, Heather Breckel ; letters, Steve Dutro.
Description: First. | Milwaukie, OR : Dark Horse Books, [2021] | Series: Plants vs. zombies ; volume 19
Identifiers: LCCN 2021018452 (print) | LCCN 2021018453 (ebook) | ISBN 9781506720920 (hardcover) | ISBN 9781506720951 (ebook)
Subjects: LCSH: Graphic novels. | CYAC: Graphic novels. | Zombies--Fiction. | Plants--Fiction.
Classification: LCC PZ7.7.T62 Dr 2021 (print) | LCC PZ7.7.T62 (ebook) | DDC 741.5/973--dc23
LC record available at https://lccn.loc.gov/2021018452
LC ebook record available at https://lccn.loc.gov/2021018453

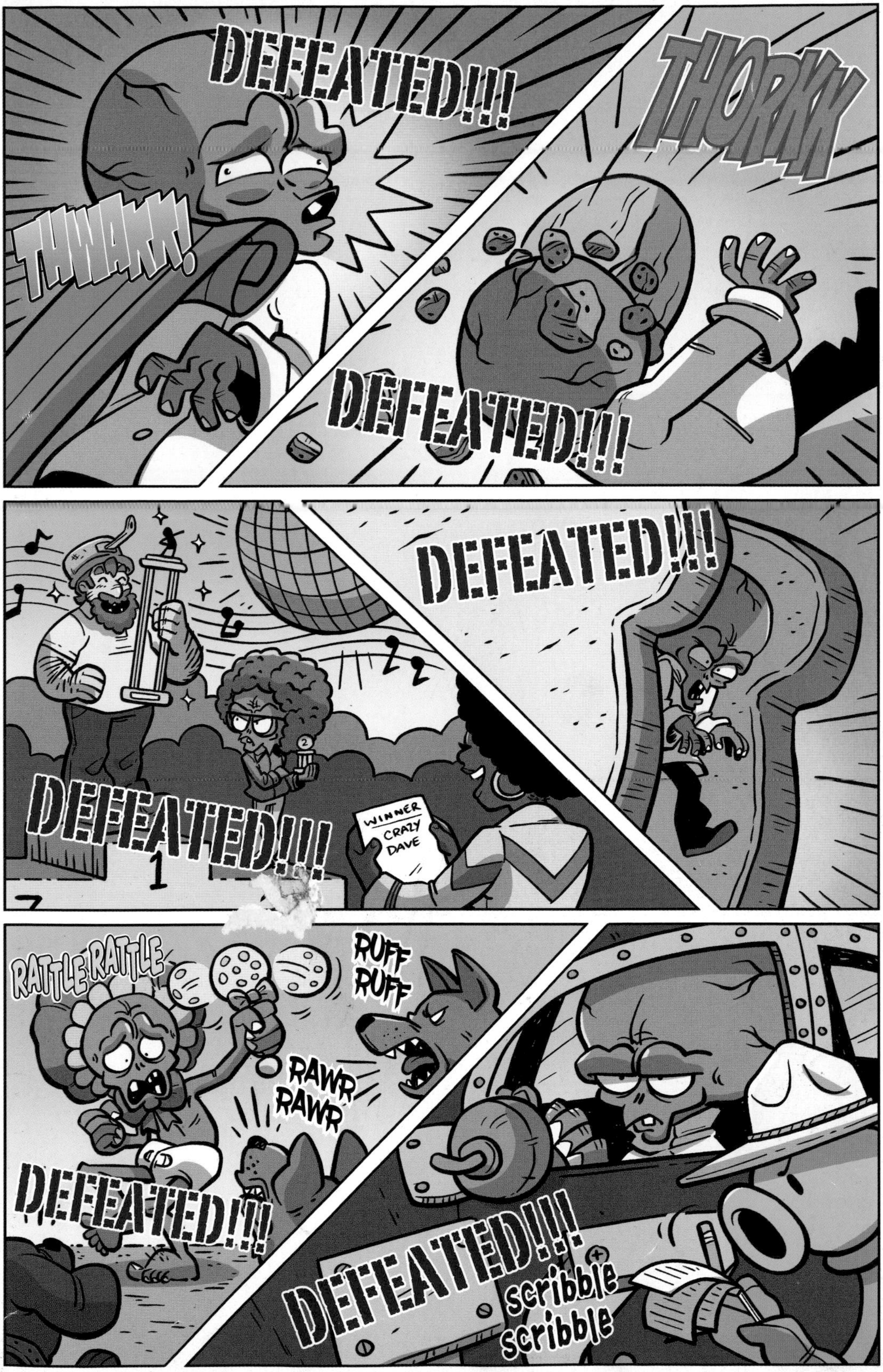

DEFEATED!!!
THWAKK!
THORKK
DEFEATED!!!
DEFEATED!!!
WINNER
CRAZY DAVE
DEFEATED!!!
1
RATTLE RATTLE
RUFF RUFF
RAWR RAWR
DEFEATED!!!
DEFEATED!!!
scribble scribble

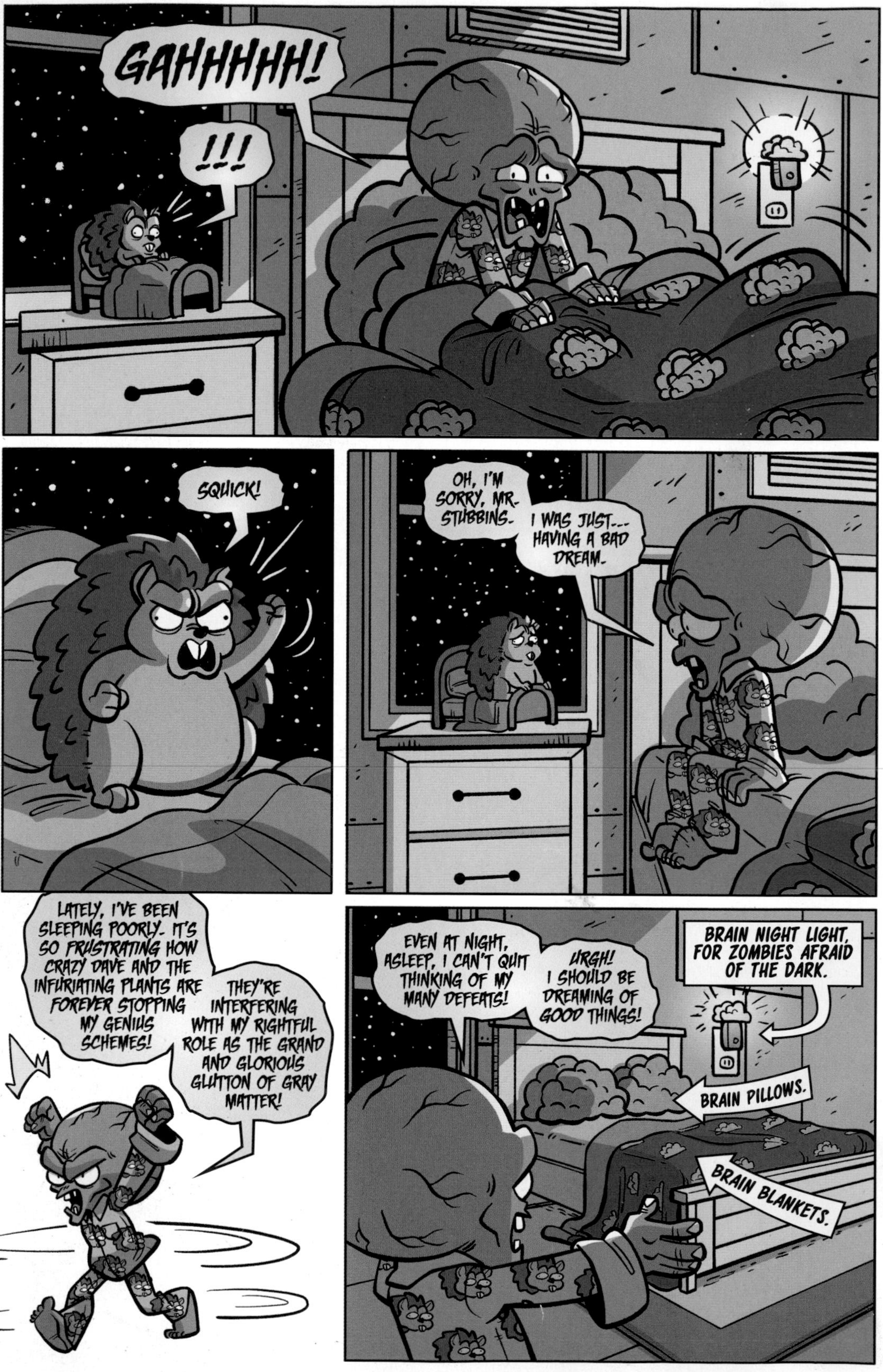
GAHHHHH!
!!!
SQUICK!
OH, I'M SORRY, MR. STUBBINS.
I WAS JUST... HAVING A BAD DREAM.
LATELY, I'VE BEEN SLEEPING POORLY. IT'S SO FRUSTRATING HOW CRAZY DAVE AND THE INFURIATING PLANTS ARE FOREVER STOPPING MY GENIUS SCHEMES!
THEY'RE INTERFERING WITH MY RIGHTFUL ROLE AS THE GRAND AND GLORIOUS GLUTTON OF GRAY MATTER!
EVEN AT NIGHT, ASLEEP, I CAN'T QUIT THINKING OF MY MANY DEFEATS!
URGH! I SHOULD BE DREAMING OF GOOD THINGS!
BRAIN NIGHT LIGHT, FOR ZOMBIES AFRAID OF THE DARK.
BRAIN PILLOWS.
BRAIN BLANKETS.

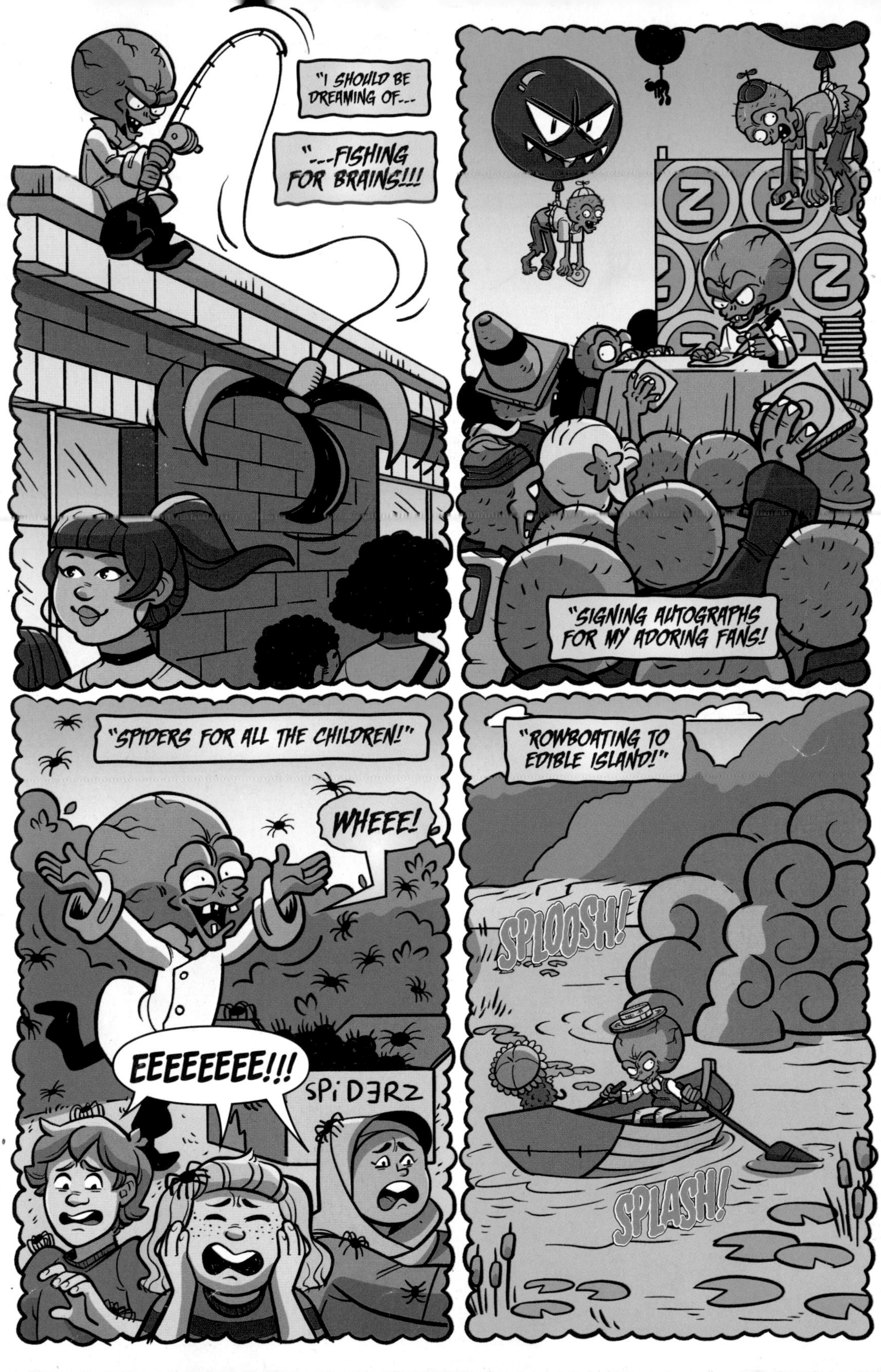
"I SHOULD BE DREAMING OF...
"...FISHING FOR BRAINS!!!
"SIGNING AUTOGRAPHS FOR MY ADORING FANS!
"SPIDERS FOR ALL THE CHILDREN!"
WHEEE!
EEEEEEEE!!!
SPiDƎRZ
"ROWBOATING TO EDIBLE ISLAND!"
SPLOOSH!
SPLASH!

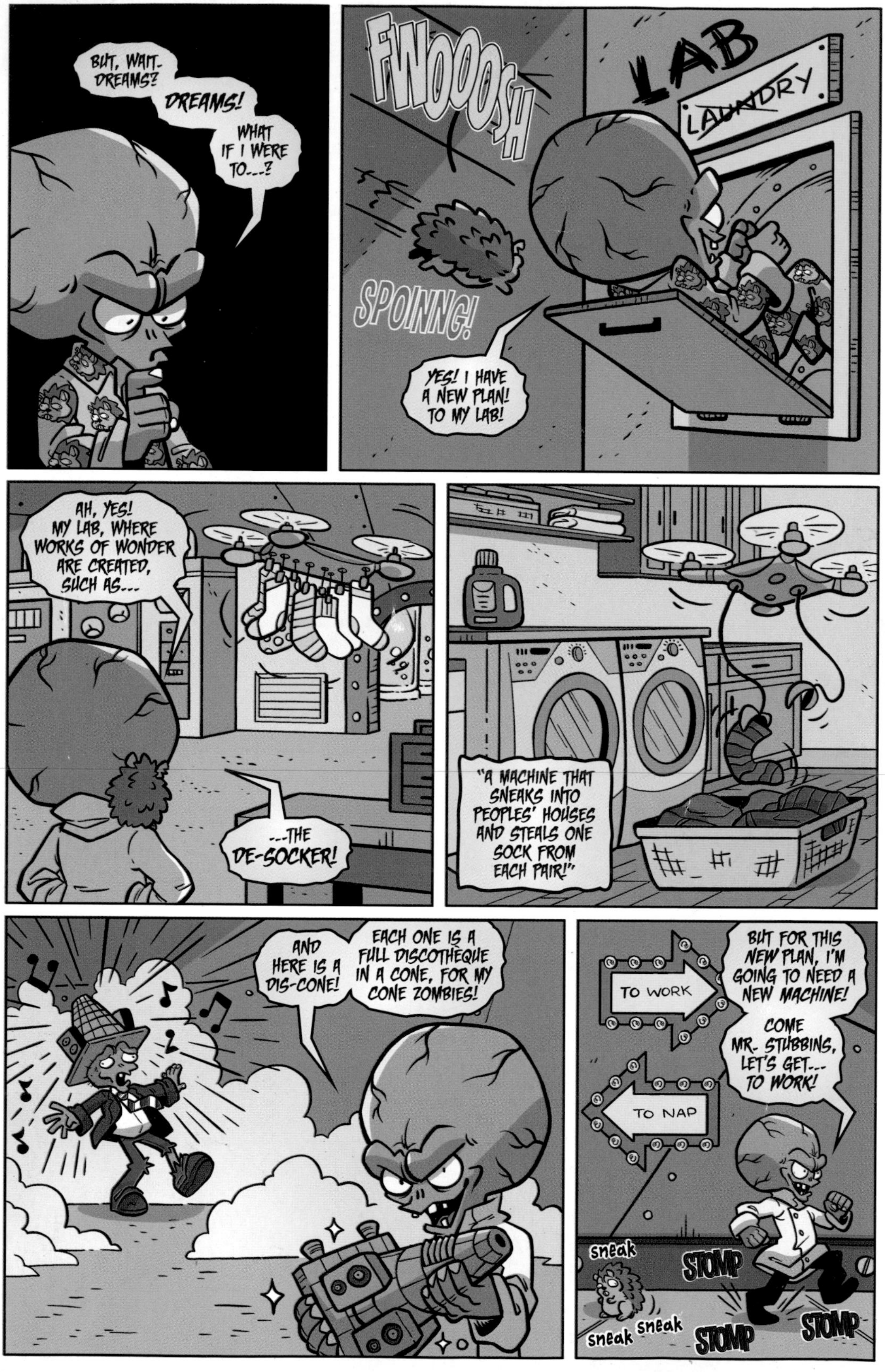
BUT, WAIT-
DREAMS?
DREAMS!
WHAT IF I WERE TO...?
FWOOOOSH
LAB
LAUNDRY
SPOINNG!
YES! I HAVE A NEW PLAN! TO MY LAB!
AH, YES! MY LAB, WHERE WORKS OF WONDER ARE CREATED, SUCH AS...
...THE DE-SOCKER!
"A MACHINE THAT SNEAKS INTO PEOPLES' HOUSES AND STEALS ONE SOCK FROM EACH PAIR!"
AND HERE IS A DIS-CONE!
EACH ONE IS A FULL DISCOTHEQUE IN A CONE, FOR MY CONE ZOMBIES!
TO WORK
TO NAP
BUT FOR THIS NEW PLAN, I'M GOING TO NEED A NEW MACHINE!
COME MR. STUBBINS, LET'S GET... TO WORK!
SNEAK
SNEAK
SNEAK
STOMP
STOMP
STOMP

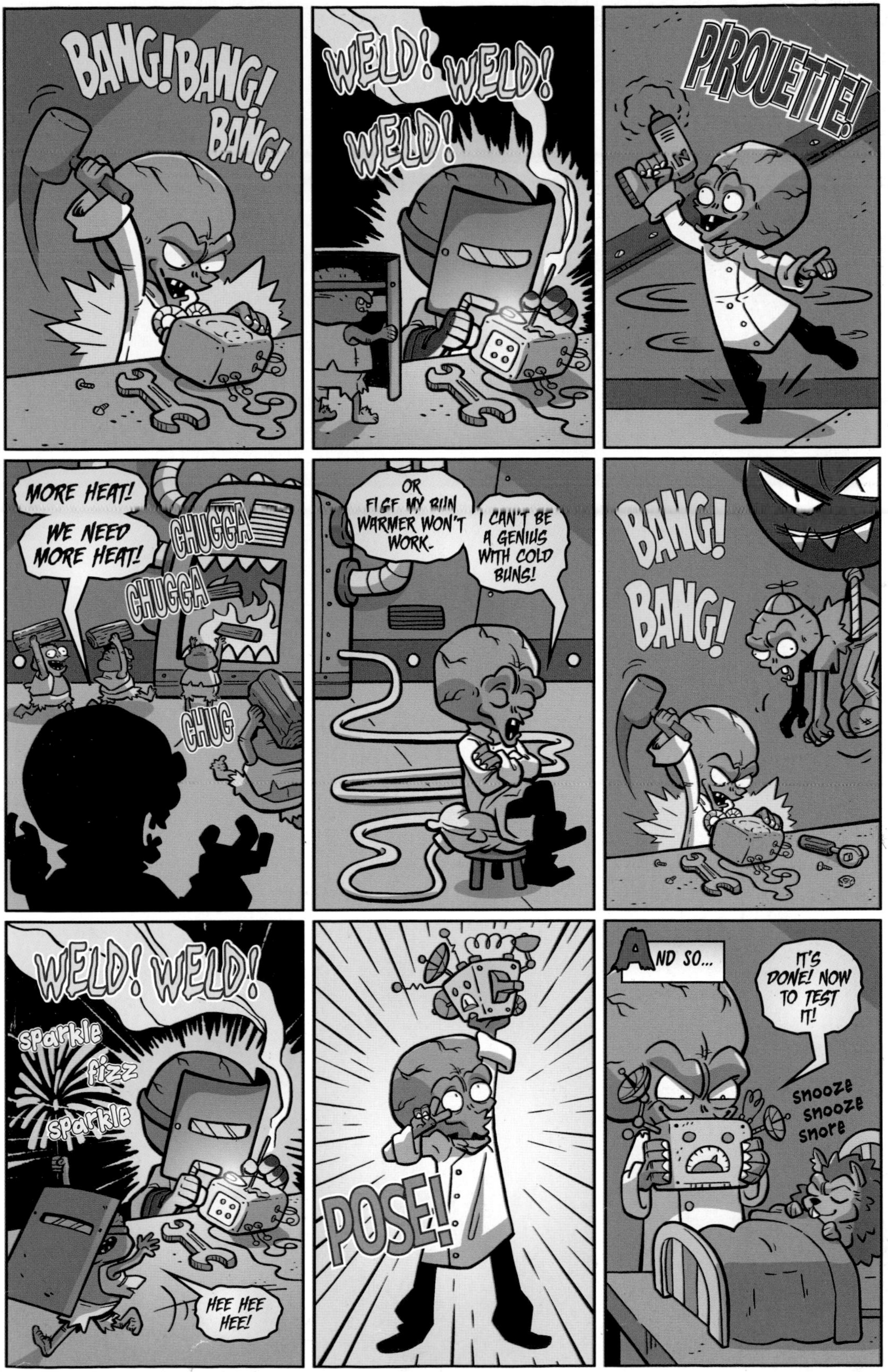
BANG! BANG! BANG!
WELD! WELD! WELD!
PIROUETTE!
MORE HEAT!
WE NEED MORE HEAT!
CHUGGA
CHUGGA
CHUG
OR ELSE MY BUN WARMER WON'T WORK.
I CAN'T BE A GENIUS WITH COLD BUNS!
BANG!
BANG!
WELD! WELD!
sparkle
fizz
sparkle
HEE HEE HEE!
POSE!
AND SO...
IT'S DONE! NOW TO TEST IT!
snooze
snooze
snore

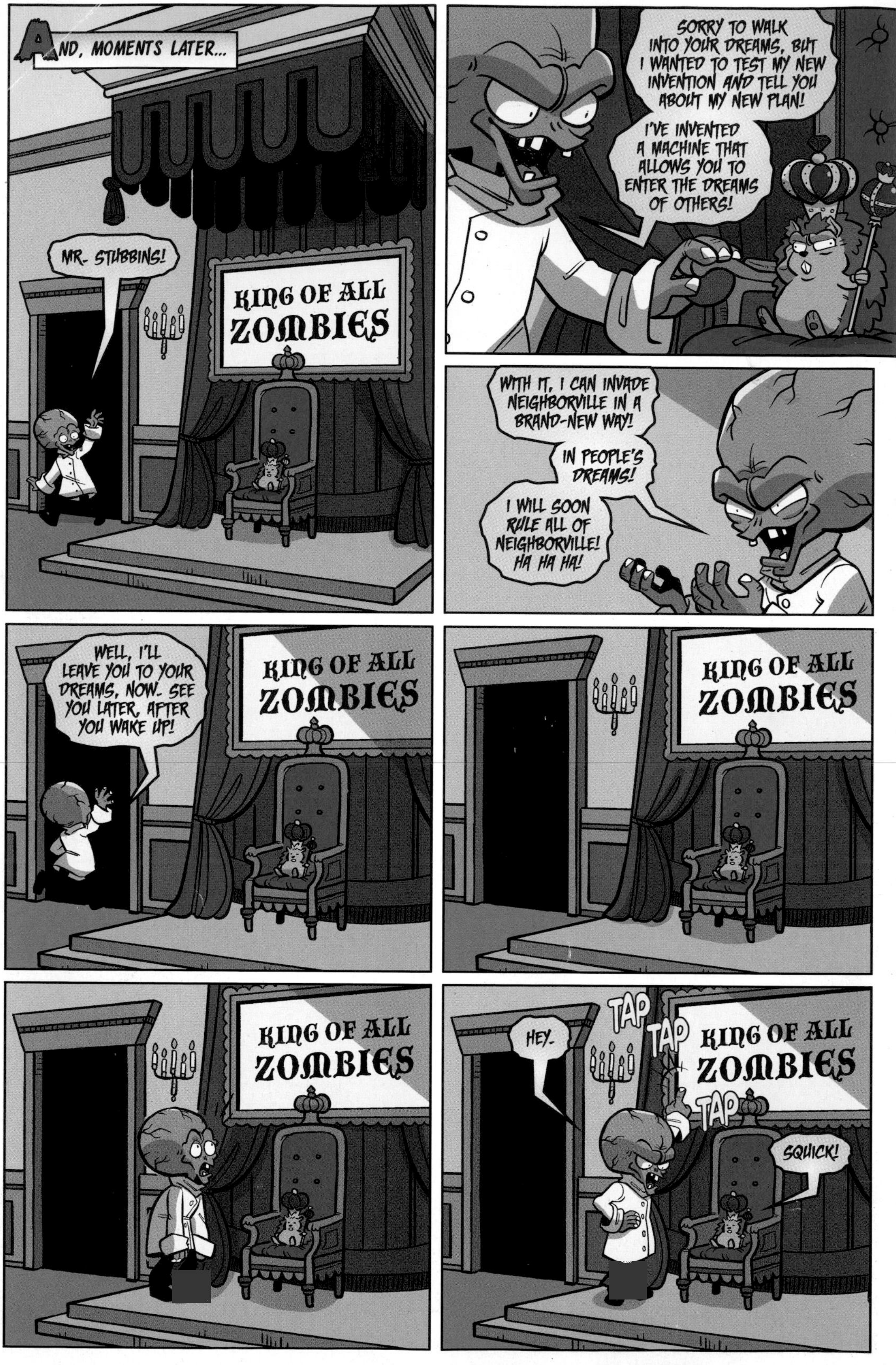
AND, MOMENTS LATER...
MR. STUBBINS!
KING OF ALL ZOMBIES
SORRY TO WALK INTO YOUR DREAMS, BUT I WANTED TO TEST MY NEW INVENTION AND TELL YOU ABOUT MY NEW PLAN!
I'VE INVENTED A MACHINE THAT ALLOWS YOU TO ENTER THE DREAMS OF OTHERS!
WITH IT, I CAN INVADE NEIGHBORVILLE IN A BRAND-NEW WAY!
IN PEOPLE'S DREAMS!
I WILL SOON RULE ALL OF NEIGHBORVILLE! HA HA HA!
WELL, I'LL LEAVE YOU TO YOUR DREAMS, NOW. SEE YOU LATER, AFTER YOU WAKE UP!
KING OF ALL ZOMBIES
KING OF ALL ZOMBIES
KING OF ALL ZOMBIES
HEY.
TAP
TAP
TAP
KING OF ALL ZOMBIES
SQUICK!

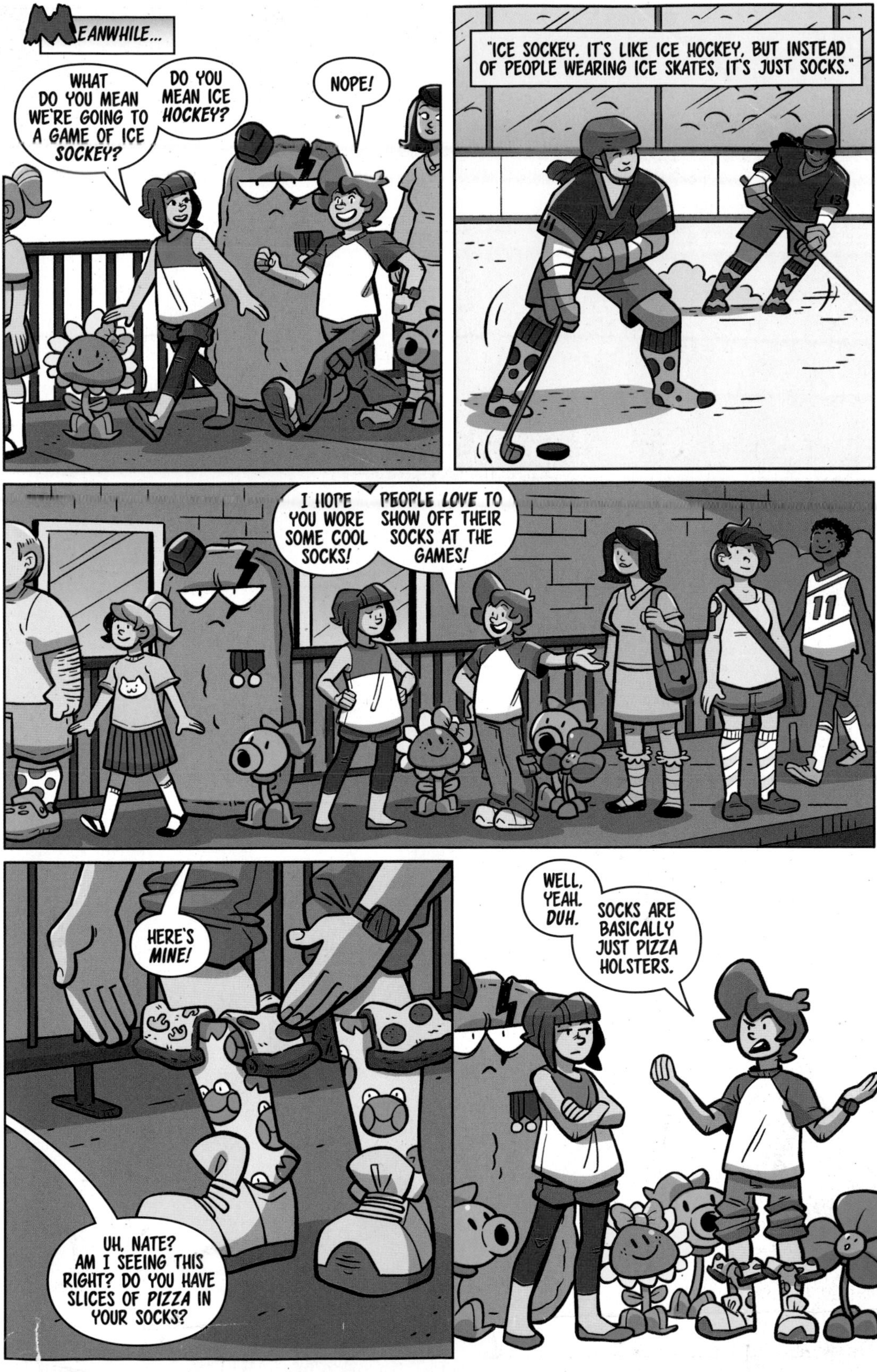
MEANWHILE...
WHAT DO YOU MEAN WE'RE GOING TO A GAME OF ICE SOCKEY?
DO YOU MEAN ICE HOCKEY?
NOPE!
"ICE SOCKEY. IT'S LIKE ICE HOCKEY, BUT INSTEAD OF PEOPLE WEARING ICE SKATES, IT'S JUST SOCKS."
I HOPE YOU WORE SOME COOL SOCKS!
PEOPLE LOVE TO SHOW OFF THEIR SOCKS AT THE GAMES!
11
HERE'S MINE!
UH, NATE? AM I SEEING THIS RIGHT? DO YOU HAVE SLICES OF PIZZA IN YOUR SOCKS?
WELL, YEAH. DUH.
SOCKS ARE BASICALLY JUST PIZZA HOLSTERS.

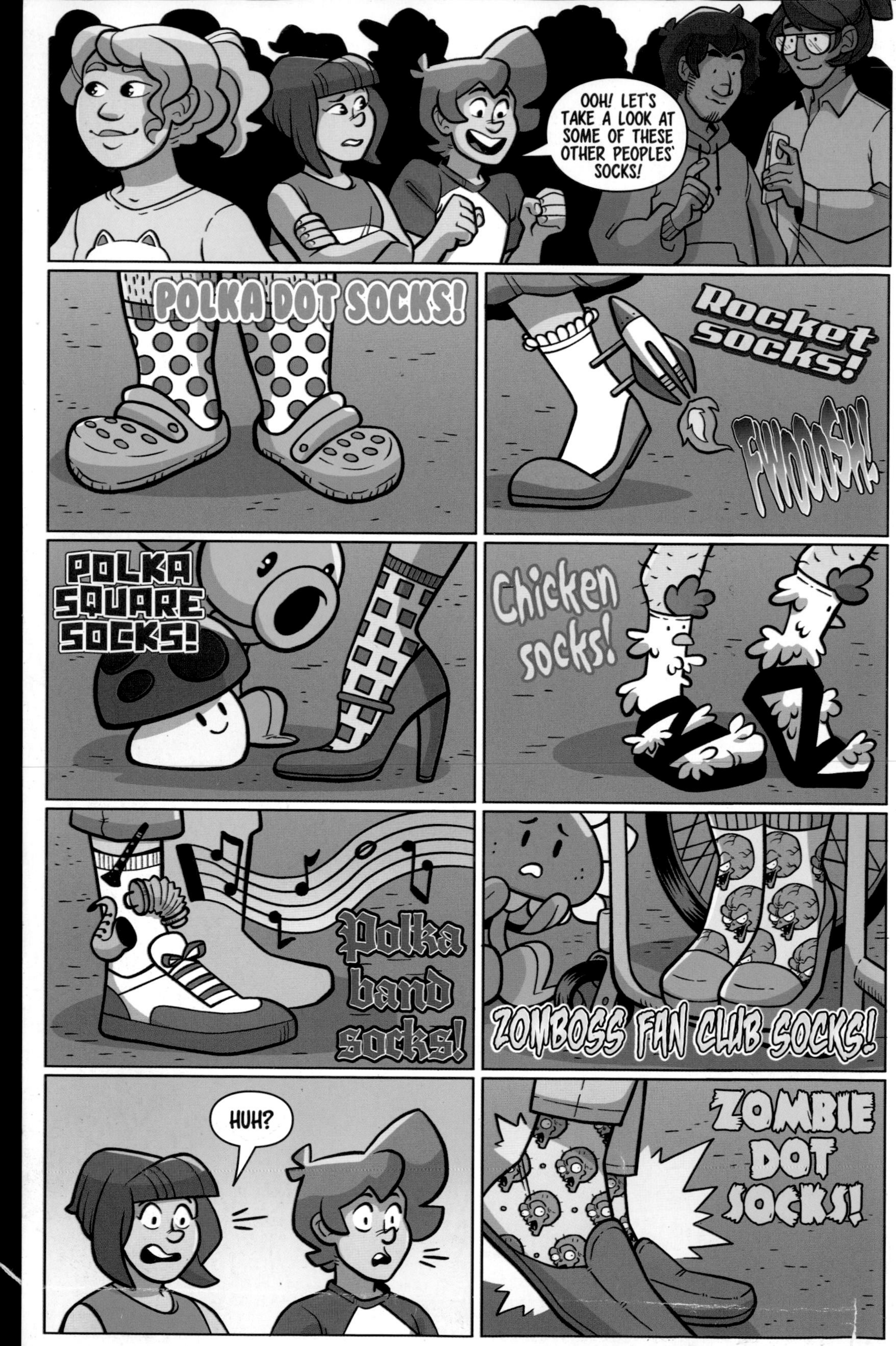
OOH! LET'S TAKE A LOOK AT SOME OF THESE OTHER PEOPLES' SOCKS!
POLKA DOT SOCKS!
Rocket socks!
FWOOOSH!
POLKA SQUARE SOCKS!
Chicken socks!
Polka band socks!
ZOMBOSS FAN CLUB SOCKS!
HUH?
ZOMBIE DOT SOCKS!

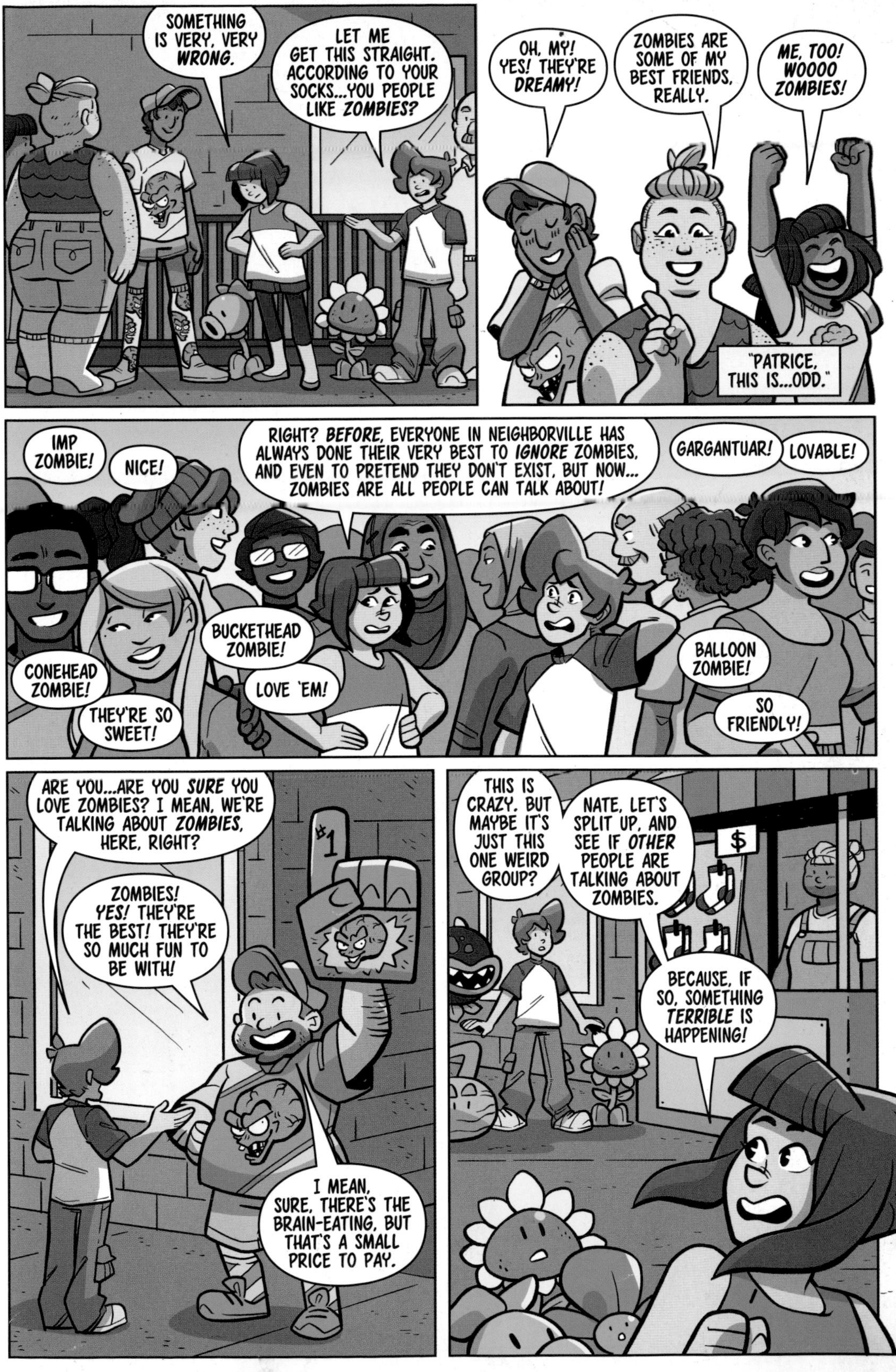
SOMETHING IS VERY, VERY *WRONG*.
LET ME GET THIS STRAIGHT. ACCORDING TO YOUR SOCKS...YOU PEOPLE LIKE *ZOMBIES*?
OH, MY! YES! THEY'RE *DREAMY*!
ZOMBIES ARE SOME OF MY BEST FRIENDS, REALLY.
ME, TOO! WOOOO ZOMBIES!
"PATRICE, THIS IS...ODD."
IMP ZOMBIE!
NICE!
RIGHT? *BEFORE*, EVERYONE IN NEIGHBORVILLE HAS ALWAYS DONE THEIR VERY BEST TO *IGNORE* ZOMBIES, AND EVEN TO PRETEND THEY DON'T EXIST, BUT NOW... ZOMBIES ARE ALL PEOPLE CAN TALK ABOUT!
GARGANTUAR!
LOVABLE!
BUCKETHEAD ZOMBIE!
CONEHEAD ZOMBIE!
LOVE 'EM!
THEY'RE SO SWEET!
BALLOON ZOMBIE!
SO FRIENDLY!
ARE YOU...ARE YOU *SURE* YOU LOVE ZOMBIES? I MEAN, WE'RE TALKING ABOUT *ZOMBIES*, HERE, RIGHT?
ZOMBIES! *YES!* THEY'RE THE BEST! THEY'RE SO MUCH FUN TO BE WITH!
#1
I MEAN, SURE, THERE'S THE BRAIN-EATING, BUT THAT'S A SMALL PRICE TO PAY.
THIS IS CRAZY. BUT MAYBE IT'S JUST THIS ONE WEIRD GROUP?
NATE, LET'S SPLIT UP, AND SEE IF *OTHER* PEOPLE ARE TALKING ABOUT ZOMBIES.
$
BECAUSE, IF SO, SOMETHING *TERRIBLE* IS HAPPENING!

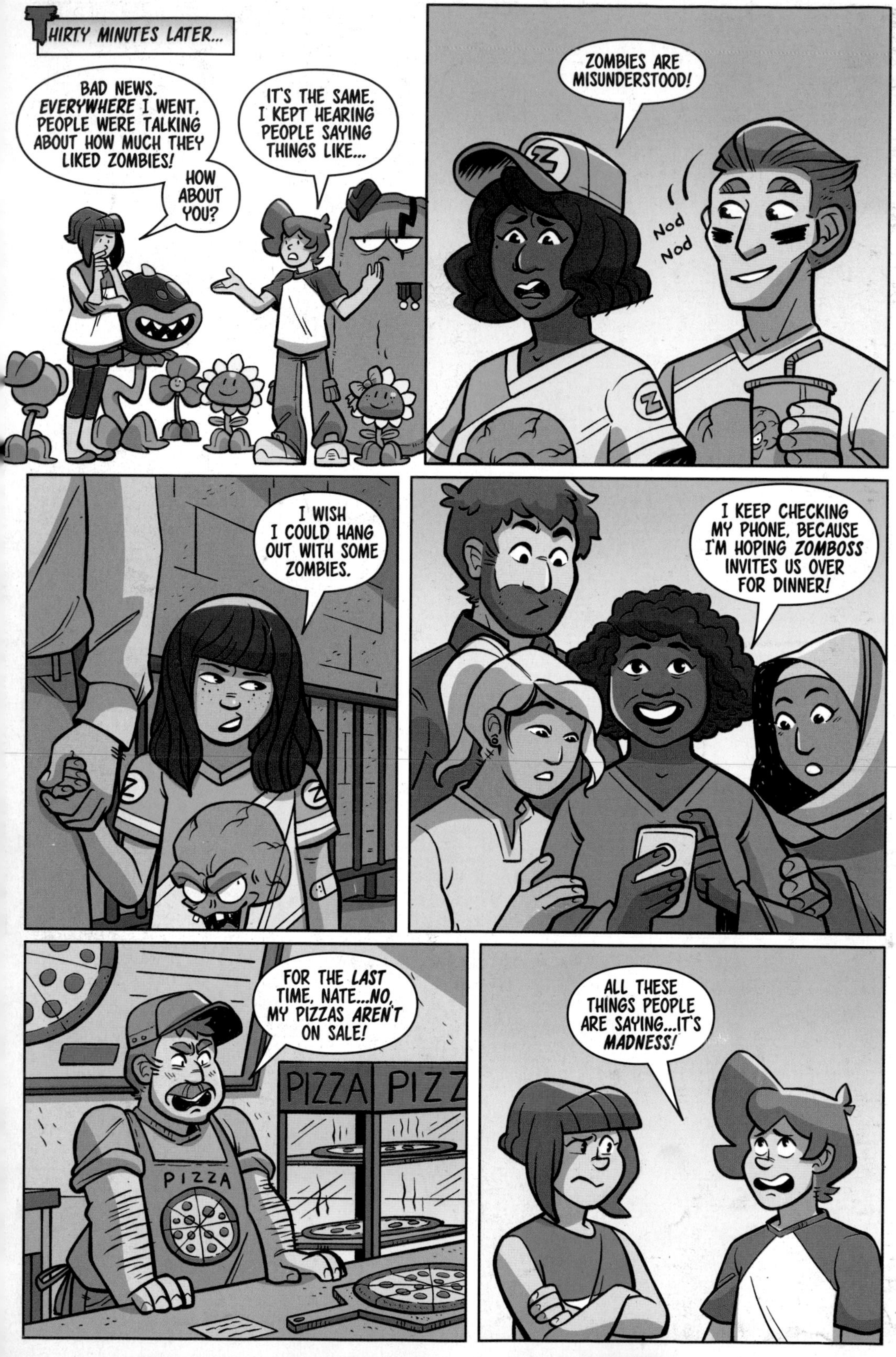
THIRTY MINUTES LATER...
BAD NEWS. EVERYWHERE I WENT, PEOPLE WERE TALKING ABOUT HOW MUCH THEY LIKED ZOMBIES!
HOW ABOUT YOU?
IT'S THE SAME. I KEPT HEARING PEOPLE SAYING THINGS LIKE...
ZOMBIES ARE MISUNDERSTOOD!
Nod Nod
I WISH I COULD HANG OUT WITH SOME ZOMBIES.
I KEEP CHECKING MY PHONE, BECAUSE I'M HOPING ZOMBOSS INVITES US OVER FOR DINNER!
FOR THE LAST TIME, NATE...NO, MY PIZZAS AREN'T ON SALE!
PIZZA PIZZ
PIZZA
ALL THESE THINGS PEOPLE ARE SAYING...IT'S MADNESS!

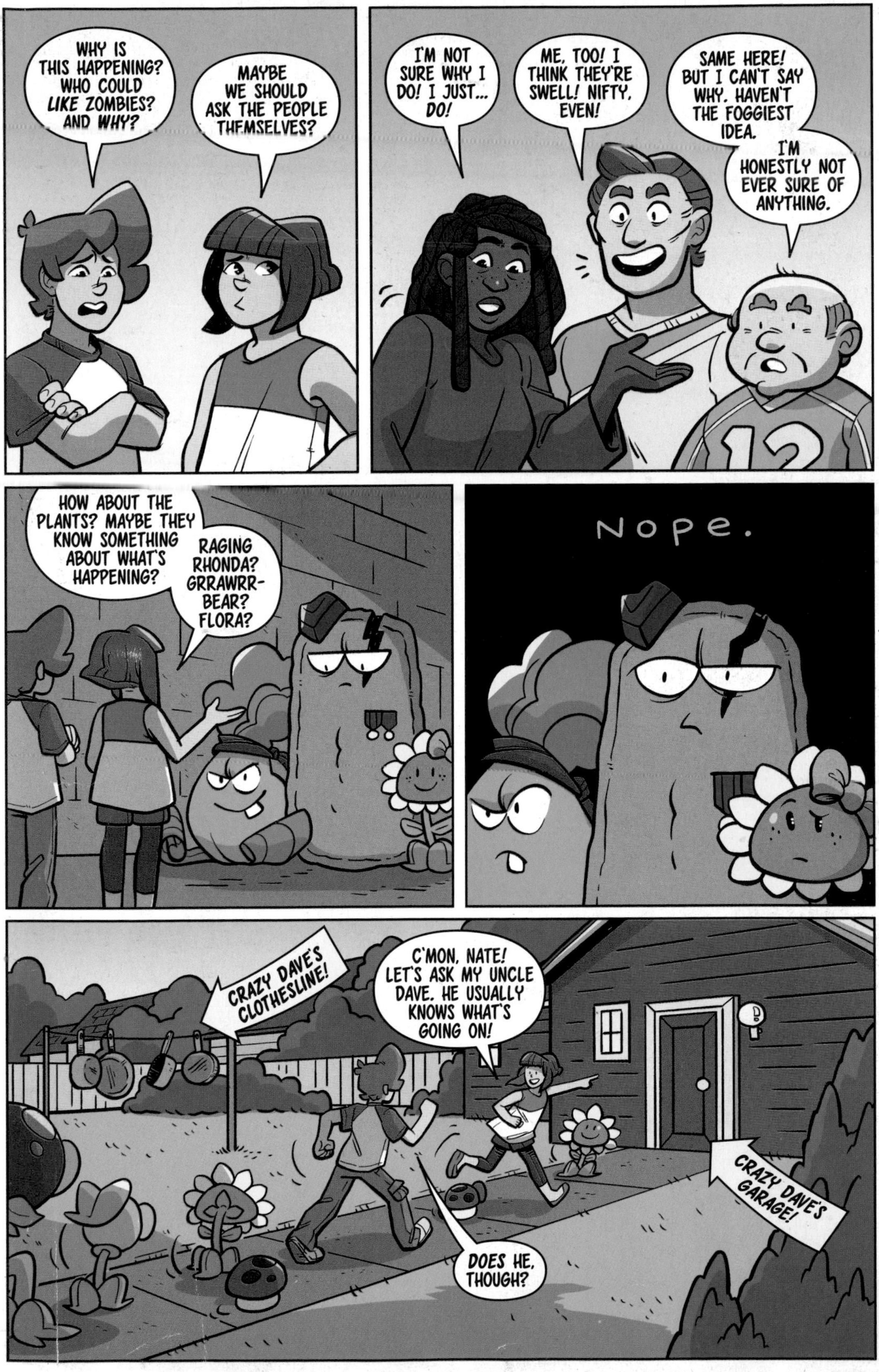
WHY IS THIS HAPPENING? WHO COULD *LIKE* ZOMBIES? AND *WHY*?
MAYBE WE SHOULD ASK THE PEOPLE THEMSELVES?
I'M NOT SURE WHY I DO! I JUST... *DO!*
ME, TOO! I THINK THEY'RE SWELL! NIFTY, EVEN!
SAME HERE! BUT I CAN'T SAY WHY. HAVEN'T THE FOGGIEST IDEA.
I'M HONESTLY NOT EVER SURE OF ANYTHING.
HOW ABOUT THE PLANTS? MAYBE THEY KNOW SOMETHING ABOUT WHAT'S HAPPENING?
RAGING RHONDA? GRRAWRR-BEAR? FLORA?
Nope.
CRAZY DAVE'S CLOTHESLINE!
C'MON, NATE! LET'S ASK MY UNCLE DAVE. HE USUALLY KNOWS WHAT'S GOING ON!
CRAZY DAVE'S GARAGE!
DOES HE, THOUGH?

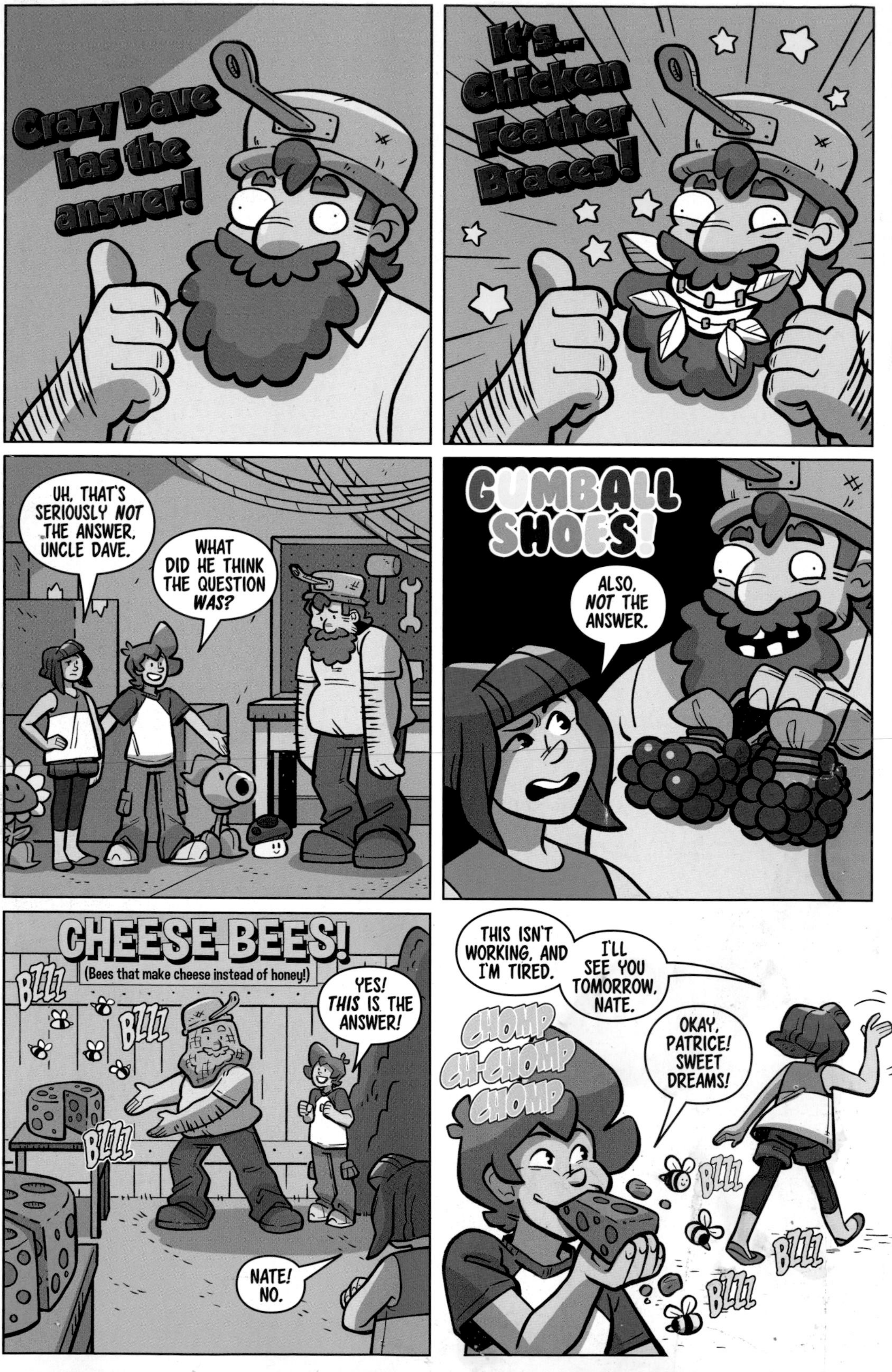

Crazy Dave has the answer!
It's... Chicken Feather Braces!
UH, THAT'S SERIOUSLY *NOT* THE ANSWER, UNCLE DAVE.
WHAT DID HE THINK THE QUESTION *WAS?*
GUMBALL SHOES!
ALSO, *NOT* THE ANSWER.
CHEESE BEES!
(Bees that make cheese instead of honey!)
BZZZ
BZZZ
BZZZ
YES! *THIS* IS THE ANSWER!
NATE! NO.
THIS ISN'T WORKING, AND I'M TIRED.
I'LL SEE YOU TOMORROW, NATE.
CHOMP CH-CHOMP CHOMP
OKAY, PATRICE! SWEET DREAMS!
BZZZ
BZZZ
BZZZ

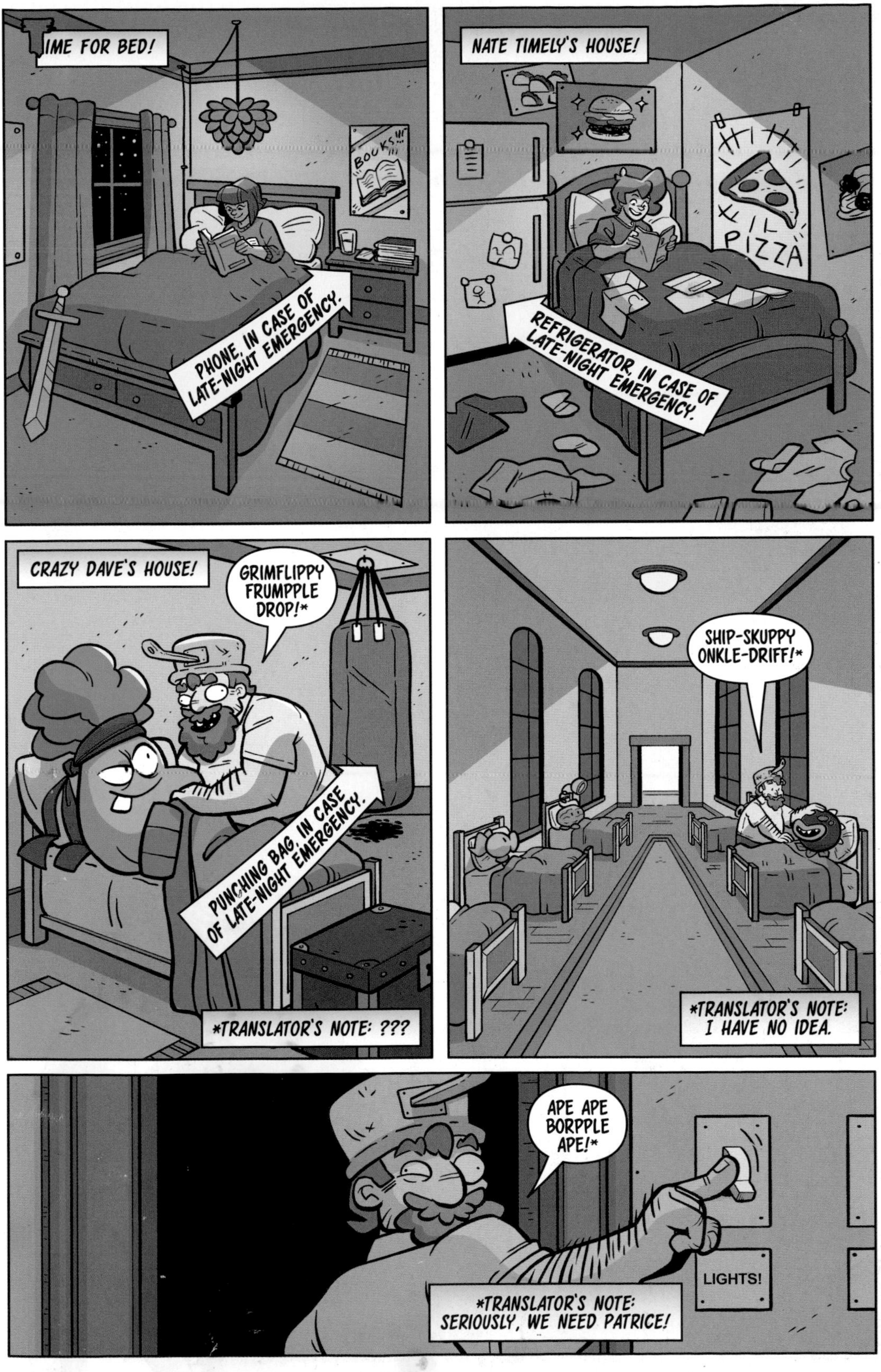
TIME FOR BED!
BOOKS!!!
PHONE, IN CASE OF LATE-NIGHT EMERGENCY.
NATE TIMELY'S HOUSE!
PIZZA
REFRIGERATOR, IN CASE OF LATE-NIGHT EMERGENCY.
CRAZY DAVE'S HOUSE!
GRIMFLIPPY FRUMPPLE DROP!*
PUNCHING BAG, IN CASE OF LATE-NIGHT EMERGENCY.
*TRANSLATOR'S NOTE: ???
SHIP-SKUPPY ONKLE-DRIFF!*
*TRANSLATOR'S NOTE: I HAVE NO IDEA.
APE APE BORPPLE APE!*
LIGHTS!
*TRANSLATOR'S NOTE: SERIOUSLY, WE NEED PATRICE!

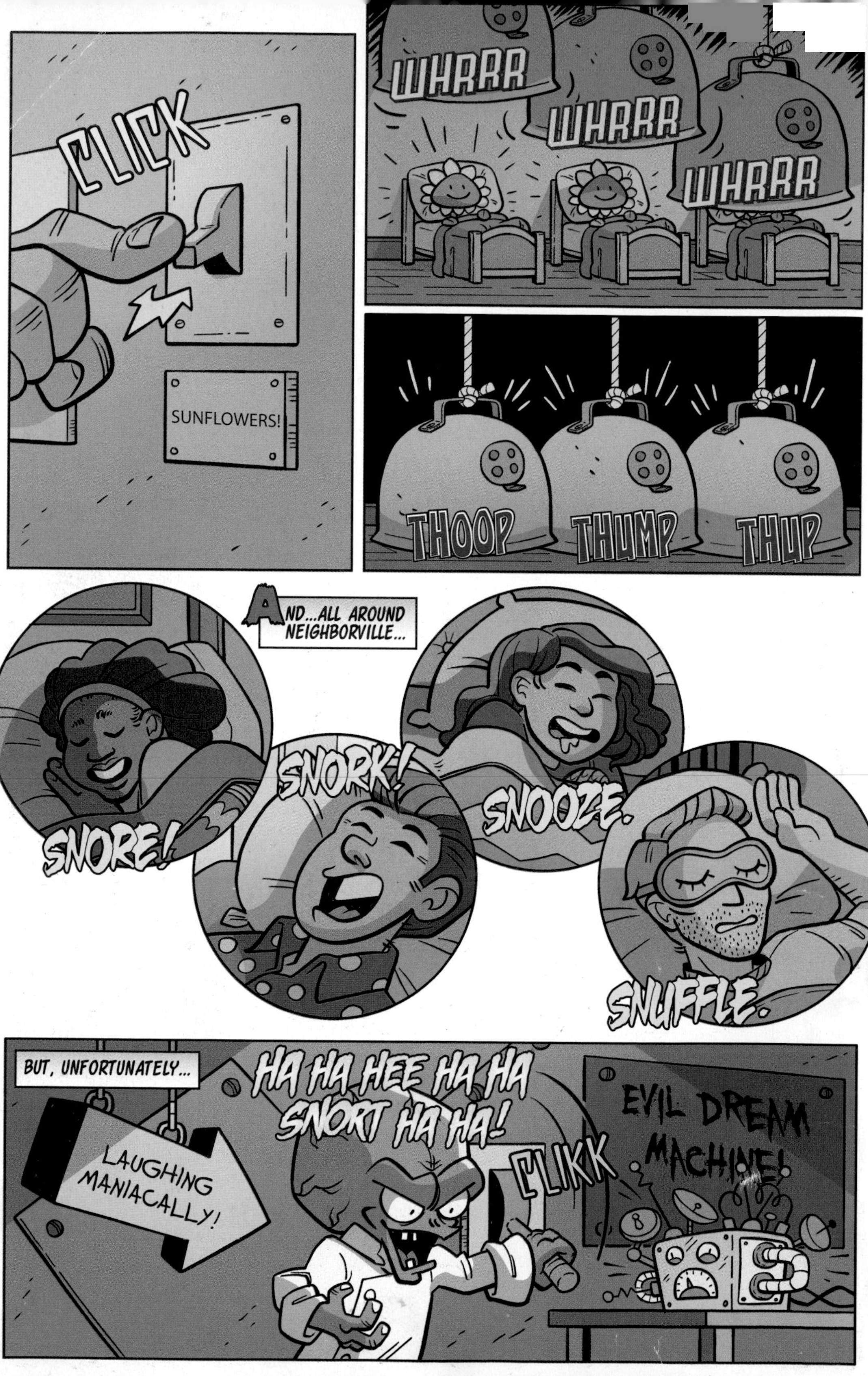
CLICK
SUNFLOWERS!
WHRRR
WHRRR
WHRRR
THOOP
THUMP
THUP
AND...ALL AROUND NEIGHBORVILLE...
SNORE!
SNORK!
SNOOZE.
SNUFFLE.
BUT, UNFORTUNATELY...
HA HA HEE HA HA SNORT HA HA!
LAUGHING MANIACALLY!
CLIKK
EVIL DREAM MACHINE!

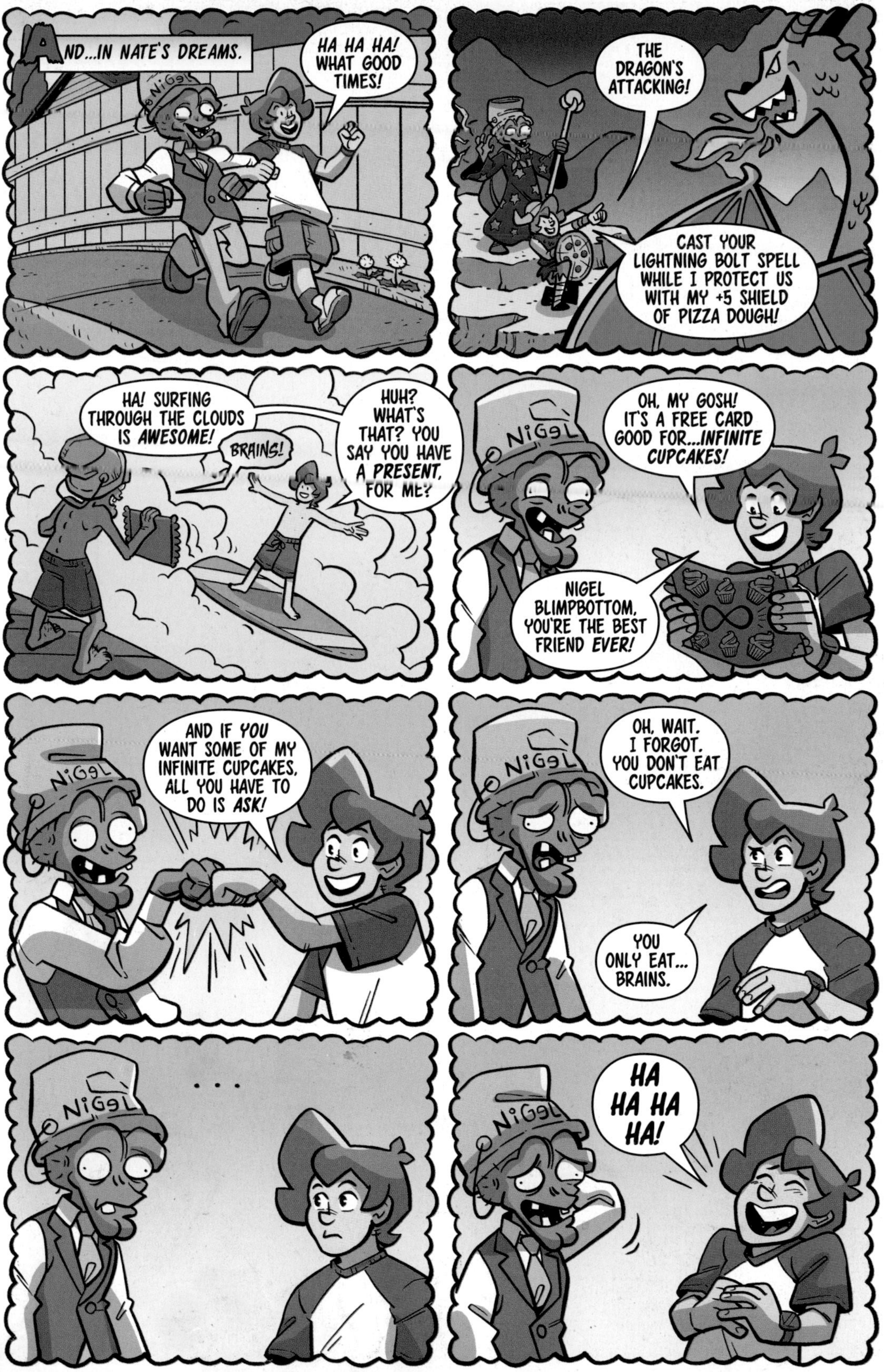
AND...IN NATE'S DREAMS.
NiGeL
HA HA HA! WHAT GOOD TIMES!
THE DRAGON'S ATTACKING!
CAST YOUR LIGHTNING BOLT SPELL WHILE I PROTECT US WITH MY +5 SHIELD OF PIZZA DOUGH!
HA! SURFING THROUGH THE CLOUDS IS AWESOME!
BRAINS!
HUH? WHAT'S THAT? YOU SAY YOU HAVE A PRESENT, FOR ME?
NiGeL
OH, MY GOSH! IT'S A FREE CARD GOOD FOR...INFINITE CUPCAKES!
NIGEL BLIMPBOTTOM, YOU'RE THE BEST FRIEND EVER!
NiGeL
AND IF YOU WANT SOME OF MY INFINITE CUPCAKES, ALL YOU HAVE TO DO IS ASK!
NiGeL
OH, WAIT. I FORGOT. YOU DON'T EAT CUPCAKES.
YOU ONLY EAT... BRAINS.
NiGeL
...
NiGeL
HA HA HA HA!

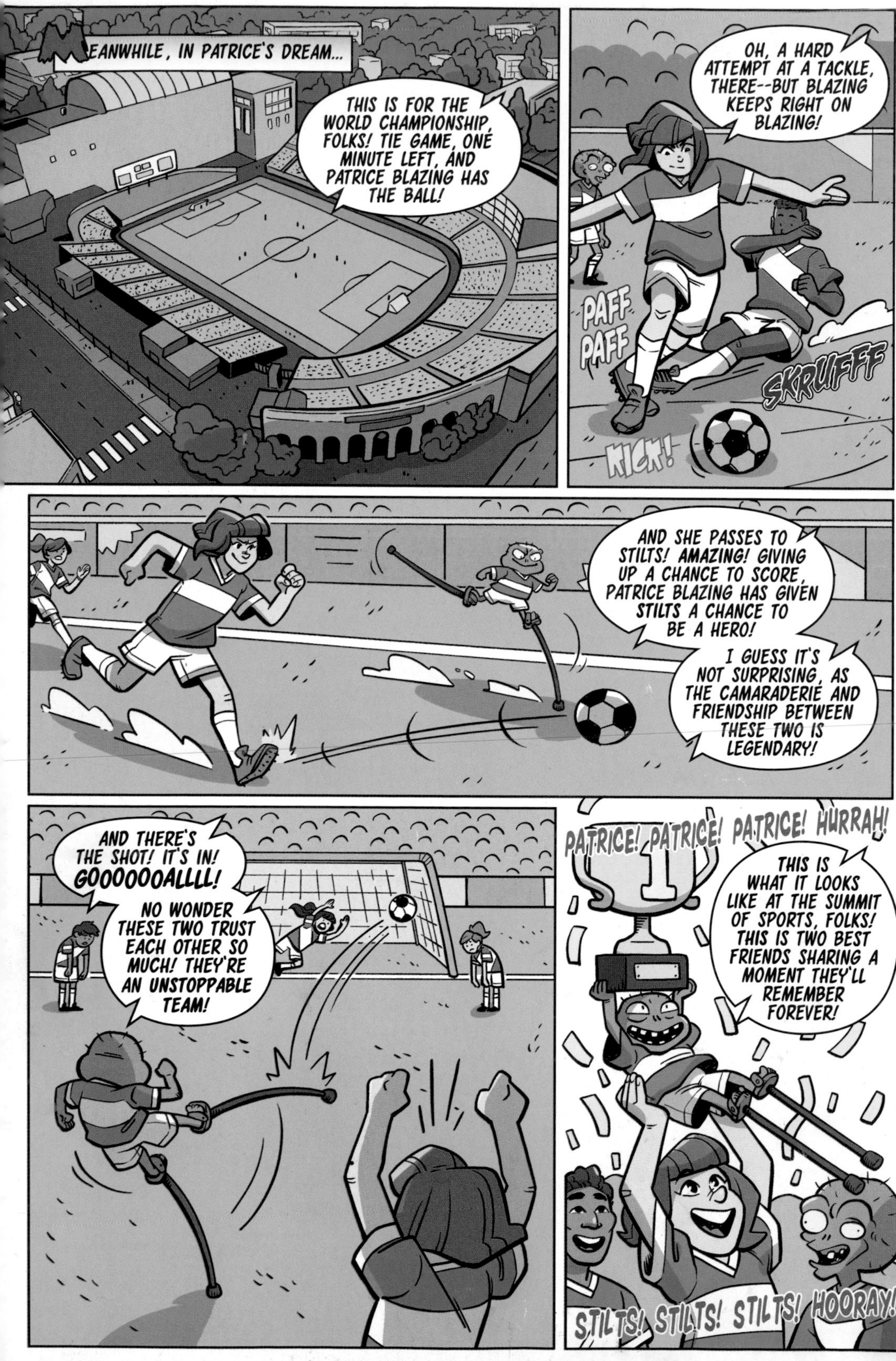
MEANWHILE, IN PATRICE'S DREAM...
THIS IS FOR THE WORLD CHAMPIONSHIP, FOLKS! TIE GAME, ONE MINUTE LEFT, AND PATRICE BLAZING HAS THE BALL!
OH, A HARD ATTEMPT AT A TACKLE, THERE--BUT BLAZING KEEPS RIGHT ON BLAZING!
PAFF PAFF
SKRUFFF
KICK!
AND SHE PASSES TO STILTS! AMAZING! GIVING UP A CHANCE TO SCORE, PATRICE BLAZING HAS GIVEN STILTS A CHANCE TO BE A HERO!
I GUESS IT'S NOT SURPRISING, AS THE CAMARADERIE AND FRIENDSHIP BETWEEN THESE TWO IS LEGENDARY!
AND THERE'S THE SHOT! IT'S IN! GOOOOOOALLLL!
NO WONDER THESE TWO TRUST EACH OTHER SO MUCH! THEY'RE AN UNSTOPPABLE TEAM!
PATRICE! PATRICE! PATRICE! HURRAH!
1
THIS IS WHAT IT LOOKS LIKE AT THE SUMMIT OF SPORTS, FOLKS! THIS IS TWO BEST FRIENDS SHARING A MOMENT THEY'LL REMEMBER FOREVER!
STILTS! STILTS! STILTS! HOORAY!

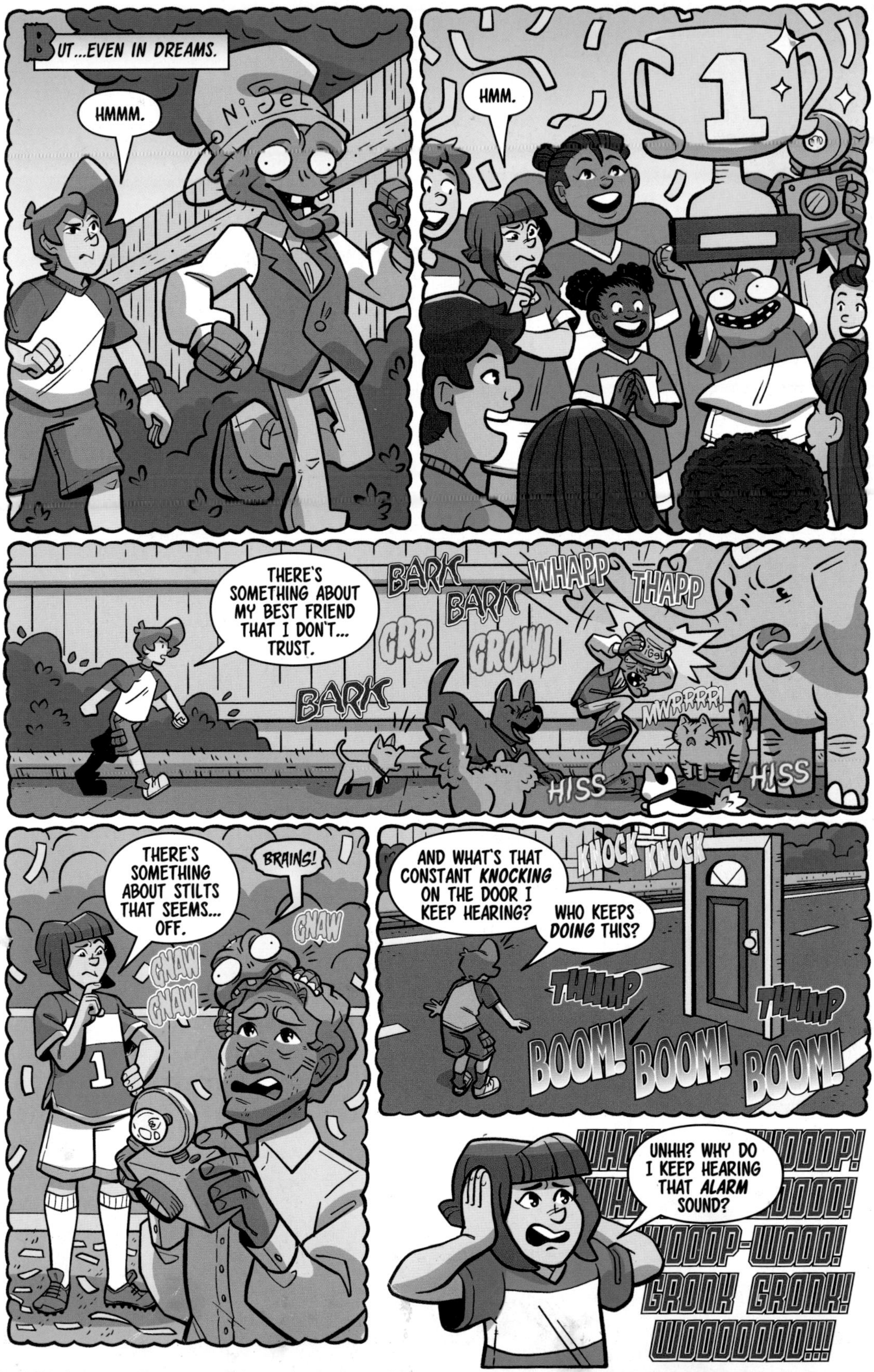
BUT...EVEN IN DREAMS.
HMMM.
NIGEL
HMM.
1
THERE'S SOMETHING ABOUT MY BEST FRIEND THAT I DON'T... TRUST.
BARK
BARK
GRR
GROWL
BARK
WHAPP
THAPP
MWRRRR!
HISS
HISS
THERE'S SOMETHING ABOUT STILTS THAT SEEMS... OFF.
BRAINS!
GNAW
GNAW
GNAW
AND WHAT'S THAT CONSTANT *KNOCKING* ON THE DOOR I KEEP HEARING?
WHO KEEPS *DOING* THIS?
KNOCK KNOCK
THUMP
THUMP
BOOM! BOOM! BOOM!
UNHH? WHY DO I KEEP HEARING THAT *ALARM* SOUND?
WOOOP-WOOO!
GRONK GRONK!
WOOOOOOO!!!

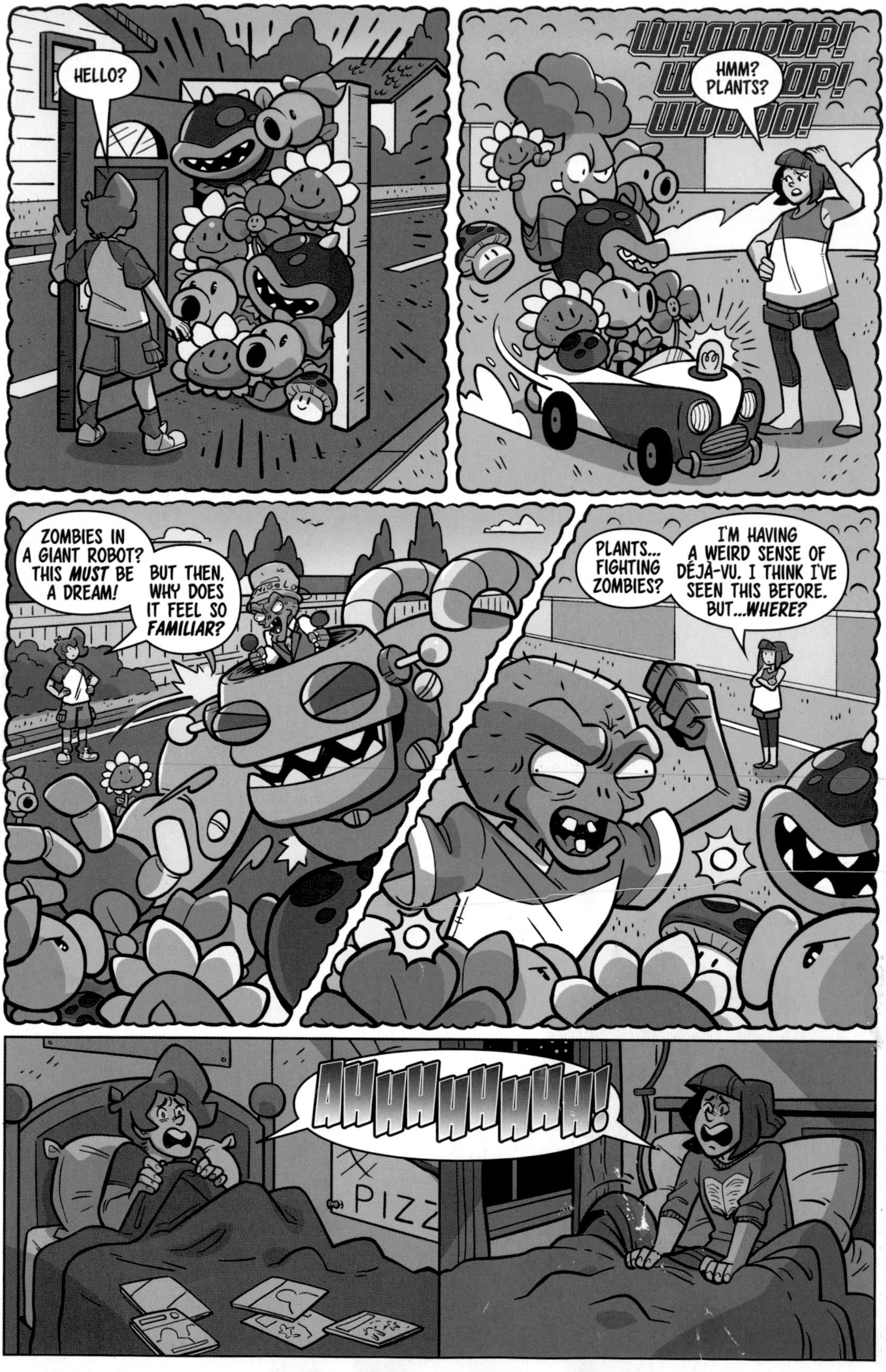
HELLO?
WHOOOOOP!
HMM? PLANTS?
ZOMBIES IN A GIANT ROBOT? THIS *MUST* BE A DREAM!
BUT THEN, WHY DOES IT FEEL SO **FAMILIAR**?
PLANTS... FIGHTING ZOMBIES?
I'M HAVING A WEIRD SENSE OF DÉJÀ-VU. I THINK I'VE SEEN THIS BEFORE. BUT...***WHERE?***
AHHHHHHHHH!
PIZZ

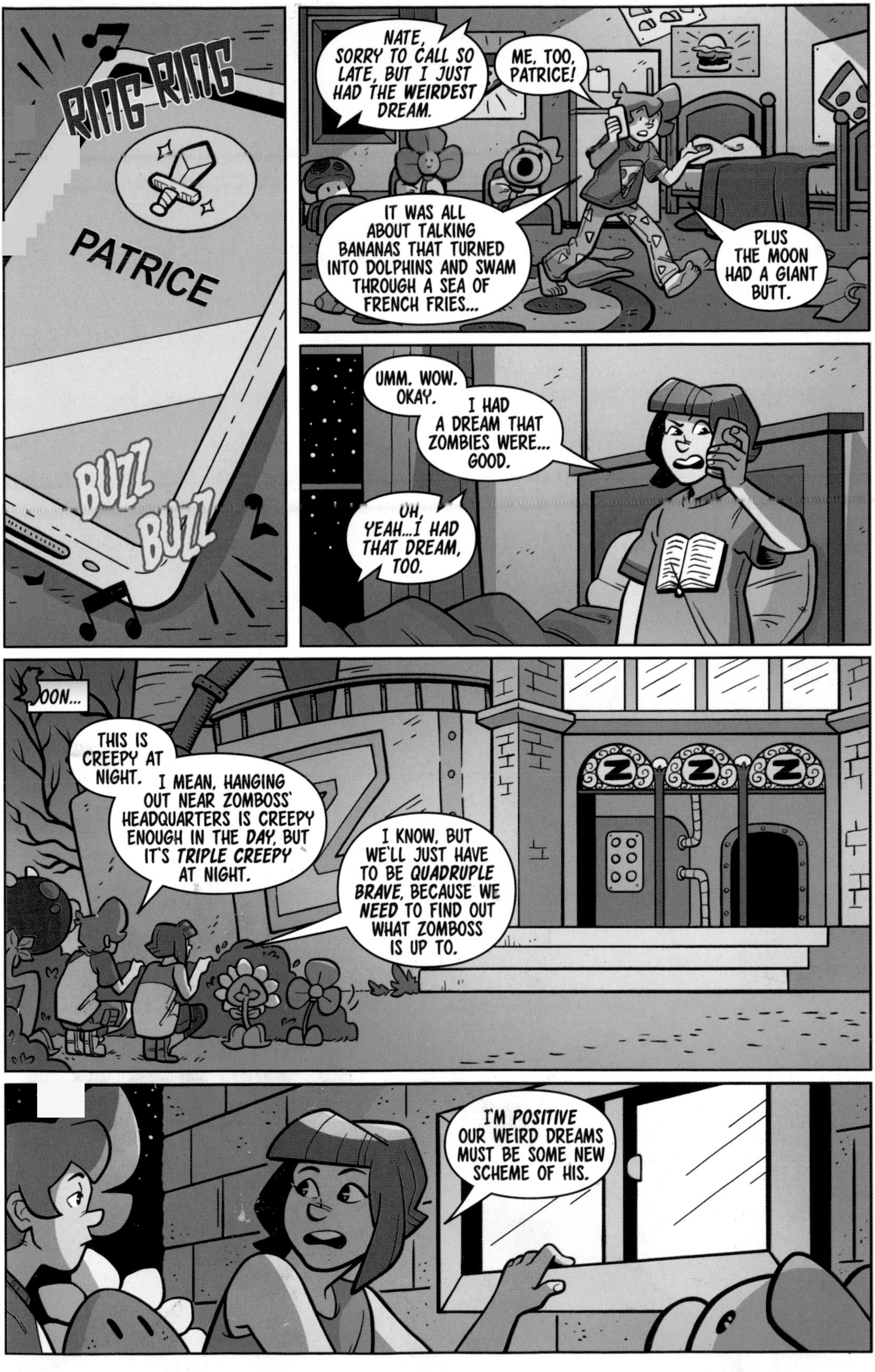

RING RING
PATRICE
BUZZ BUZZ
NATE, SORRY TO CALL SO LATE, BUT I JUST HAD THE WEIRDEST DREAM.
ME, TOO, PATRICE!
IT WAS ALL ABOUT TALKING BANANAS THAT TURNED INTO DOLPHINS AND SWAM THROUGH A SEA OF FRENCH FRIES...
PLUS THE MOON HAD A GIANT BUTT.
UMM. WOW. OKAY.
I HAD A DREAM THAT ZOMBIES WERE... GOOD.
OH, YEAH...I HAD THAT DREAM, TOO.
OON...
THIS IS CREEPY AT NIGHT.
I MEAN, HANGING OUT NEAR ZOMBOSS' HEADQUARTERS IS CREEPY ENOUGH IN THE DAY, BUT IT'S TRIPLE CREEPY AT NIGHT.
I KNOW, BUT WE'LL JUST HAVE TO BE QUADRUPLE BRAVE, BECAUSE WE NEED TO FIND OUT WHAT ZOMBOSS IS UP TO.
I'M POSITIVE OUR WEIRD DREAMS MUST BE SOME NEW SCHEME OF HIS.

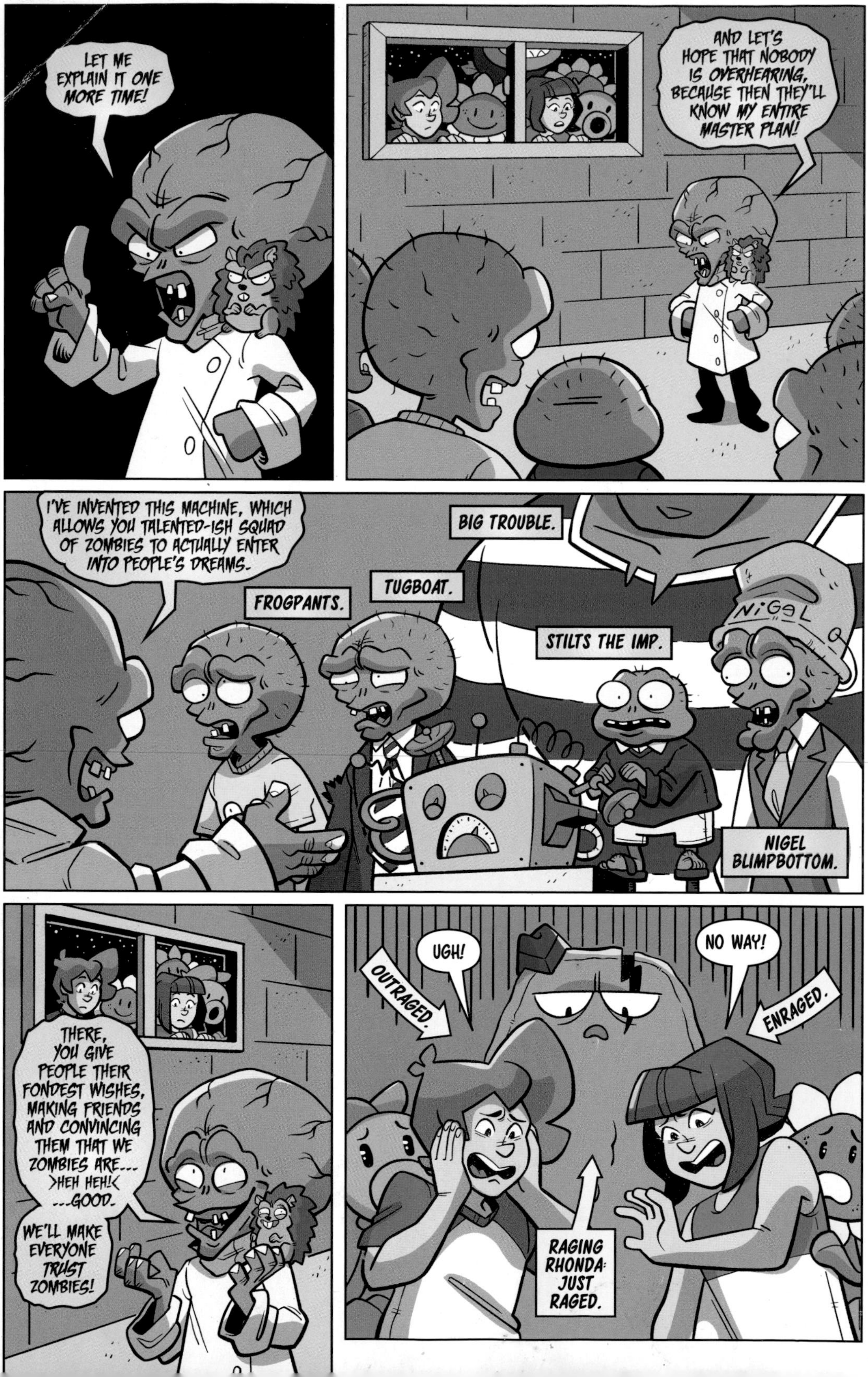

LET ME EXPLAIN IT ONE MORE TIME!
AND LET'S HOPE THAT NOBODY IS OVERHEARING, BECAUSE THEN THEY'LL KNOW MY ENTIRE MASTER PLAN!
I'VE INVENTED THIS MACHINE, WHICH ALLOWS YOU TALENTED-ISH SQUAD OF ZOMBIES TO ACTUALLY ENTER INTO PEOPLE'S DREAMS.
FROGPANTS.
TUGBOAT.
BIG TROUBLE.
STILTS THE IMP.
NIGEL
NIGEL BLIMPBOTTOM.
THERE, YOU GIVE PEOPLE THEIR FONDEST WISHES, MAKING FRIENDS AND CONVINCING THEM THAT WE ZOMBIES ARE... >HEH HEH!< ...GOOD.
WE'LL MAKE EVERYONE TRUST ZOMBIES!
UGH!
OUTRAGED.
NO WAY!
ENRAGED.
RAGING RHONDA: JUST RAGED.

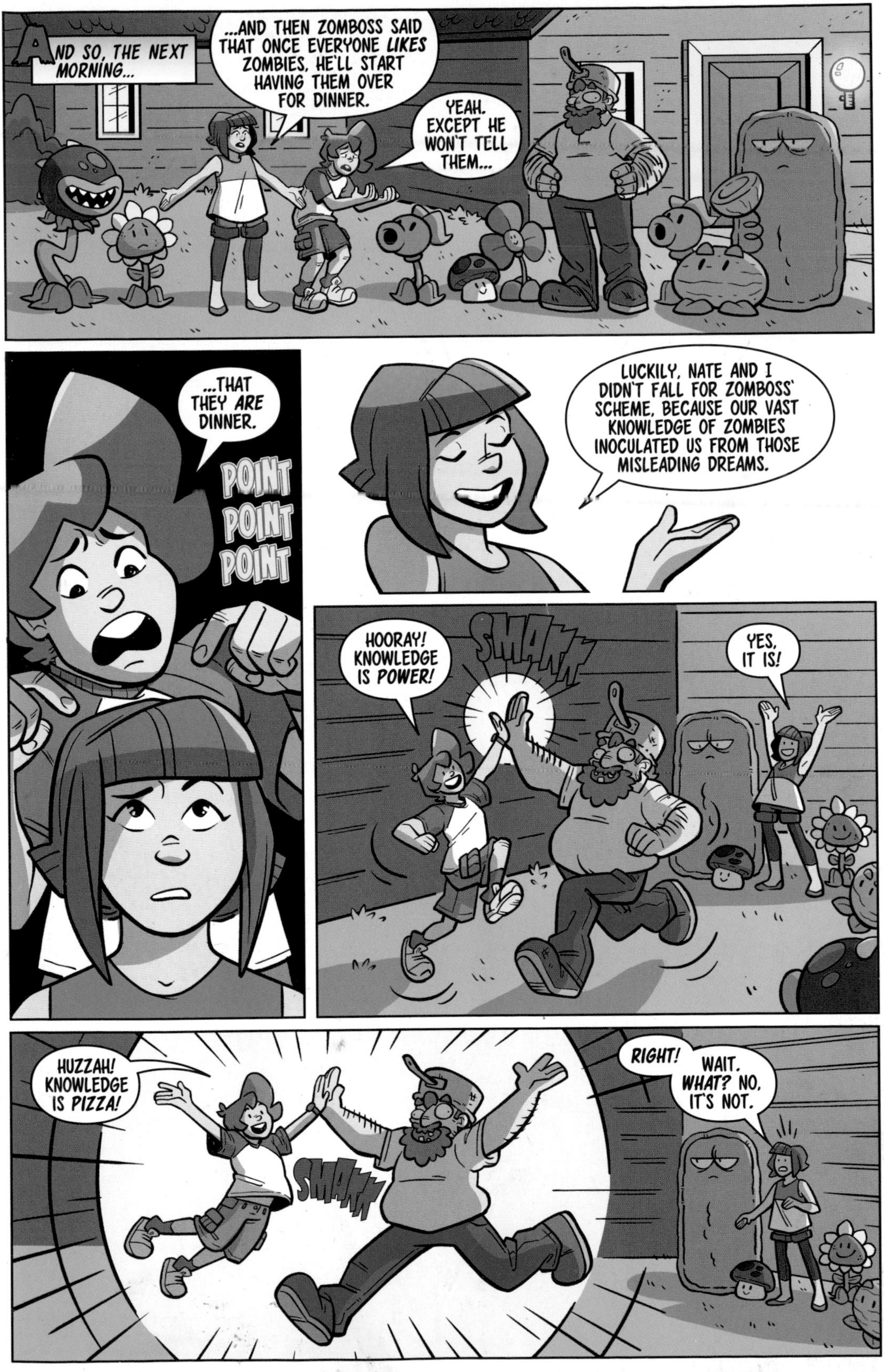
AND SO, THE NEXT MORNING...
...AND THEN ZOMBOSS SAID THAT ONCE EVERYONE LIKES ZOMBIES, HE'LL START HAVING THEM OVER FOR DINNER.
YEAH. EXCEPT HE WON'T TELL THEM...
...THAT THEY ARE DINNER.
POINT POINT POINT
LUCKILY, NATE AND I DIDN'T FALL FOR ZOMBOSS' SCHEME, BECAUSE OUR VAST KNOWLEDGE OF ZOMBIES INOCULATED US FROM THOSE MISLEADING DREAMS.
HOORAY! KNOWLEDGE IS POWER!
SMAKK
YES, IT IS!
HUZZAH! KNOWLEDGE IS PIZZA!
SMAKK
RIGHT!
WAIT. WHAT? NO, IT'S NOT.

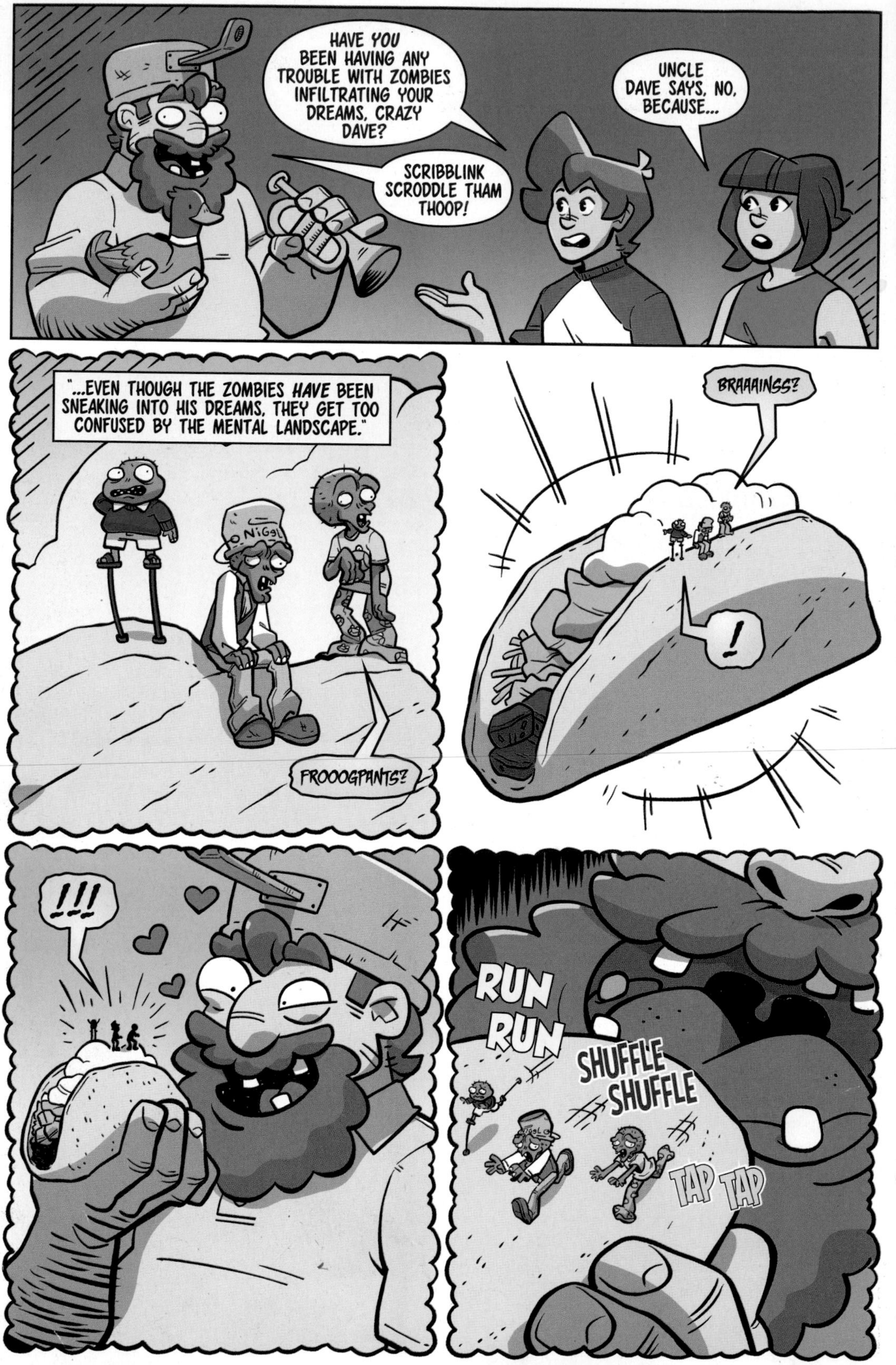
HAVE YOU BEEN HAVING ANY TROUBLE WITH ZOMBIES INFILTRATING YOUR DREAMS, CRAZY DAVE?
SCRIBBLINK SCRODDLE THAM THOOP!
UNCLE DAVE SAYS, NO, BECAUSE...
"...EVEN THOUGH THE ZOMBIES HAVE BEEN SNEAKING INTO HIS DREAMS, THEY GET TOO CONFUSED BY THE MENTAL LANDSCAPE."
NiGgL
FROOOGPANTS?
BRAAAINSS?
!
!!!
RUN
RUN
SHUFFLE
SHUFFLE
TAP TAP

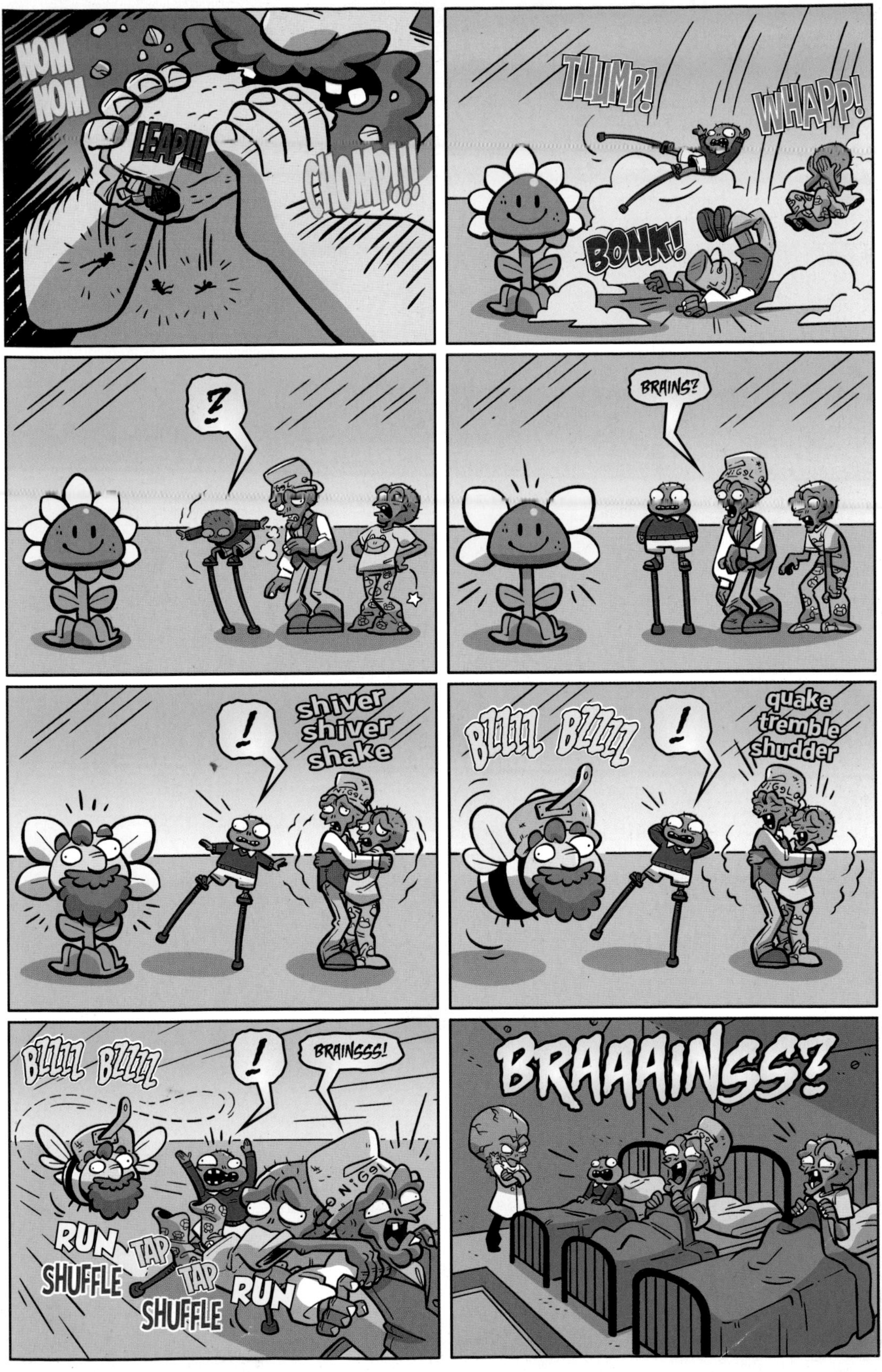
NOM NOM
LEAP!!!
CHOMP!!!
THUMP!
WHAPP!
BONK!
?
BRAINS?
!
shiver shiver shake
BZZZZ BZZZZ
!
quake tremble shudder
BZZZZ BZZZZ
!
BRAINSSS!
RUN
SHUFFLE
TAP
TAP
RUN
SHUFFLE
BRAAAINSS?

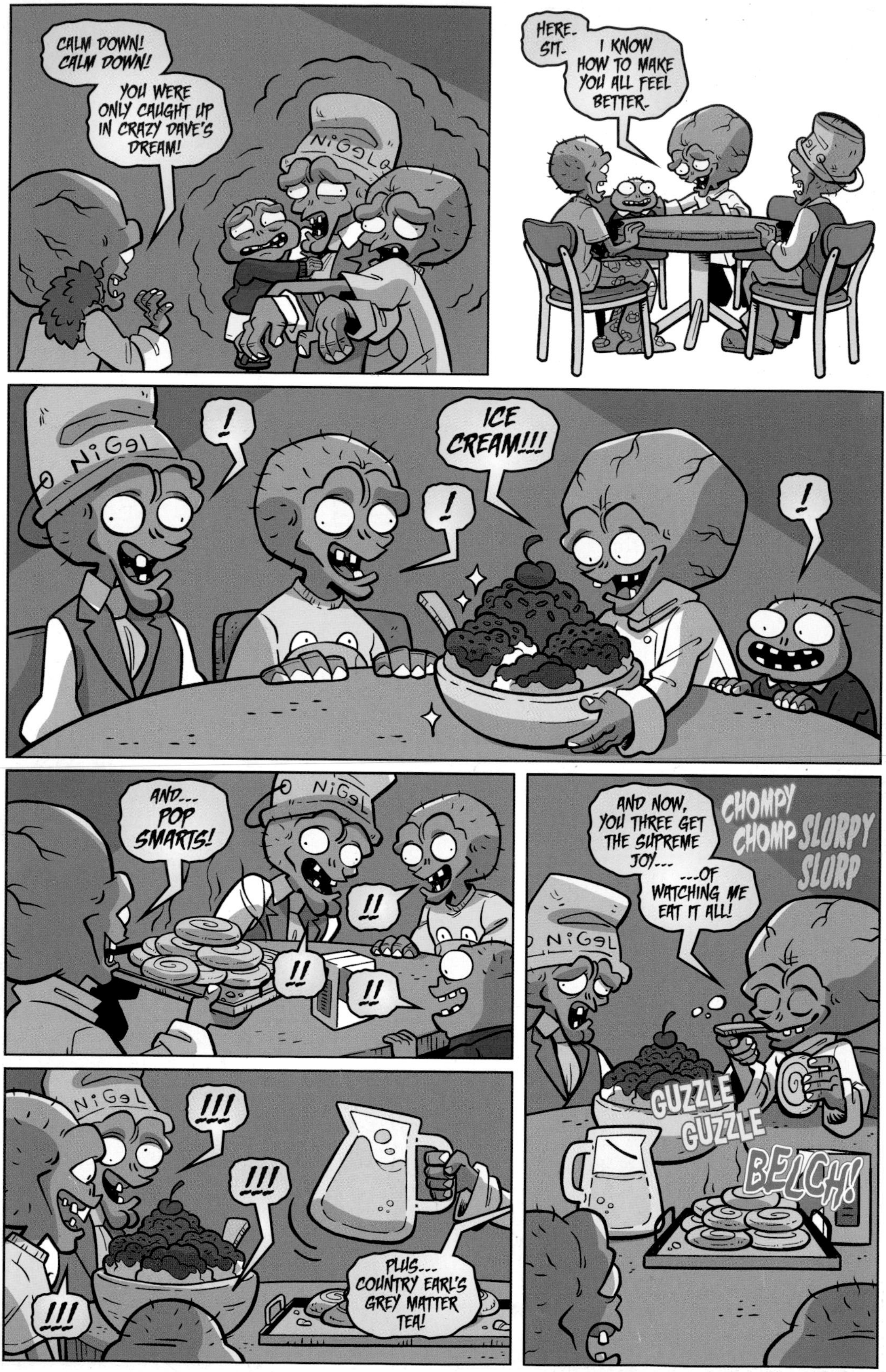
CALM DOWN! CALM DOWN!
YOU WERE ONLY CAUGHT UP IN CRAZY DAVE'S DREAM!
NiGeL
HERE. SIT.
I KNOW HOW TO MAKE YOU ALL FEEL BETTER.
NiGeL
!
ICE CREAM!!!
!
!
AND... POP SMARTS!
NiGeL
!!
!!
!!
AND NOW, YOU THREE GET THE SUPREME JOY...
...OF WATCHING ME EAT IT ALL!
CHOMPY CHOMP
SLURPY SLURP
NiGeL
GUZZLE GUZZLE
BELCH!
NiGeL
!!!
!!!
!!!
PLUS... COUNTRY EARL'S GREY MATTER TEA!

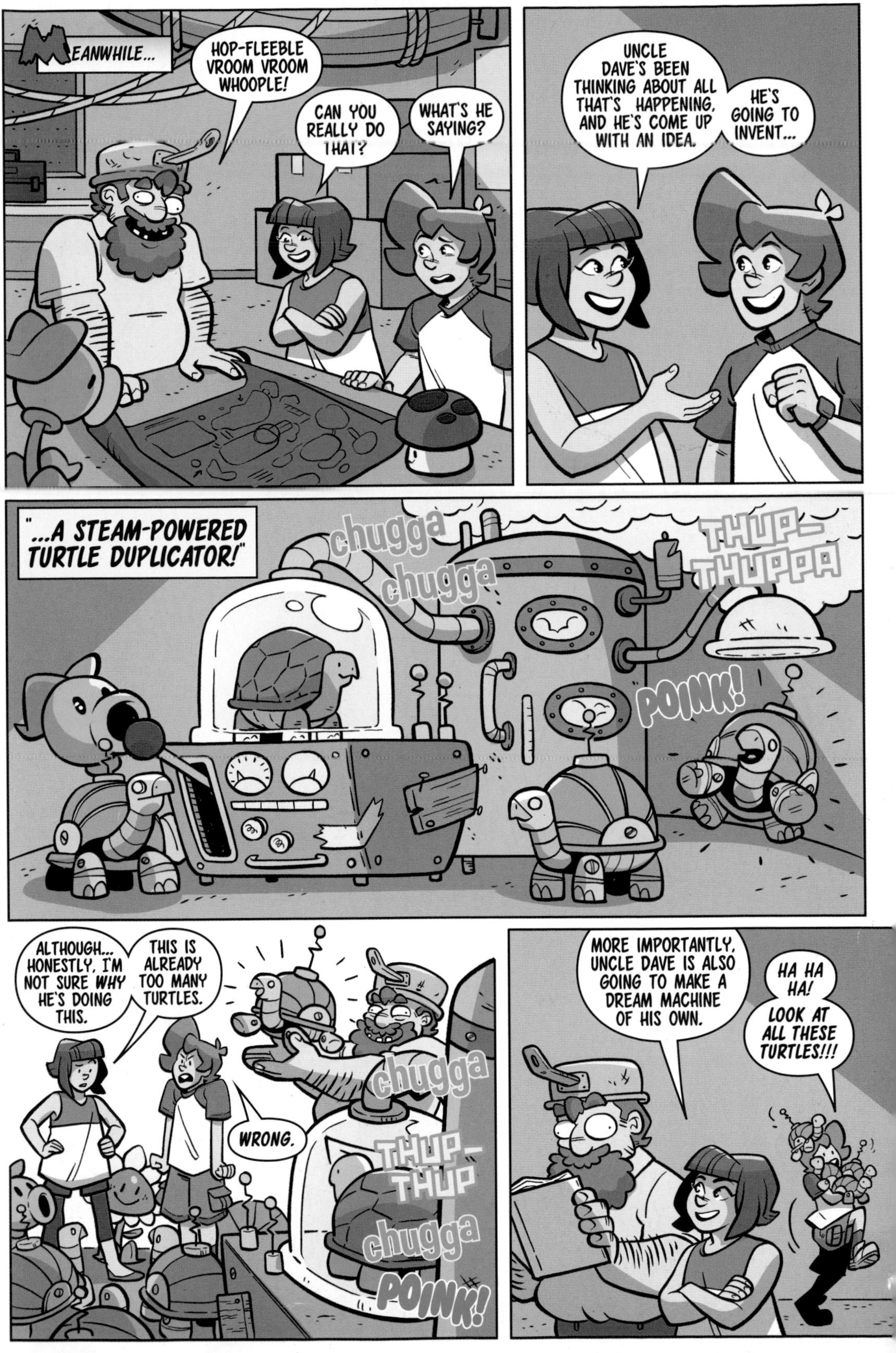
MEANWHILE...
HOP-FLEEBLE VROOM VROOM WHOOPLE!
CAN YOU REALLY DO THAT?
WHAT'S HE SAYING?
UNCLE DAVE'S BEEN THINKING ABOUT ALL THAT'S HAPPENING, AND HE'S COME UP WITH AN IDEA.
HE'S GOING TO INVENT...
"...A STEAM-POWERED TURTLE DUPLICATOR!"
chugga
chugga
THUP-THUPPA
POINK!
ALTHOUGH... HONESTLY, I'M NOT SURE WHY HE'S DOING THIS.
THIS IS ALREADY TOO MANY TURTLES.
WRONG.
chugga
THUP-THUP
chugga
POINK!
MORE IMPORTANTLY, UNCLE DAVE IS ALSO GOING TO MAKE A DREAM MACHINE OF HIS OWN.
HA HA HA!
LOOK AT ALL THESE TURTLES!!!

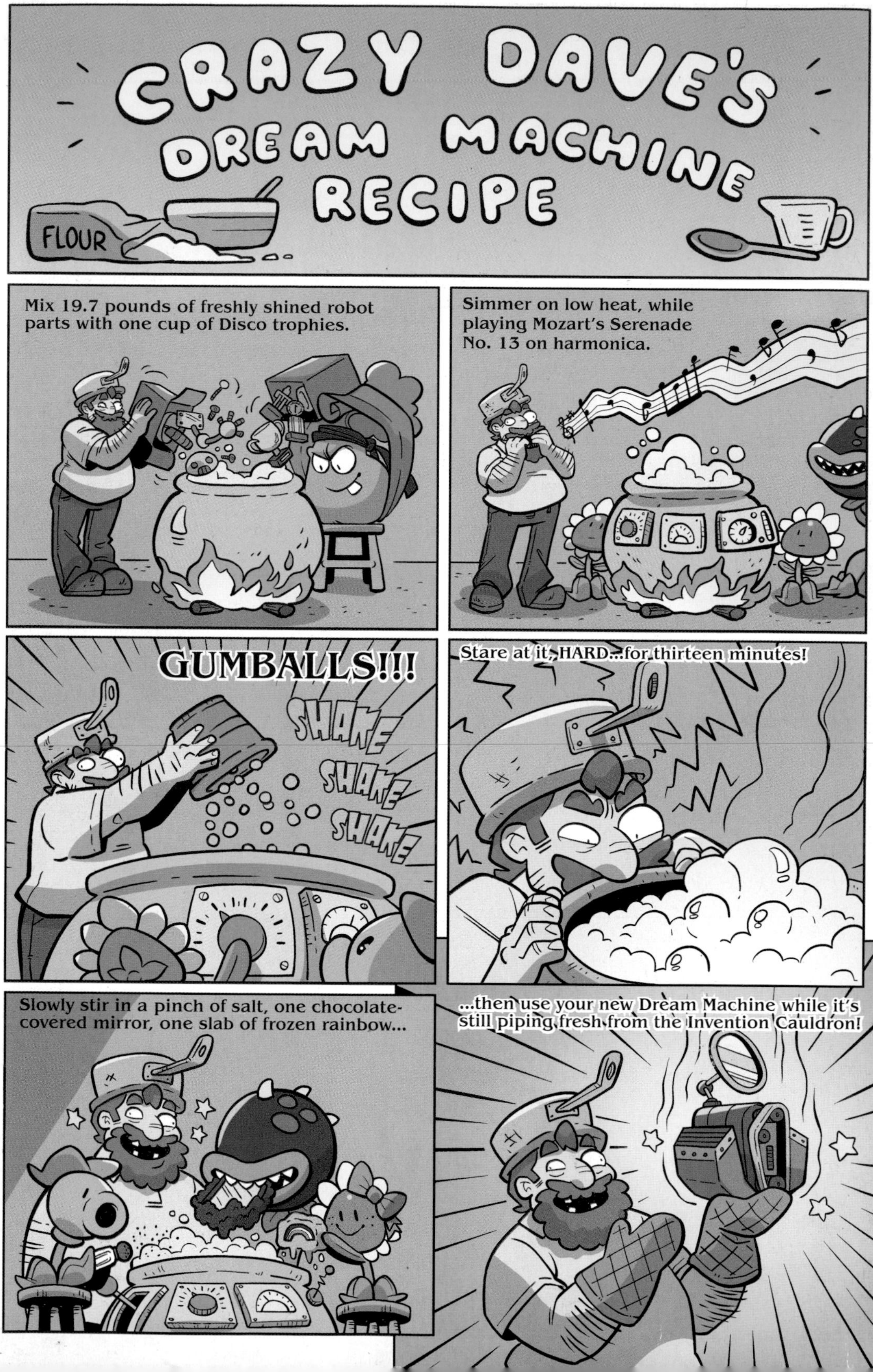
CRAZY DAVE'S DREAM MACHINE RECIPE
FLOUR
Mix 19.7 pounds of freshly shined robot parts with one cup of Disco trophies.
Simmer on low heat, while playing Mozart's Serenade No. 13 on harmonica.
GUMBALLS!!!
SHAKE
SHAKE
SHAKE
Stare at it, HARD...for thirteen minutes!
Slowly stir in a pinch of salt, one chocolate-covered mirror, one slab of frozen rainbow...
...then use your new Dream Machine while it's still piping fresh from the Invention Cauldron!

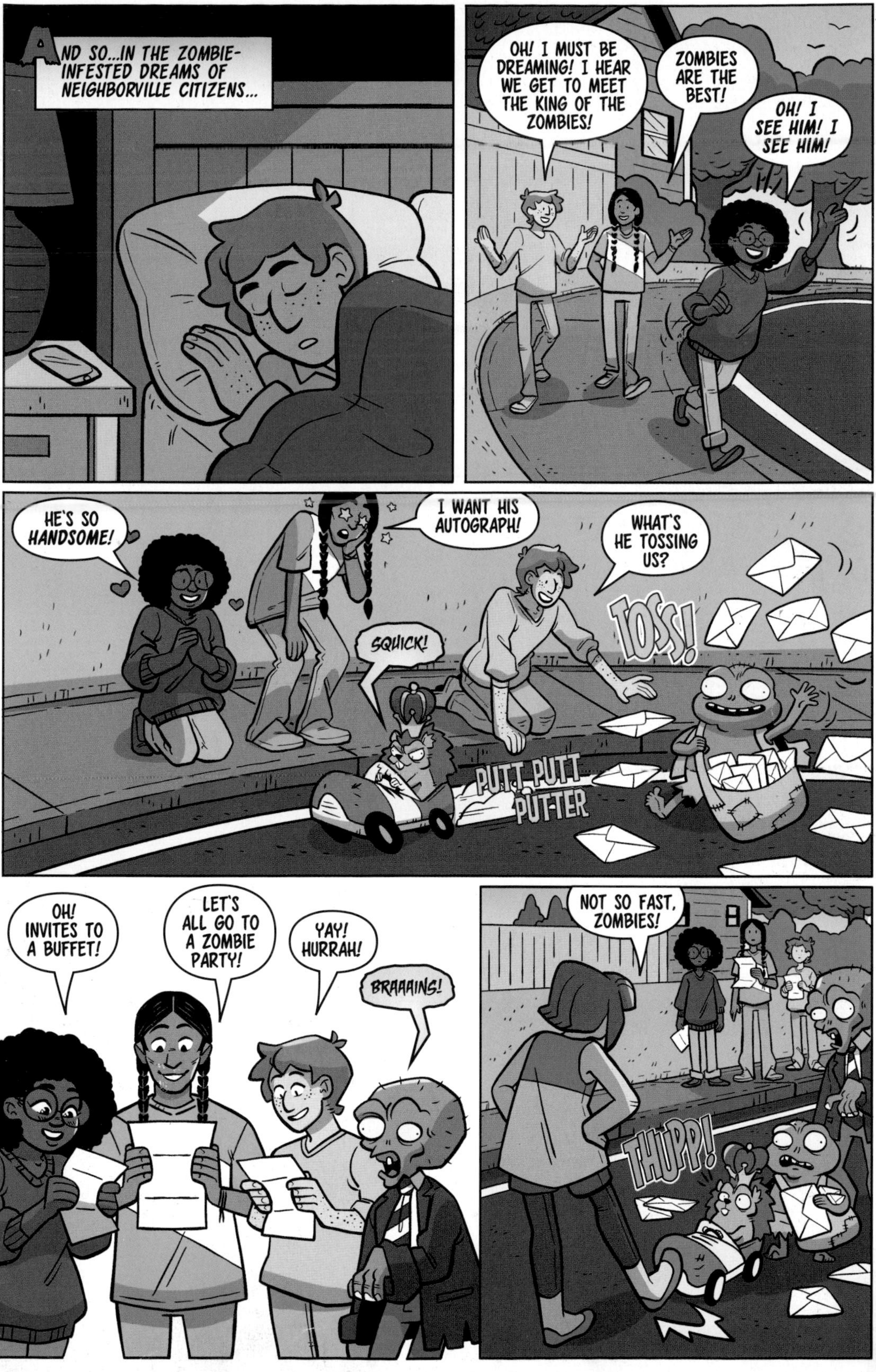
AND SO...IN THE ZOMBIE-INFESTED DREAMS OF NEIGHBORVILLE CITIZENS...
OH! I MUST BE DREAMING! I HEAR WE GET TO MEET THE KING OF THE ZOMBIES!
ZOMBIES ARE THE BEST!
OH! I SEE HIM! I SEE HIM!
HE'S SO HANDSOME!
I WANT HIS AUTOGRAPH!
WHAT'S HE TOSSING US?
TOSS!
SQUICK!
PUTT PUTT PUTTER
OH! INVITES TO A BUFFET!
LET'S ALL GO TO A ZOMBIE PARTY!
YAY! HURRAH!
BRAAAINS!
NOT SO FAST, ZOMBIES!
THUPP!

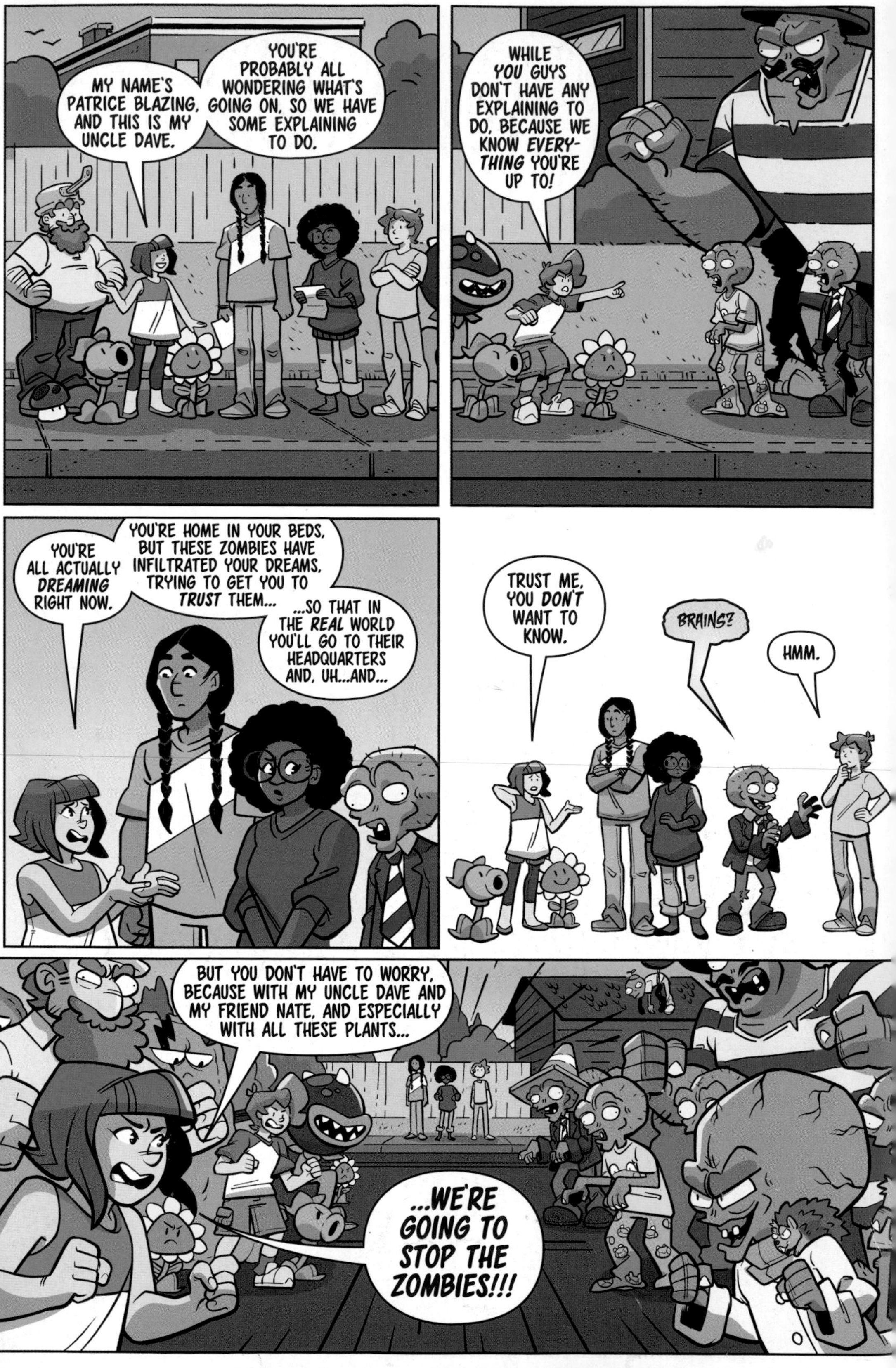
MY NAME'S PATRICE BLAZING, AND THIS IS MY UNCLE DAVE.
YOU'RE PROBABLY ALL WONDERING WHAT'S GOING ON, SO WE HAVE SOME EXPLAINING TO DO.
WHILE *YOU* GUYS DON'T HAVE ANY EXPLAINING TO DO, BECAUSE WE KNOW *EVERY-THING* YOU'RE UP TO!
YOU'RE ALL ACTUALLY *DREAMING* RIGHT NOW.
YOU'RE HOME IN YOUR BEDS, BUT THESE ZOMBIES HAVE INFILTRATED YOUR DREAMS, TRYING TO GET YOU TO *TRUST* THEM...
...SO THAT IN THE *REAL* WORLD YOU'LL GO TO THEIR HEADQUARTERS AND, UH...AND...
TRUST ME, YOU *DON'T* WANT TO KNOW.
BRAINS?
HMM.
BUT YOU DON'T HAVE TO WORRY, BECAUSE WITH MY UNCLE DAVE AND MY FRIEND NATE, AND ESPECIALLY WITH ALL THESE PLANTS...
...WE'RE GOING TO STOP THE ZOMBIES!!!

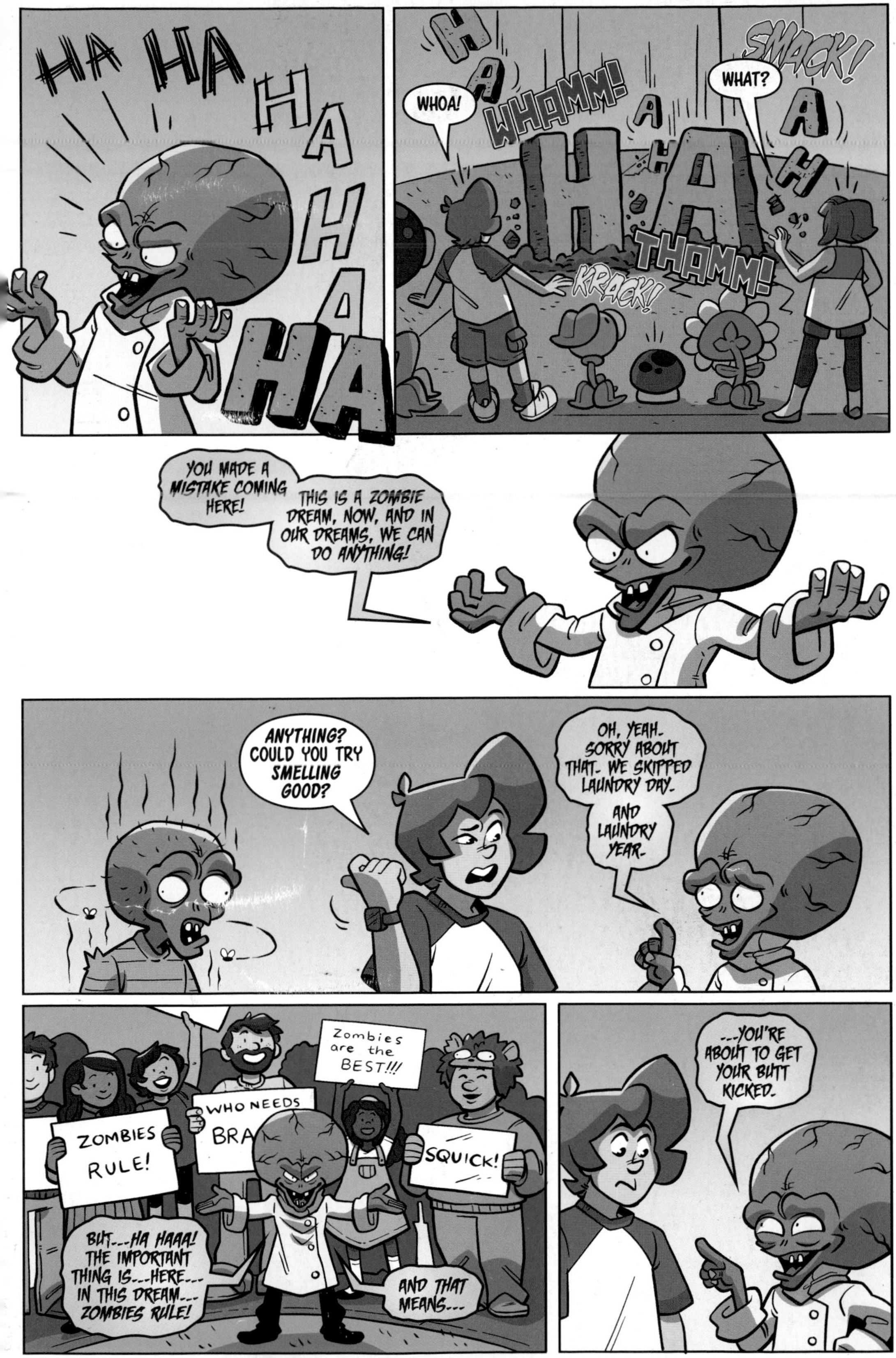
HA HA HA HA HA HA HA HA
WHOA!
H A WHAMM! A H H A
WHAT?
SMACK!
A H
KRACK!
THAMM!
YOU MADE A MISTAKE COMING HERE!
THIS IS A ZOMBIE DREAM, NOW, AND IN OUR DREAMS, WE CAN DO ANYTHING!
ANYTHING? COULD YOU TRY SMELLING GOOD?
OH, YEAH. SORRY ABOUT THAT. WE SKIPPED LAUNDRY DAY.
AND LAUNDRY YEAR.
Zombies are the BEST!!!
WHO NEEDS BRA
ZOMBIES RULE!
SQUICK!
BUT...HA HAAA! THE IMPORTANT THING IS...HERE... IN THIS DREAM... ZOMBIES RULE!
AND THAT MEANS...
...YOU'RE ABOUT TO GET YOUR BUTT KICKED.

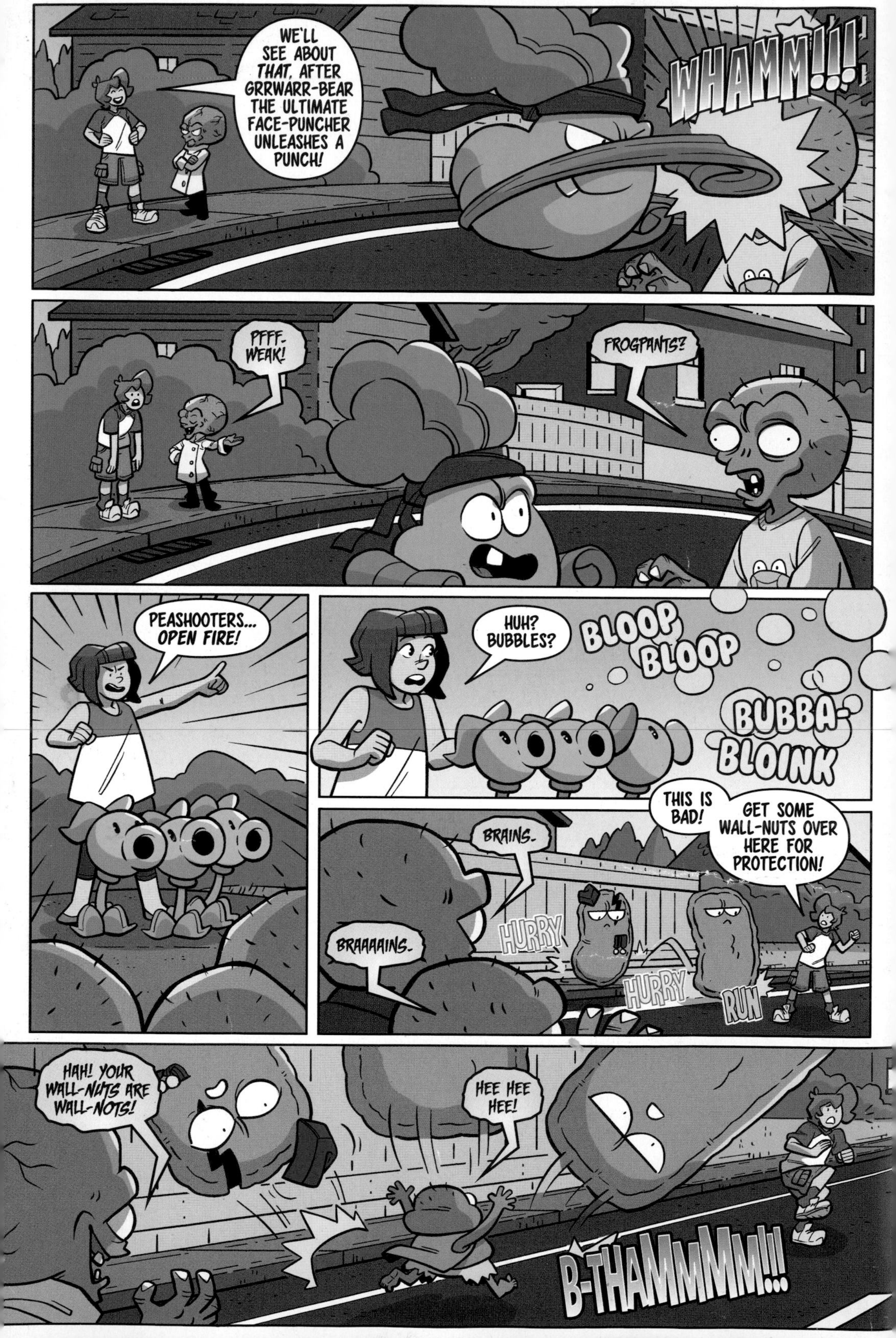
WE'LL SEE ABOUT THAT, AFTER GRRWARR-BEAR THE ULTIMATE FACE-PUNCHER UNLEASHES A PUNCH!
WHAMM!!!
PFFF. WEAK!
FROGPANTS?
PEASHOOTERS... OPEN FIRE!
HUH? BUBBLES?
BLOOP BLOOP
BUBBA-BLOINK
BRAINS.
BRAAAAINS.
HURRY
HURRY
RUN
THIS IS BAD!
GET SOME WALL-NUTS OVER HERE FOR PROTECTION!
HAH! YOUR WALL-NUTS ARE WALL-NOTS!
HEE HEE HEE!
B-THAMMMM!!!

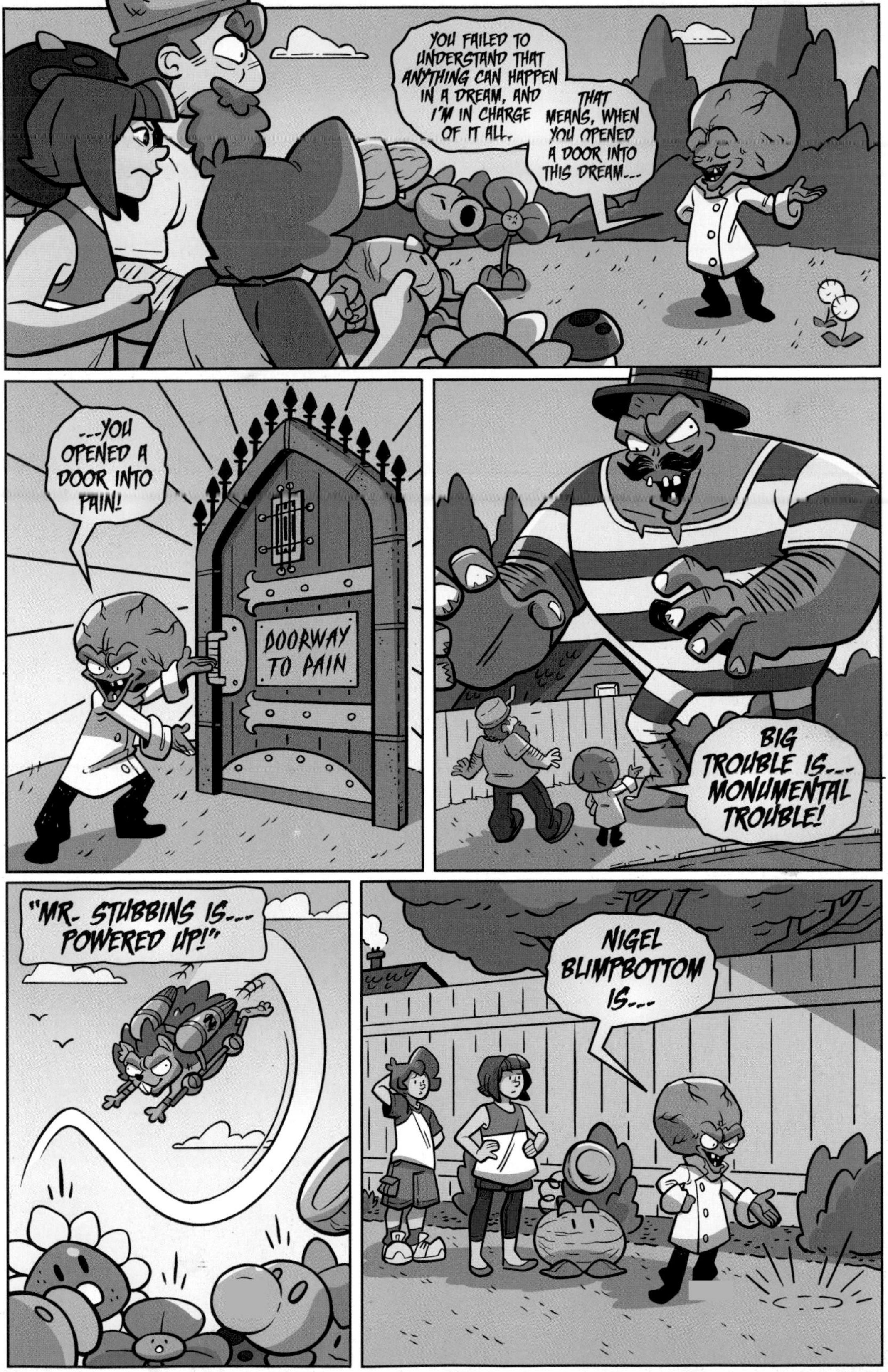
YOU FAILED TO UNDERSTAND THAT ANYTHING CAN HAPPEN IN A DREAM, AND I'M IN CHARGE OF IT ALL...
THAT MEANS, WHEN YOU OPENED A DOOR INTO THIS DREAM...
...YOU OPENED A DOOR INTO PAIN!
DOORWAY TO PAIN
BIG TROUBLE IS... MONUMENTAL TROUBLE!
"MR. STUBBINS IS... POWERED UP!"
NIGEL BLIMPBOTTOM IS...

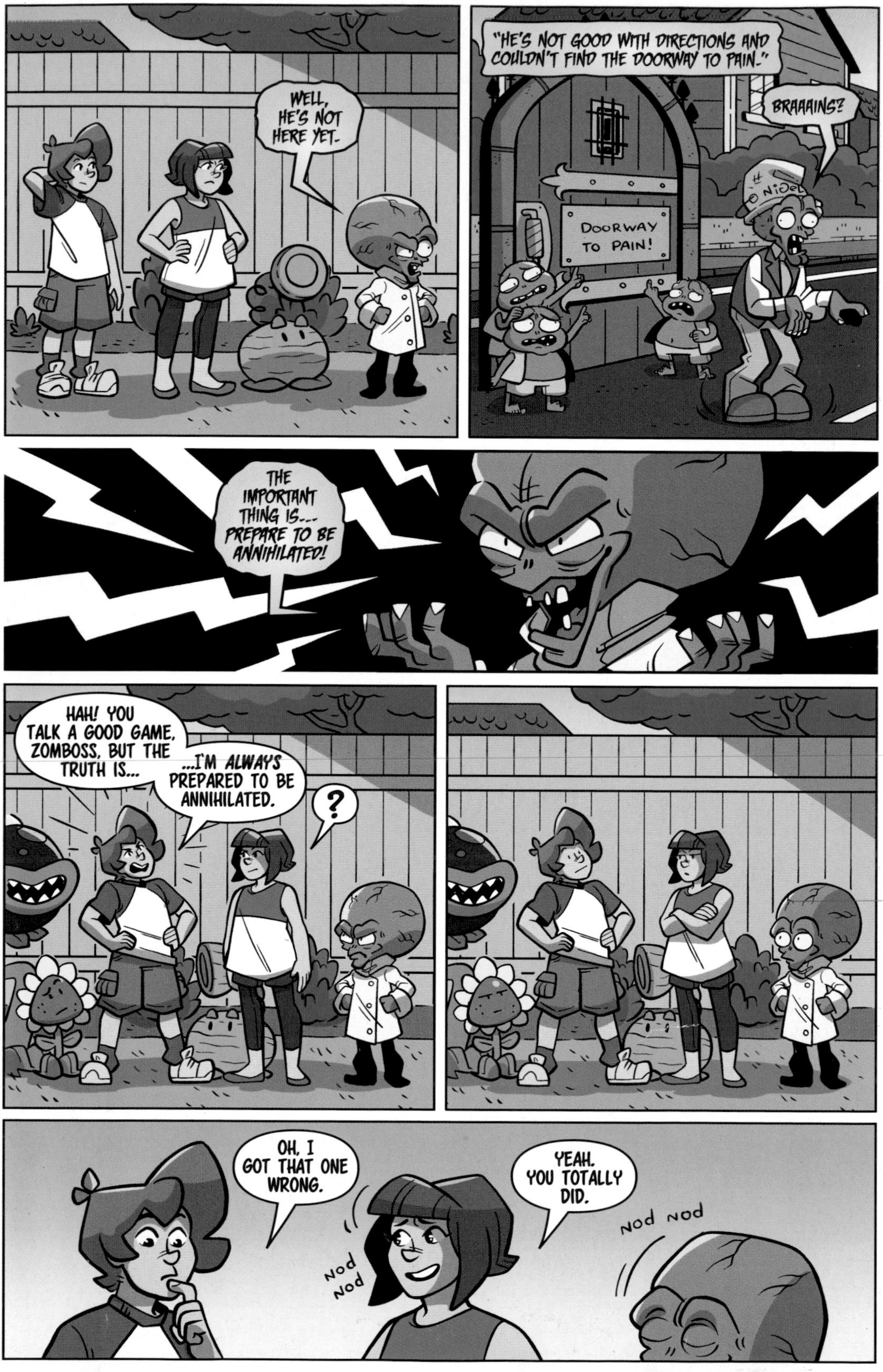
WELL, HE'S NOT HERE YET.
"HE'S NOT GOOD WITH DIRECTIONS AND COULDN'T FIND THE DOORWAY TO PAIN."
DOORWAY TO PAIN!
BRAAAINS?
NIGEL
THE IMPORTANT THING IS... PREPARE TO BE ANNIHILATED!
HAH! YOU TALK A GOOD GAME, ZOMBOSS, BUT THE TRUTH IS...
...I'M ALWAYS PREPARED TO BE ANNIHILATED.
?
OH, I GOT THAT ONE WRONG.
YEAH. YOU TOTALLY DID.
Nod Nod
Nod Nod

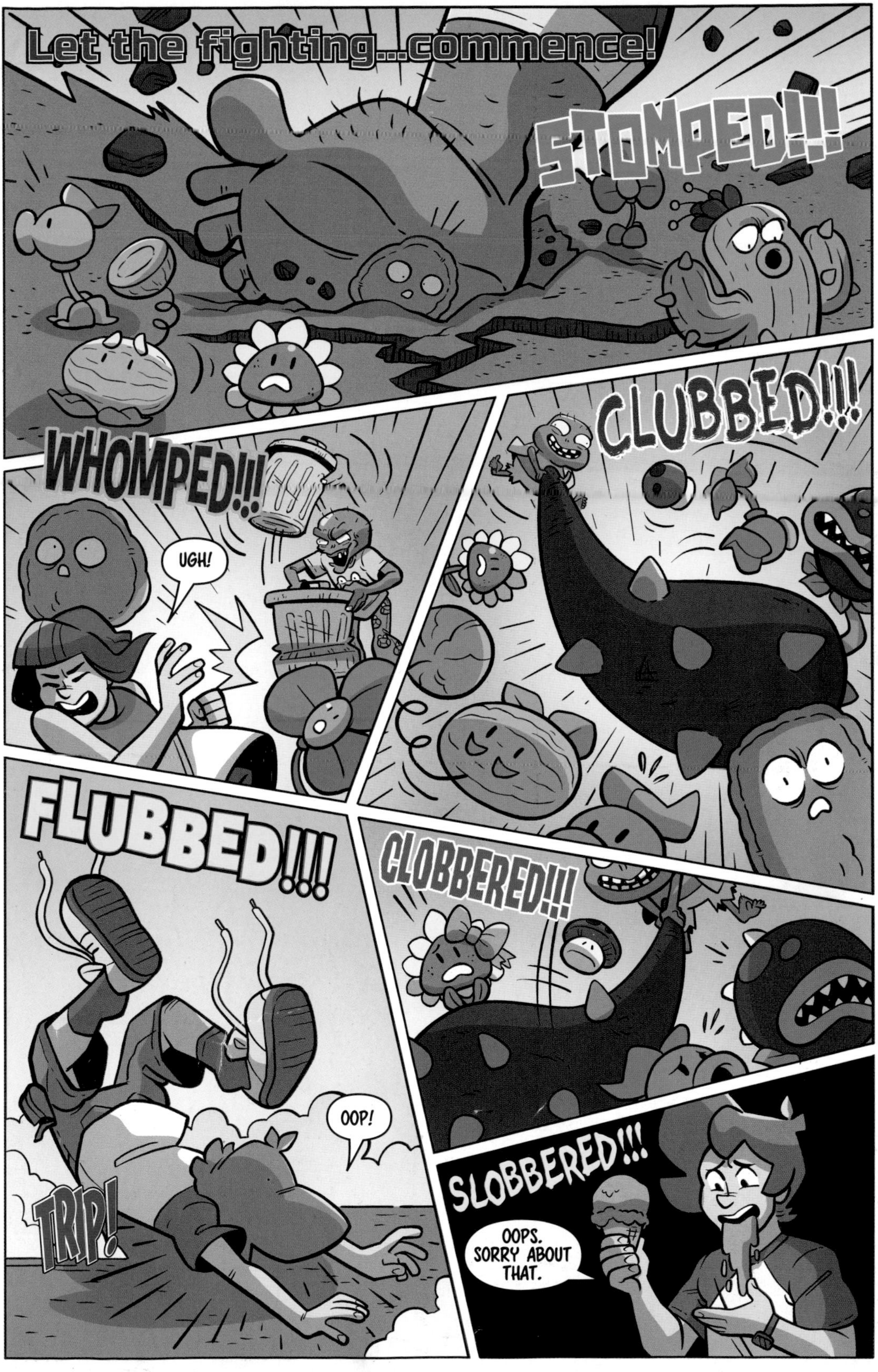
Let the fighting...commence!
STOMPED!!!
WHOMPED!!!
UGH!
CLUBBED!!!
FLUBBED!!!
OOP!
TRIP!
CLOBBERED!!!
SLOBBERED!!!
OOPS. SORRY ABOUT THAT.

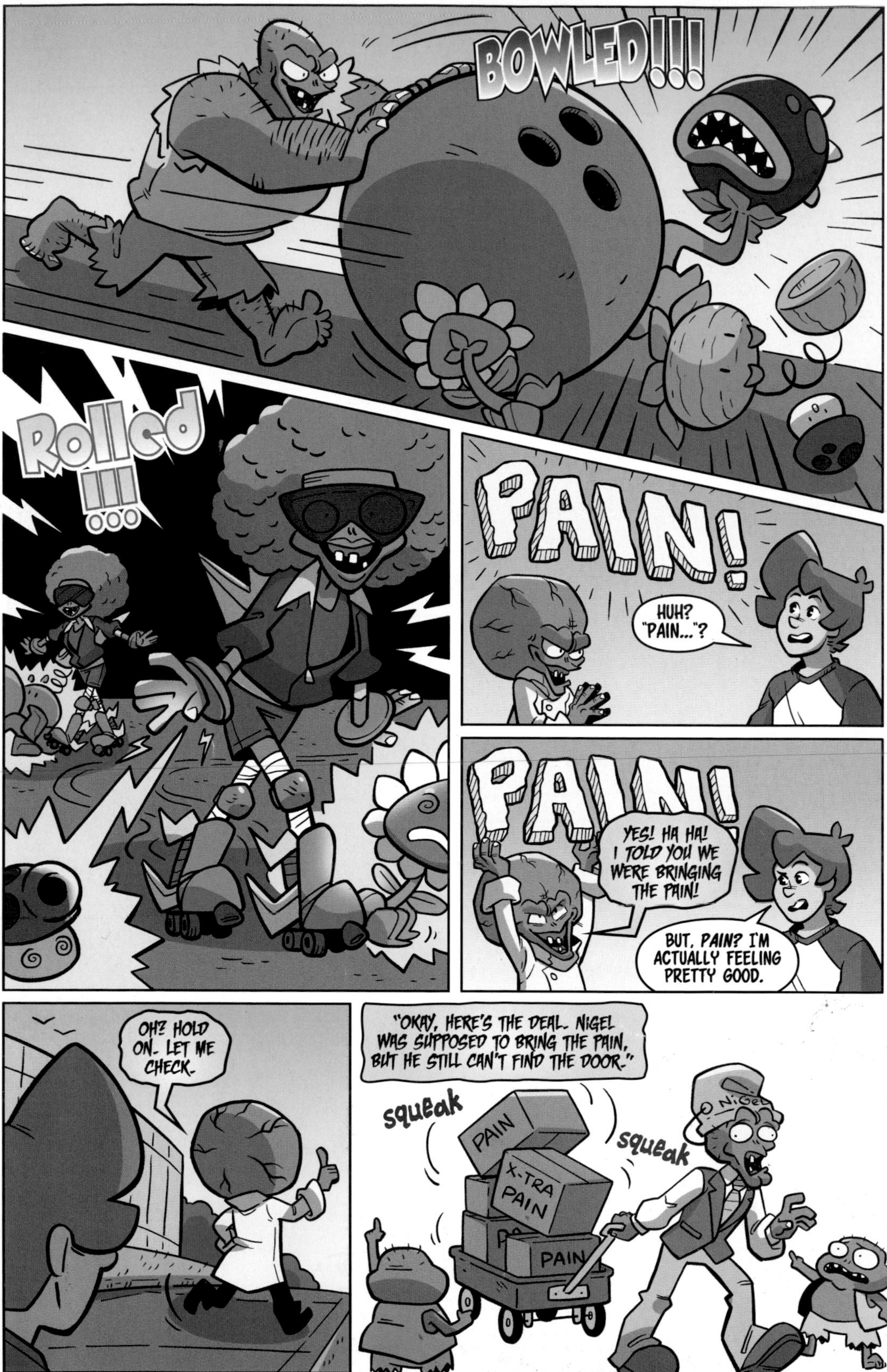
BOWLED!!!
Rolled!!!
PAIN!
HUH? "PAIN..."?
PAIN!
YES! HA HA! I TOLD YOU WE WERE BRINGING THE PAIN!
BUT, PAIN? I'M ACTUALLY FEELING PRETTY GOOD.
OH? HOLD ON. LET ME CHECK.
"OKAY, HERE'S THE DEAL. NIGEL WAS SUPPOSED TO BRING THE PAIN, BUT HE STILL CAN'T FIND THE DOOR."
squeak
squeak
PAIN
X-TRA PAIN
PAIN
NIGEL

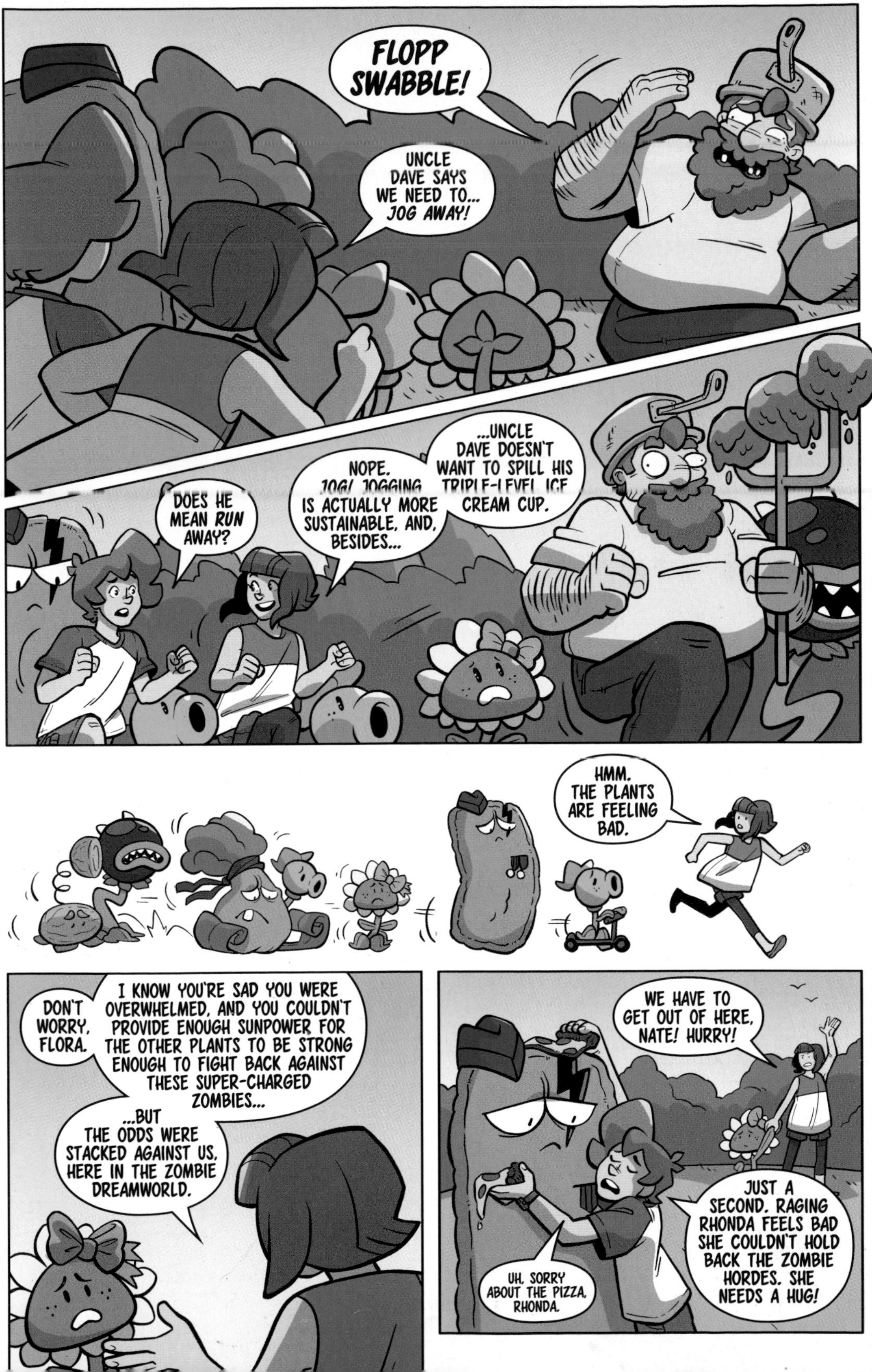
FLOPP SWABBLE!
UNCLE DAVE SAYS WE NEED TO... JOG AWAY!
DOES HE MEAN RUN AWAY?
NOPE. JOG! JOGGING IS ACTUALLY MORE SUSTAINABLE, AND, BESIDES...
...UNCLE DAVE DOESN'T WANT TO SPILL HIS TRIPLE-LEVEL ICE CREAM CUP.
HMM. THE PLANTS ARE FEELING BAD.
DON'T WORRY, FLORA.
I KNOW YOU'RE SAD YOU WERE OVERWHELMED, AND YOU COULDN'T PROVIDE ENOUGH SUNPOWER FOR THE OTHER PLANTS TO BE STRONG ENOUGH TO FIGHT BACK AGAINST THESE SUPER-CHARGED ZOMBIES...
...BUT THE ODDS WERE STACKED AGAINST US, HERE IN THE ZOMBIE DREAMWORLD.
WE HAVE TO GET OUT OF HERE, NATE! HURRY!
JUST A SECOND. RAGING RHONDA FEELS BAD SHE COULDN'T HOLD BACK THE ZOMBIE HORDES. SHE NEEDS A HUG!
UH, SORRY ABOUT THE PIZZA, RHONDA.

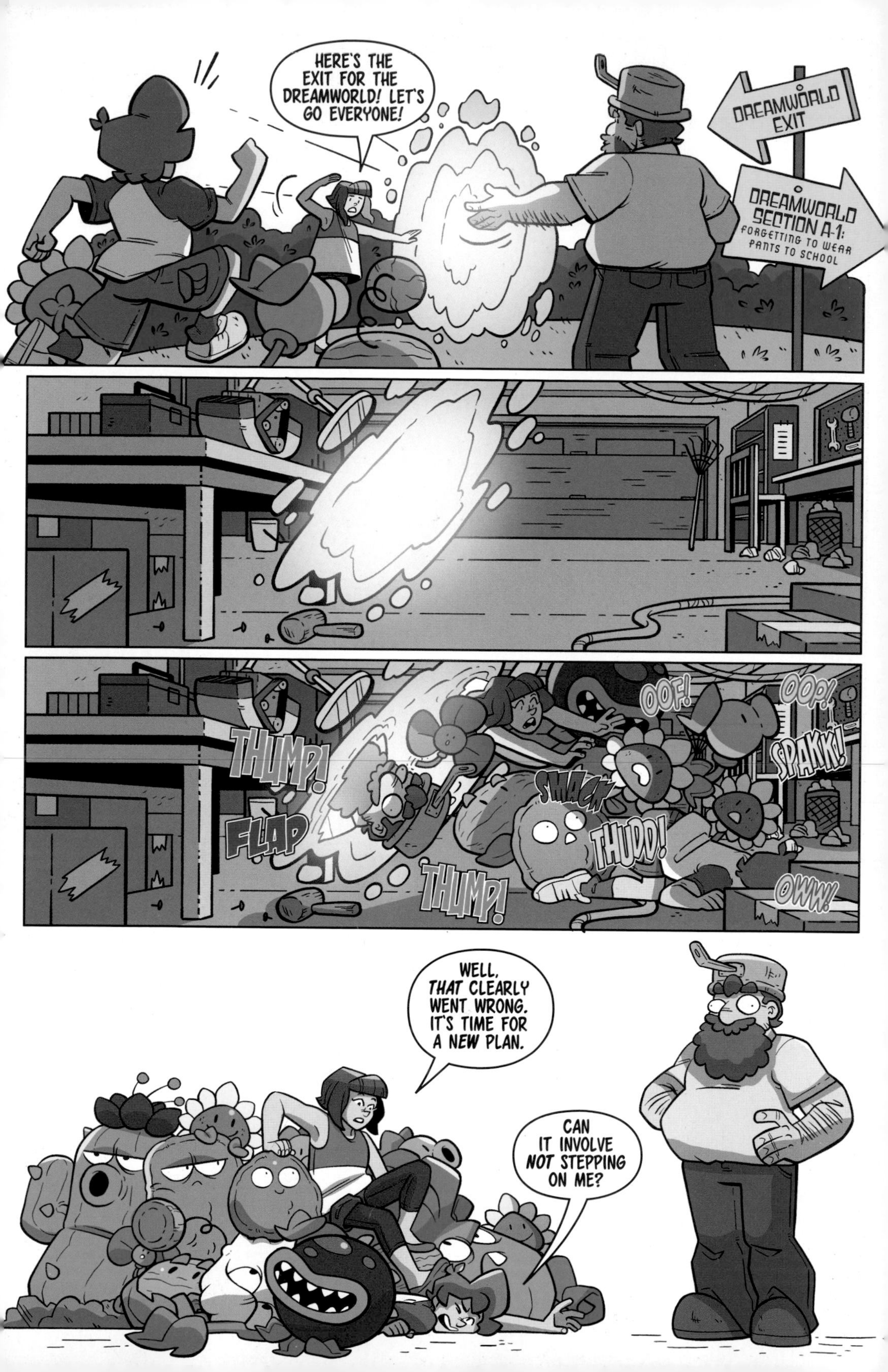
HERE'S THE EXIT FOR THE DREAMWORLD! LET'S GO EVERYONE!
DREAMWORLD EXIT
DREAMWORLD SECTION A-1: FORGETTING TO WEAR PANTS TO SCHOOL
THUMP!
OOF!
OOP!
SPAKK!
SMACK
FLAP
THUDD!
THUMP!
OWW!
WELL, THAT CLEARLY WENT WRONG. IT'S TIME FOR A NEW PLAN.
CAN IT INVOLVE NOT STEPPING ON ME?

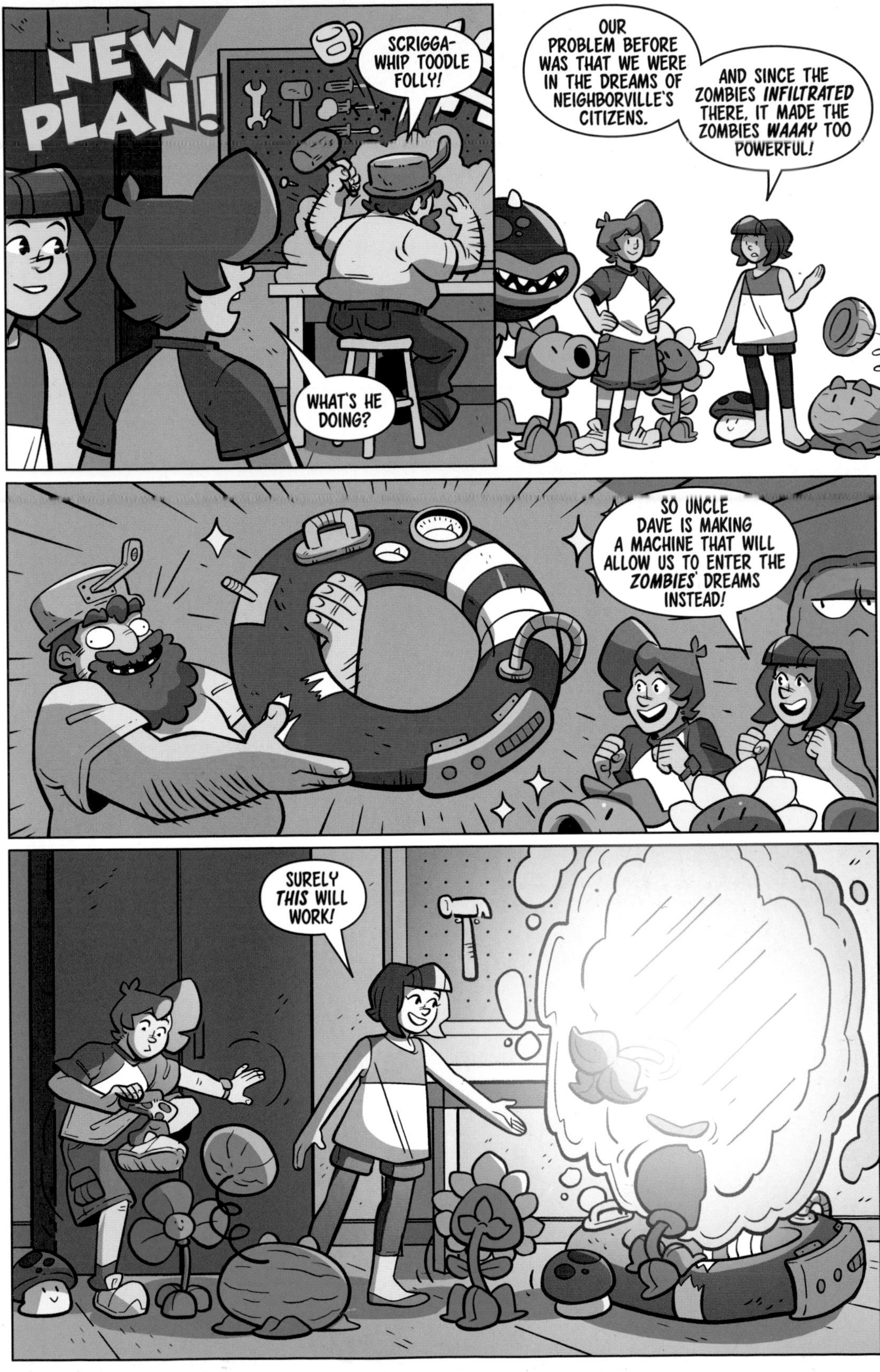
NEW PLAN!
SCRIGGA-WHIP TOODLE FOLLY!
WHAT'S HE DOING?
OUR PROBLEM BEFORE WAS THAT WE WERE IN THE DREAMS OF NEIGHBORVILLE'S CITIZENS.
AND SINCE THE ZOMBIES *INFILTRATED* THERE, IT MADE THE ZOMBIES *WAAAY* TOO POWERFUL!
SO UNCLE DAVE IS MAKING A MACHINE THAT WILL ALLOW US TO ENTER THE *ZOMBIES'* DREAMS INSTEAD!
SURELY *THIS* WILL WORK!

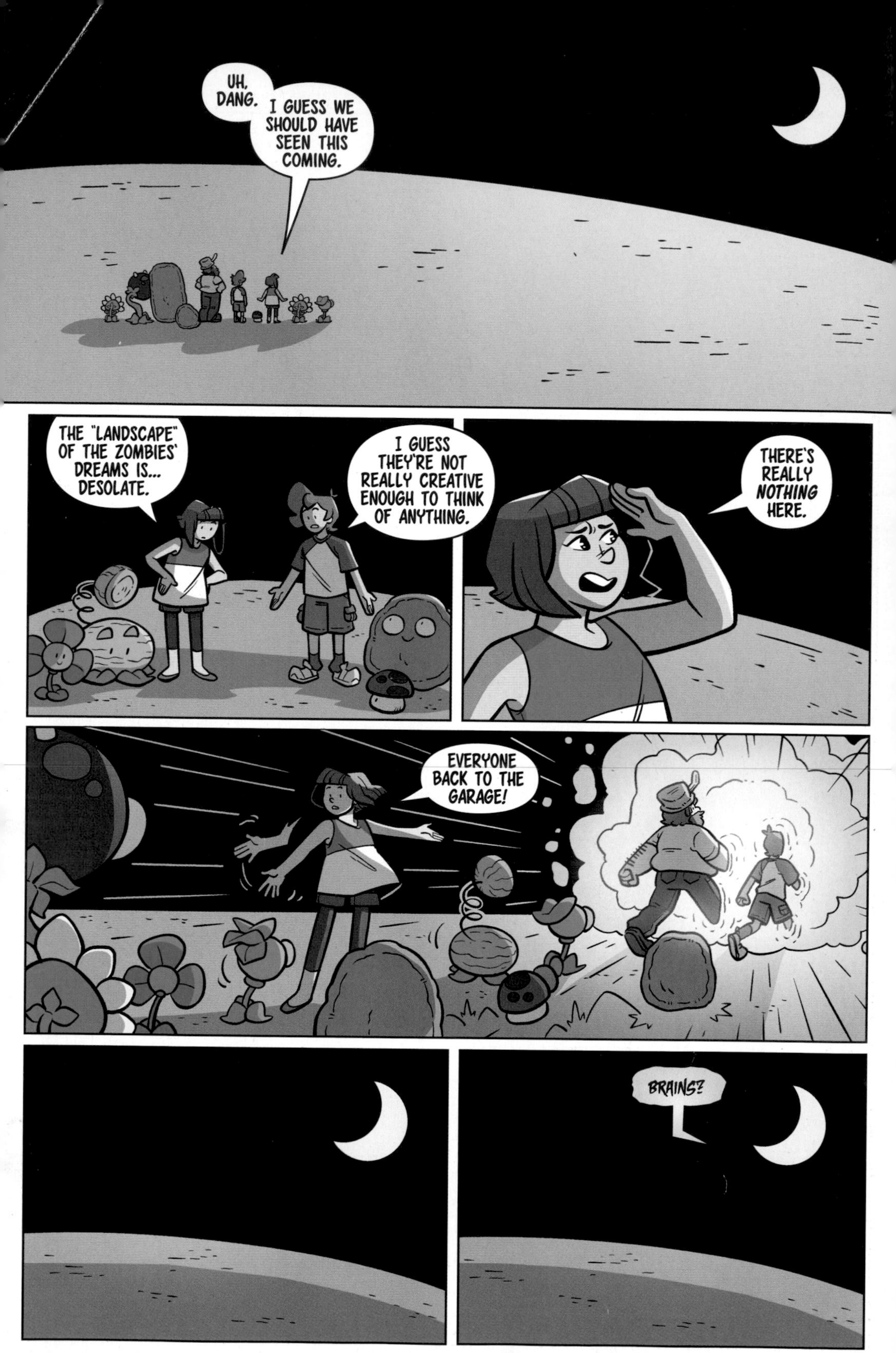
UH, DANG.
I GUESS WE SHOULD HAVE SEEN THIS COMING.
THE "LANDSCAPE" OF THE ZOMBIES' DREAMS IS... DESOLATE.
I GUESS THEY'RE NOT REALLY CREATIVE ENOUGH TO THINK OF ANYTHING.
THERE'S REALLY NOTHING HERE.
EVERYONE BACK TO THE GARAGE!
BRAINS?

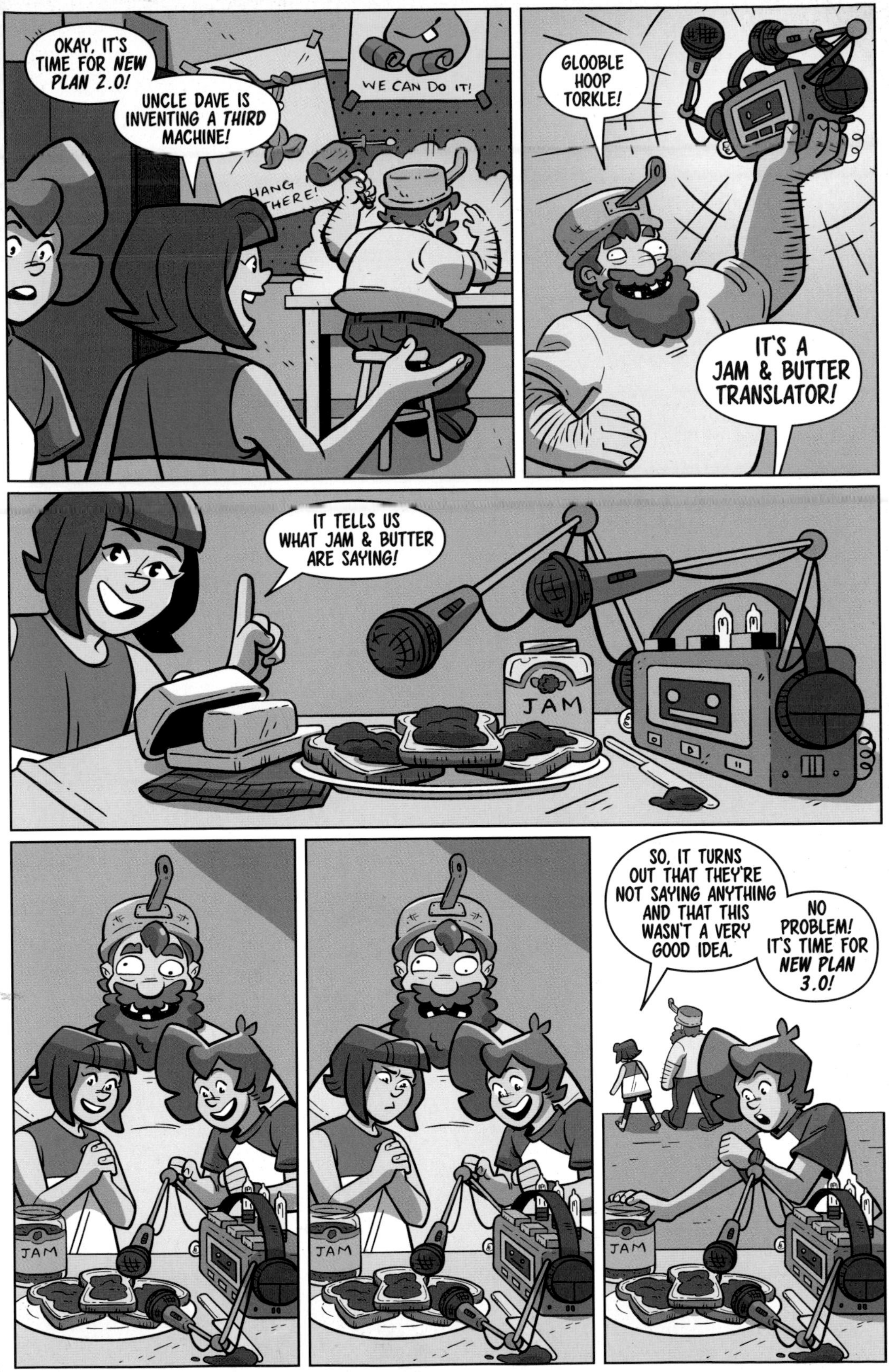
OKAY, IT'S TIME FOR NEW PLAN 2.0!
UNCLE DAVE IS INVENTING A THIRD MACHINE!
WE CAN DO IT!
HANG IN THERE!
GLOOBLE HOOP TORKLE!
IT'S A JAM & BUTTER TRANSLATOR!
IT TELLS US WHAT JAM & BUTTER ARE SAYING!
JAM
SO, IT TURNS OUT THAT THEY'RE NOT SAYING ANYTHING AND THAT THIS WASN'T A VERY GOOD IDEA.
NO PROBLEM! IT'S TIME FOR NEW PLAN 3.0!

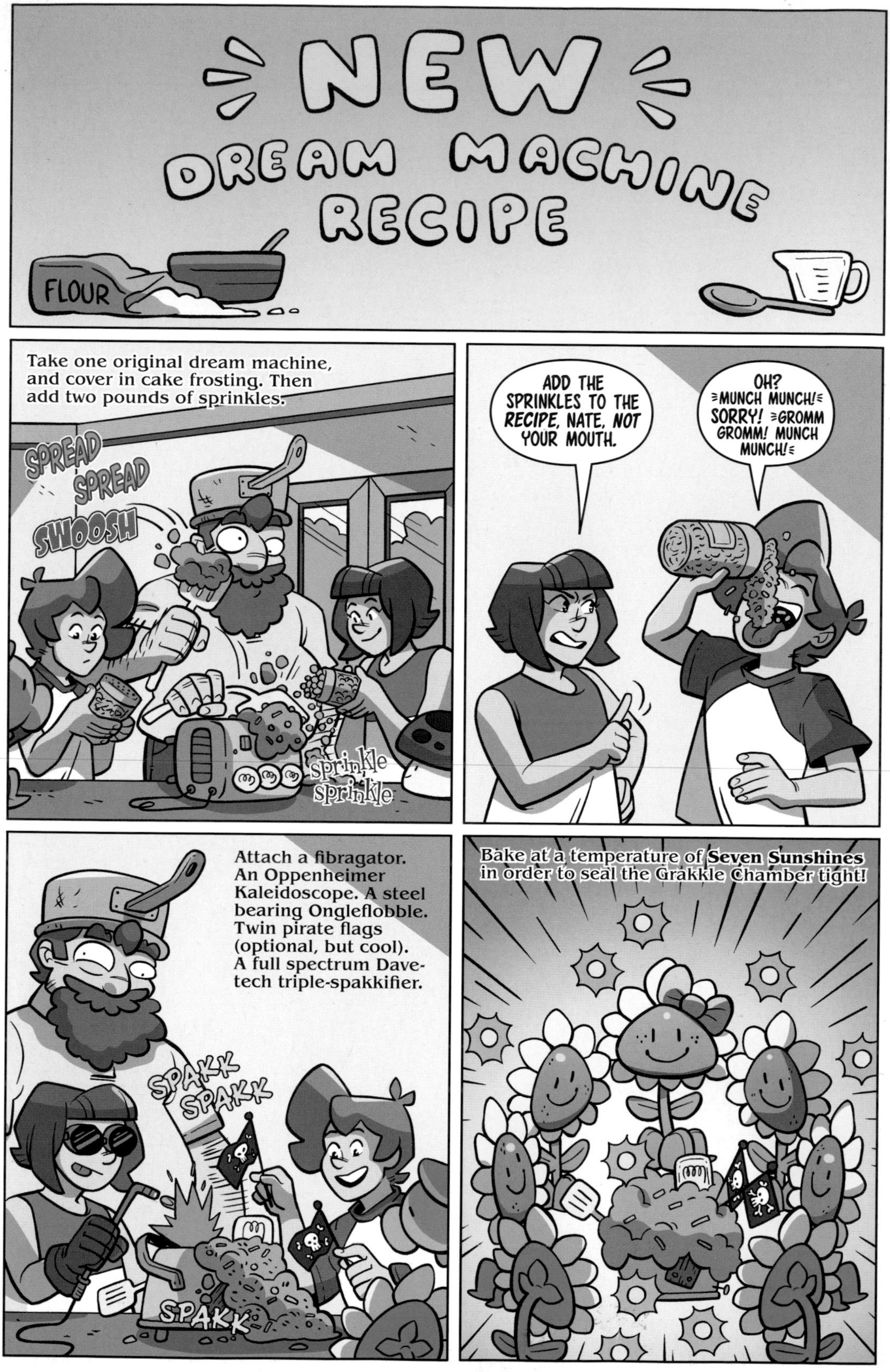
NEW
DREAM MACHINE
RECIPE
FLOUR
Take one original dream machine, and cover in cake frosting. Then add two pounds of sprinkles.
SPREAD
SPREAD
SWOOSH
sprinkle
sprinkle
ADD THE SPRINKLES TO THE *RECIPE*, NATE, *NOT* YOUR MOUTH.
OH? MUNCH MUNCH! SORRY! GROMM GROMM! MUNCH MUNCH!
Attach a fibragator. An Oppenheimer Kaleidoscope. A steel bearing Ongleflobble. Twin pirate flags (optional, but cool). A full spectrum Davetech triple-spakkifier.
SPAKK
SPAKK
SPAKK
Bake at a temperature of **Seven Sunshines** in order to seal the Grakkle Chamber tight!

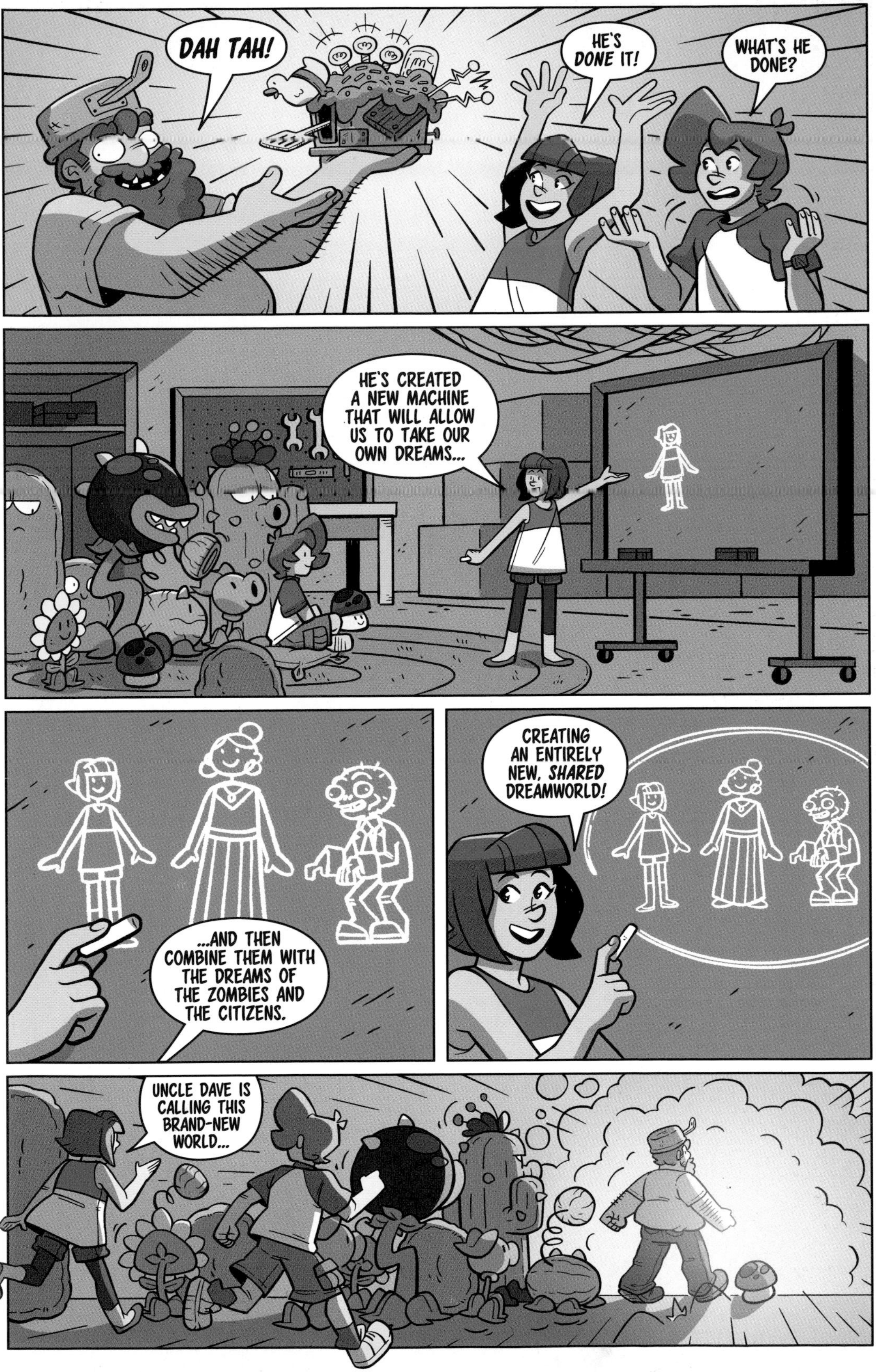
DAH TAH!
HE'S DONE IT!
WHAT'S HE DONE?
HE'S CREATED A NEW MACHINE THAT WILL ALLOW US TO TAKE OUR OWN DREAMS...
...AND THEN COMBINE THEM WITH THE DREAMS OF THE ZOMBIES AND THE CITIZENS.
CREATING AN ENTIRELY NEW, SHARED DREAMWORLD!
UNCLE DAVE IS CALLING THIS BRAND-NEW WORLD...

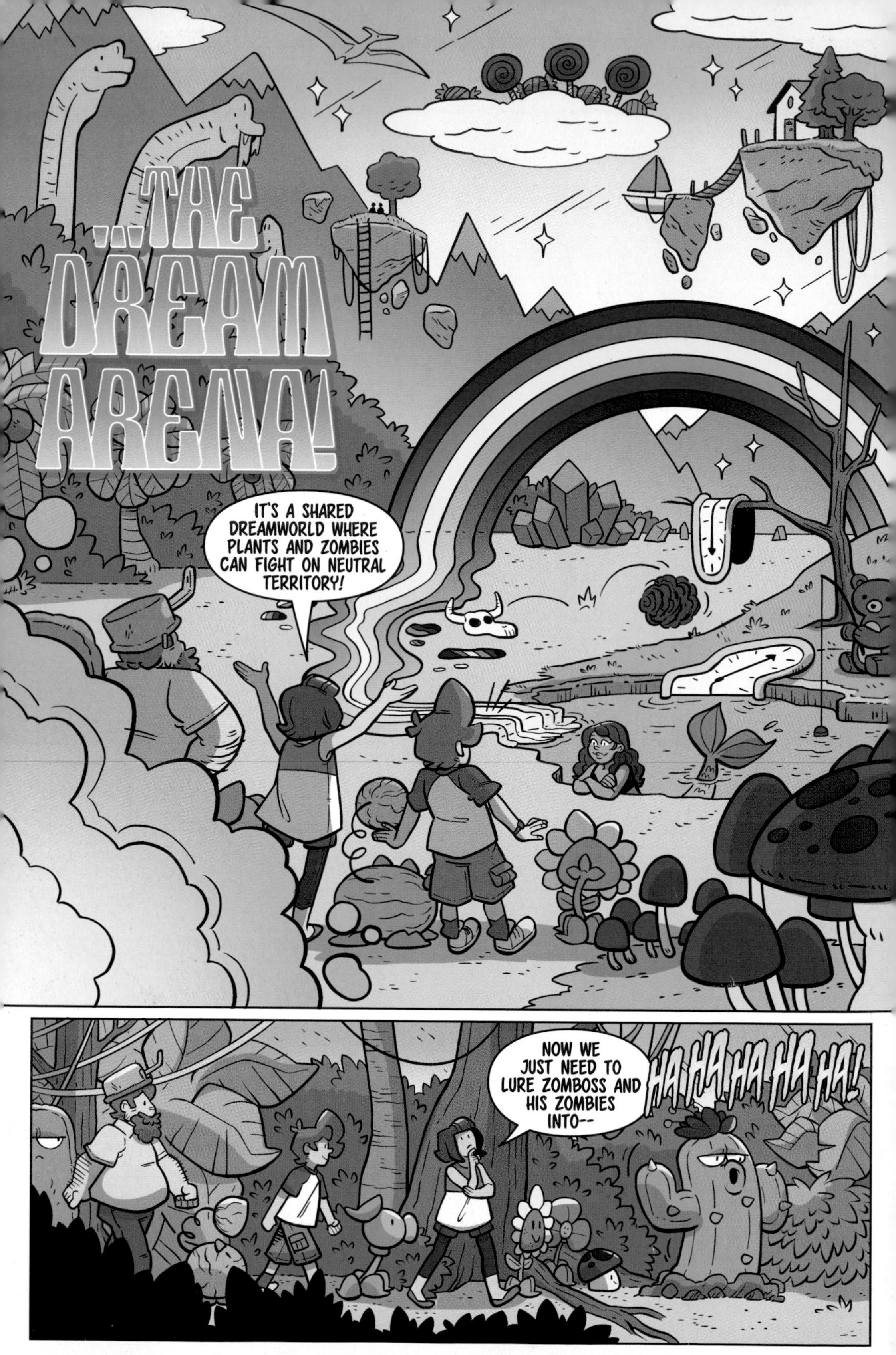

...THE DREAM ARENA!
IT'S A SHARED DREAMWORLD WHERE PLANTS AND ZOMBIES CAN FIGHT ON NEUTRAL TERRITORY!
NOW WE JUST NEED TO LURE ZOMBOSS AND HIS ZOMBIES INTO--
HA HA HA HA HA!

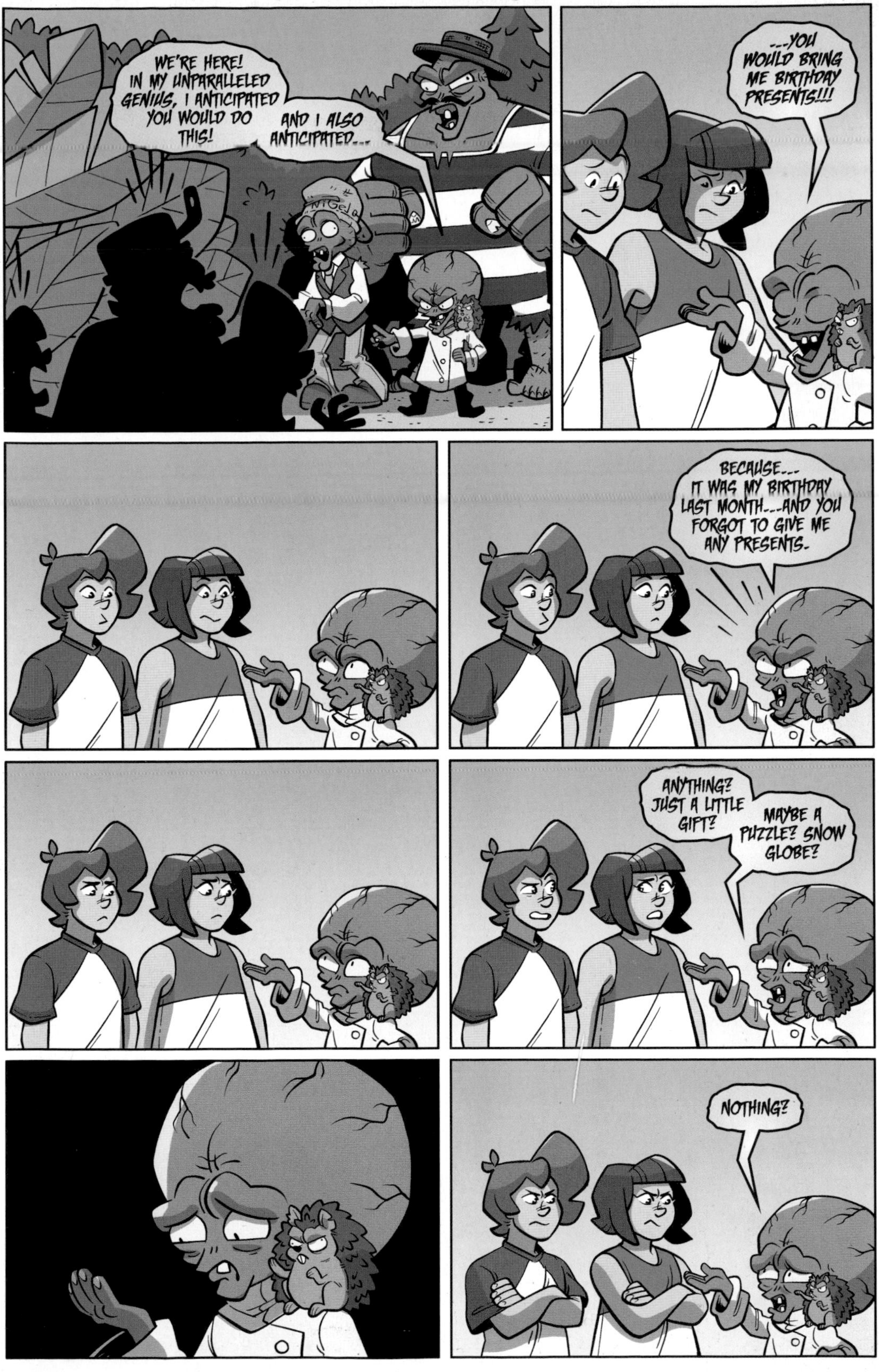
WE'RE HERE! IN MY UNPARALLELED GENIUS, I ANTICIPATED YOU WOULD DO THIS!
AND I ALSO ANTICIPATED...
...YOU WOULD BRING ME BIRTHDAY PRESENTS!!!
BECAUSE... IT WAS MY BIRTHDAY LAST MONTH...AND YOU FORGOT TO GIVE ME ANY PRESENTS.
ANYTHING? JUST A LITTLE GIFT?
MAYBE A PUZZLE? SNOW GLOBE?
NOTHING?

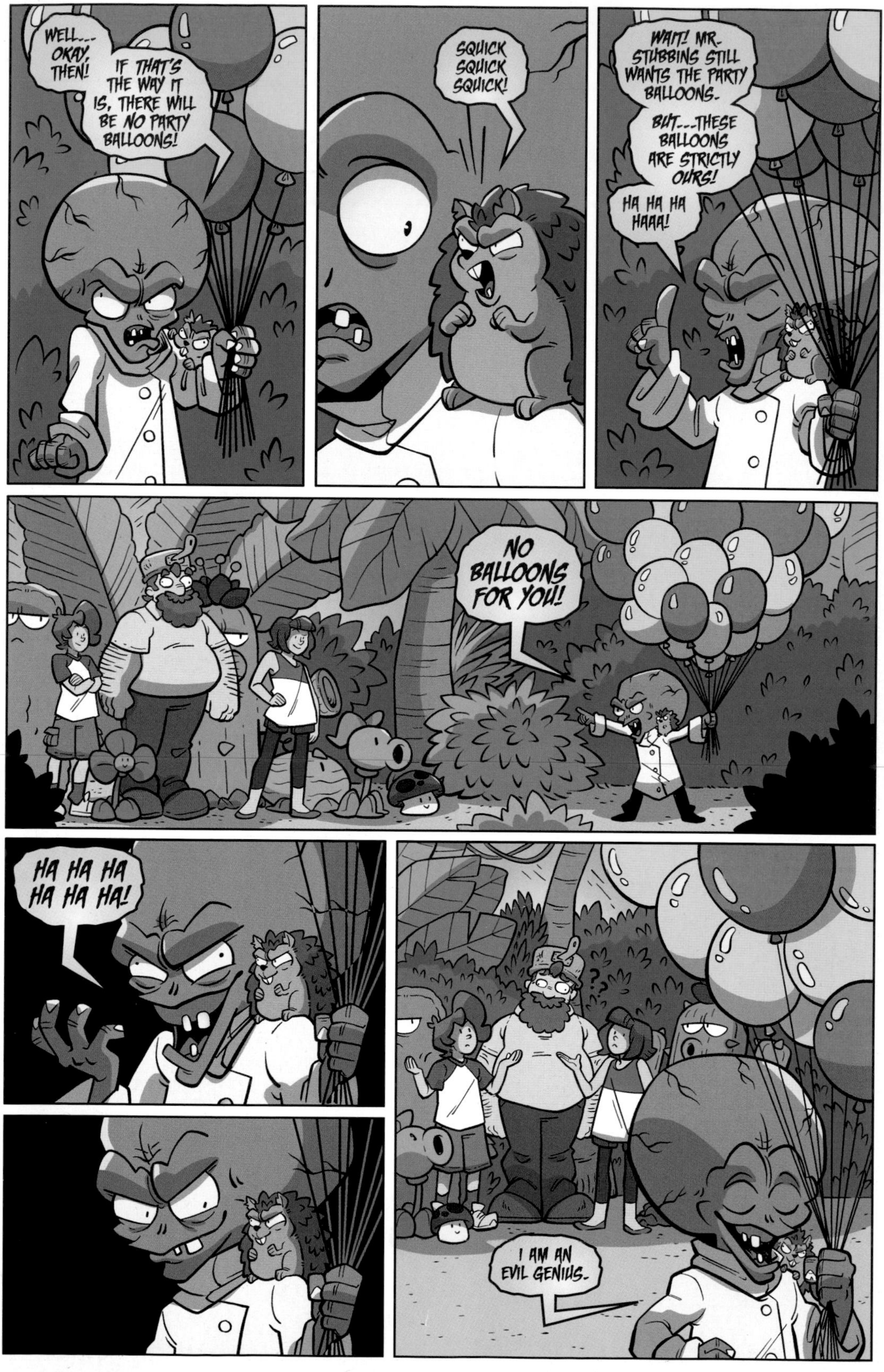
WELL... OKAY, THEN!
IF THAT'S THE WAY IT IS, THERE WILL BE NO PARTY BALLOONS!
SQUICK SQUICK SQUICK!
WAIT! MR. STUBBINS STILL WANTS THE PARTY BALLOONS.
BUT...THESE BALLOONS ARE STRICTLY OURS!
HA HA HA HAAA!
NO BALLOONS FOR YOU!
HA HA HA HA HA HA!
?
I AM AN EVIL GENIUS.

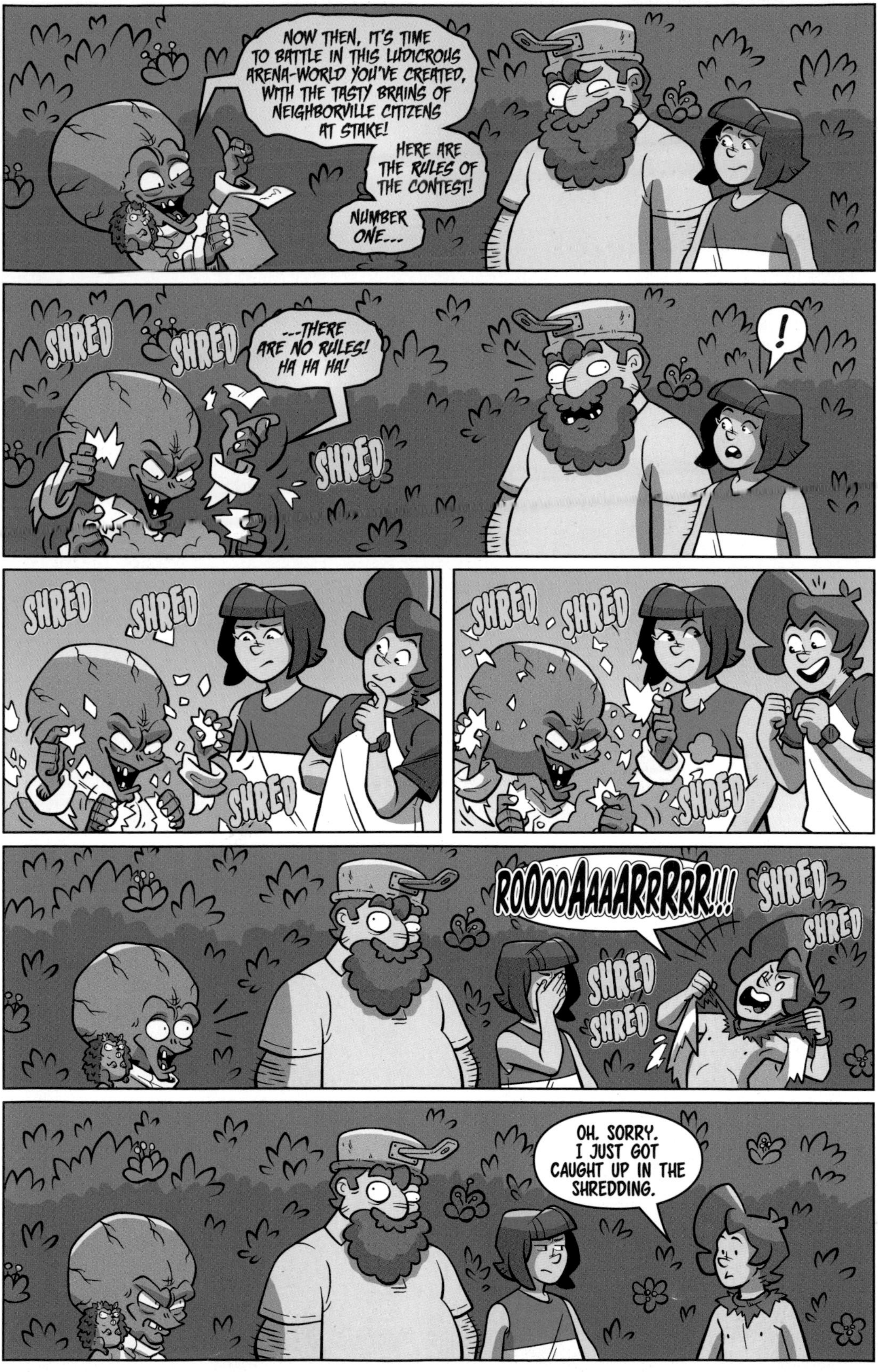
NOW THEN, IT'S TIME TO BATTLE IN THIS LUDICROUS ARENA-WORLD YOU'VE CREATED, WITH THE TASTY BRAINS OF NEIGHBORVILLE CITIZENS AT STAKE!
HERE ARE THE RULES OF THE CONTEST!
NUMBER ONE...
SHRED
SHRED
...THERE ARE NO RULES! HA HA HA!
SHRED
!
SHRED
SHRED
SHRED
SHRED
SHRED
SHRED
ROOOOAAAARRRRR!!!
SHRED
SHRED
SHRED
SHRED
OH. SORRY. I JUST GOT CAUGHT UP IN THE SHREDDING.

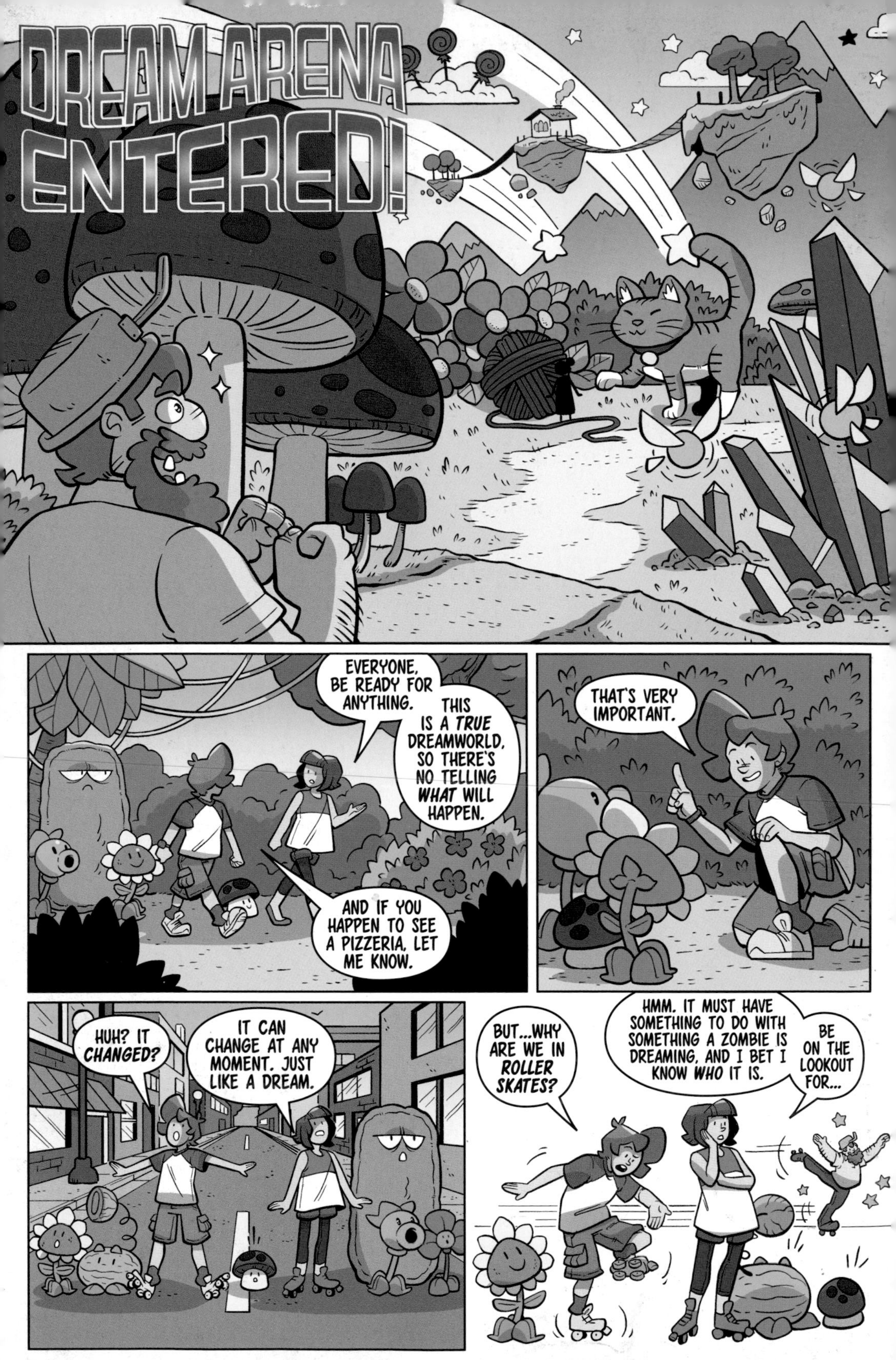
DREAM ARENA ENTERED!
EVERYONE, BE READY FOR ANYTHING.
THIS IS A TRUE DREAMWORLD, SO THERE'S NO TELLING WHAT WILL HAPPEN.
AND IF YOU HAPPEN TO SEE A PIZZERIA, LET ME KNOW.
THAT'S VERY IMPORTANT.
HUH? IT CHANGED?
IT CAN CHANGE AT ANY MOMENT. JUST LIKE A DREAM.
BUT...WHY ARE WE IN ROLLER SKATES?
HMM. IT MUST HAVE SOMETHING TO DO WITH SOMETHING A ZOMBIE IS DREAMING, AND I BET I KNOW WHO IT IS.
BE ON THE LOOKOUT FOR...

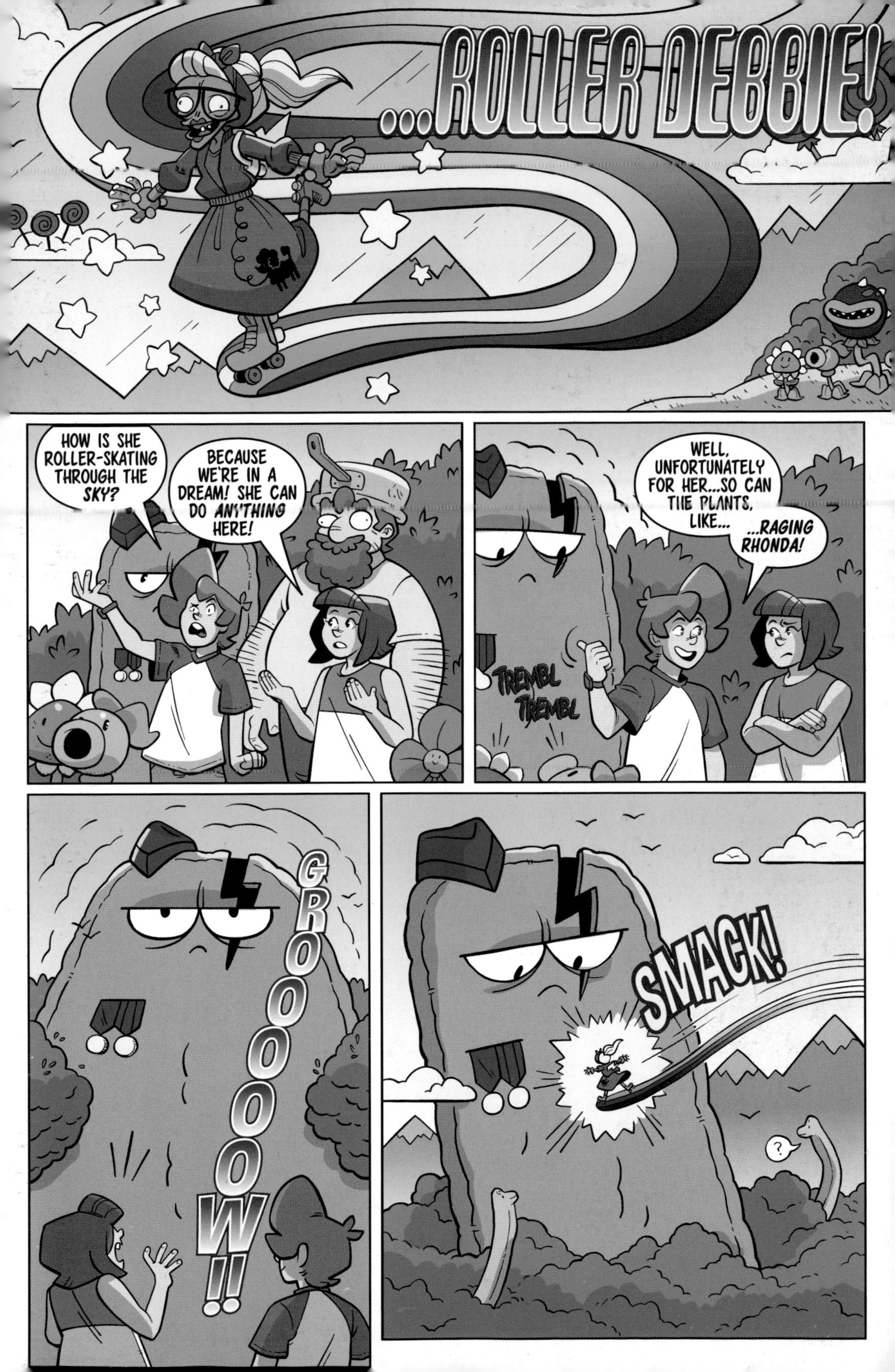
...ROLLER DEBBIE!
HOW IS SHE ROLLER-SKATING THROUGH THE SKY?
BECAUSE WE'RE IN A DREAM! SHE CAN DO ANYTHING HERE!
WELL, UNFORTUNATELY FOR HER...SO CAN THE PLANTS, LIKE...
...RAGING RHONDA!
TREMBL TREMBL
GROOOOOOOW!!
SMACK!
?

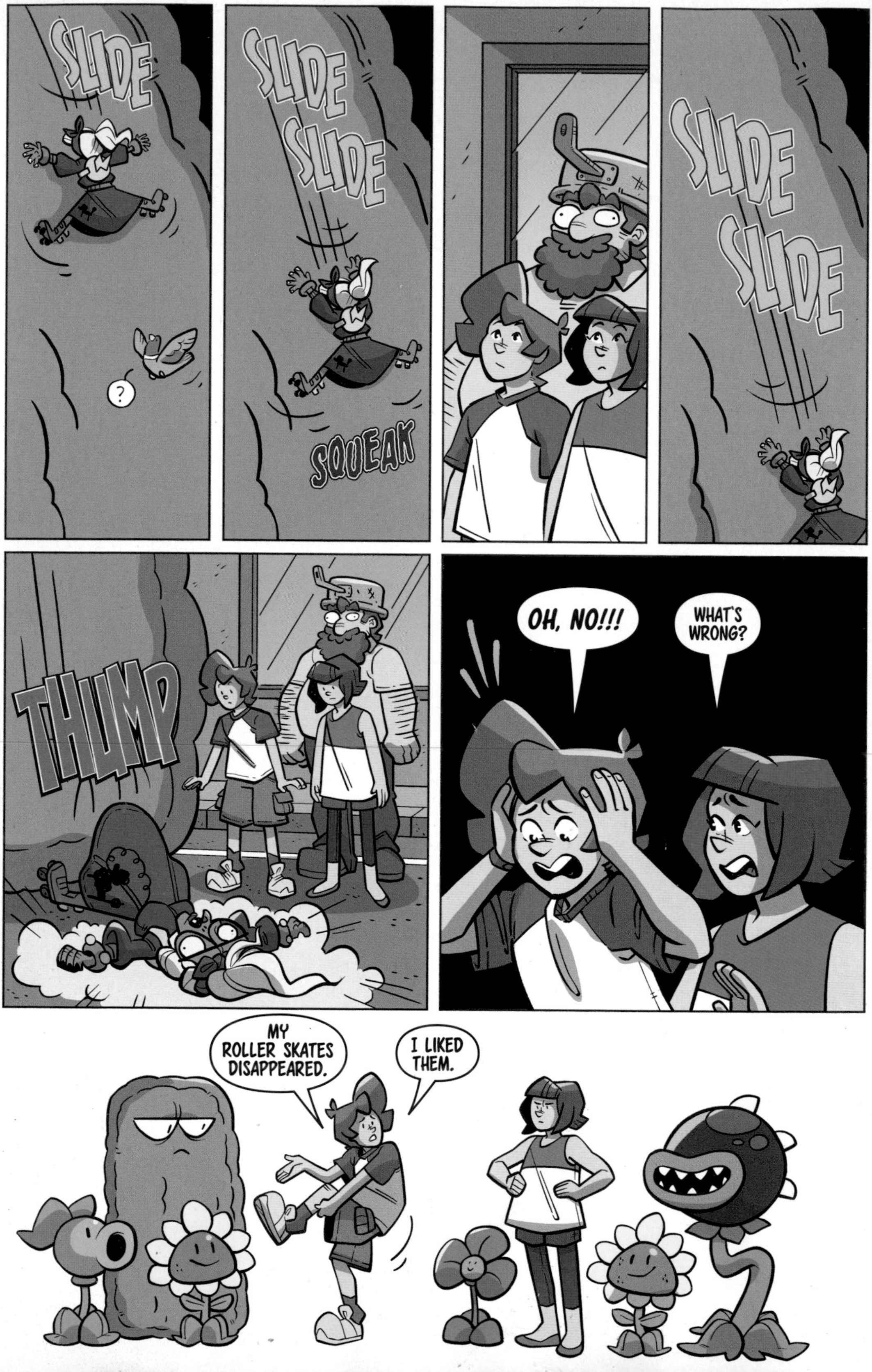
SLIDE
?
SLIDE
SLIDE
SQUEAK
SLIDE
SLIDE
THUMP
OH, NO!!!
WHAT'S WRONG?
MY ROLLER SKATES DISAPPEARED.
I LIKED THEM.

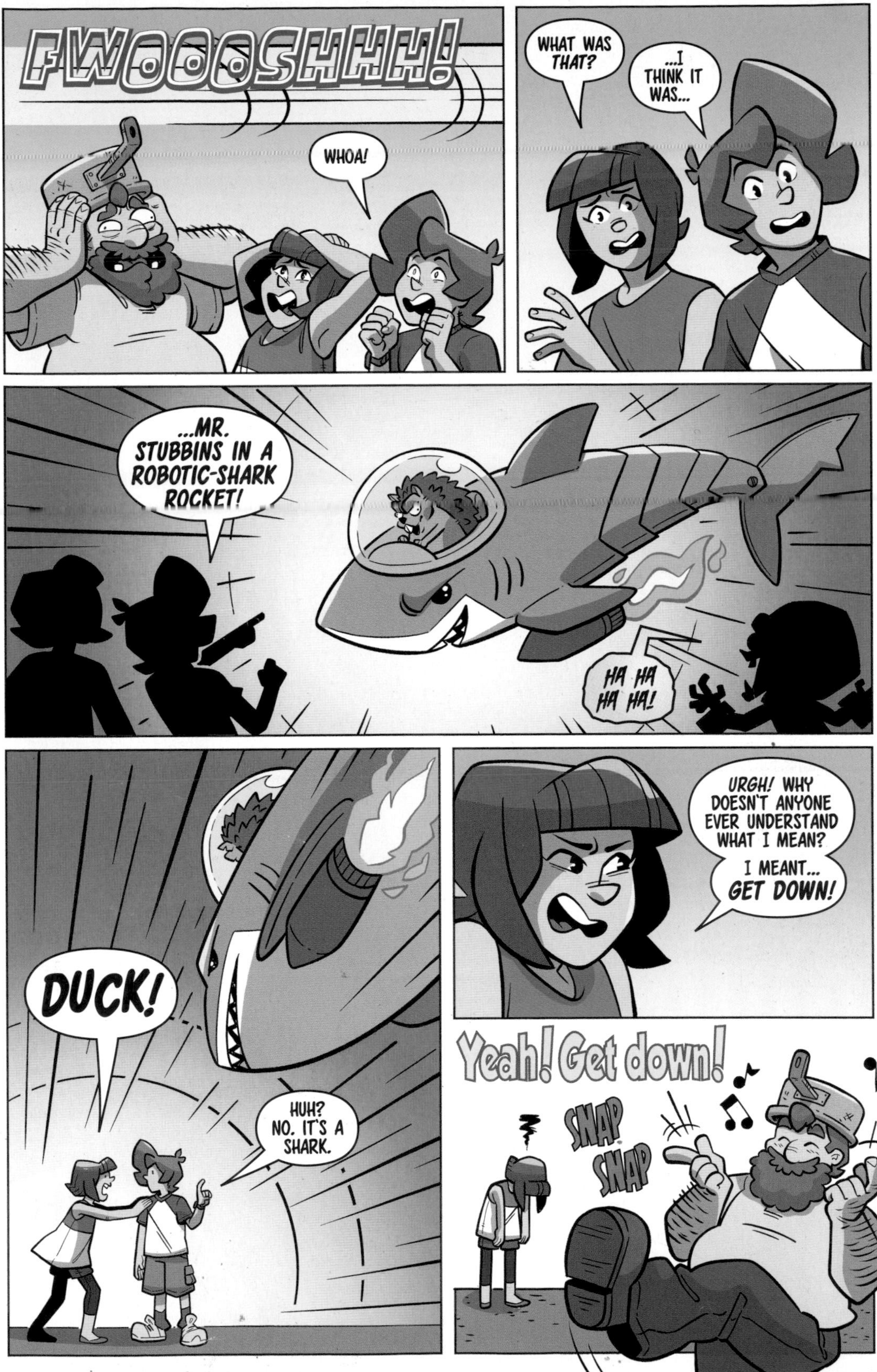

FWOOOOSHHH!
WHOA!
WHAT WAS THAT?
...I THINK IT WAS...
...MR. STUBBINS IN A ROBOTIC-SHARK ROCKET!
HA HA HA HA!
DUCK!
HUH? NO. IT'S A SHARK.
URGH! WHY DOESN'T ANYONE EVER UNDERSTAND WHAT I MEAN?
I MEANT... GET DOWN!
Yeah! Get down!
SNAP SNAP

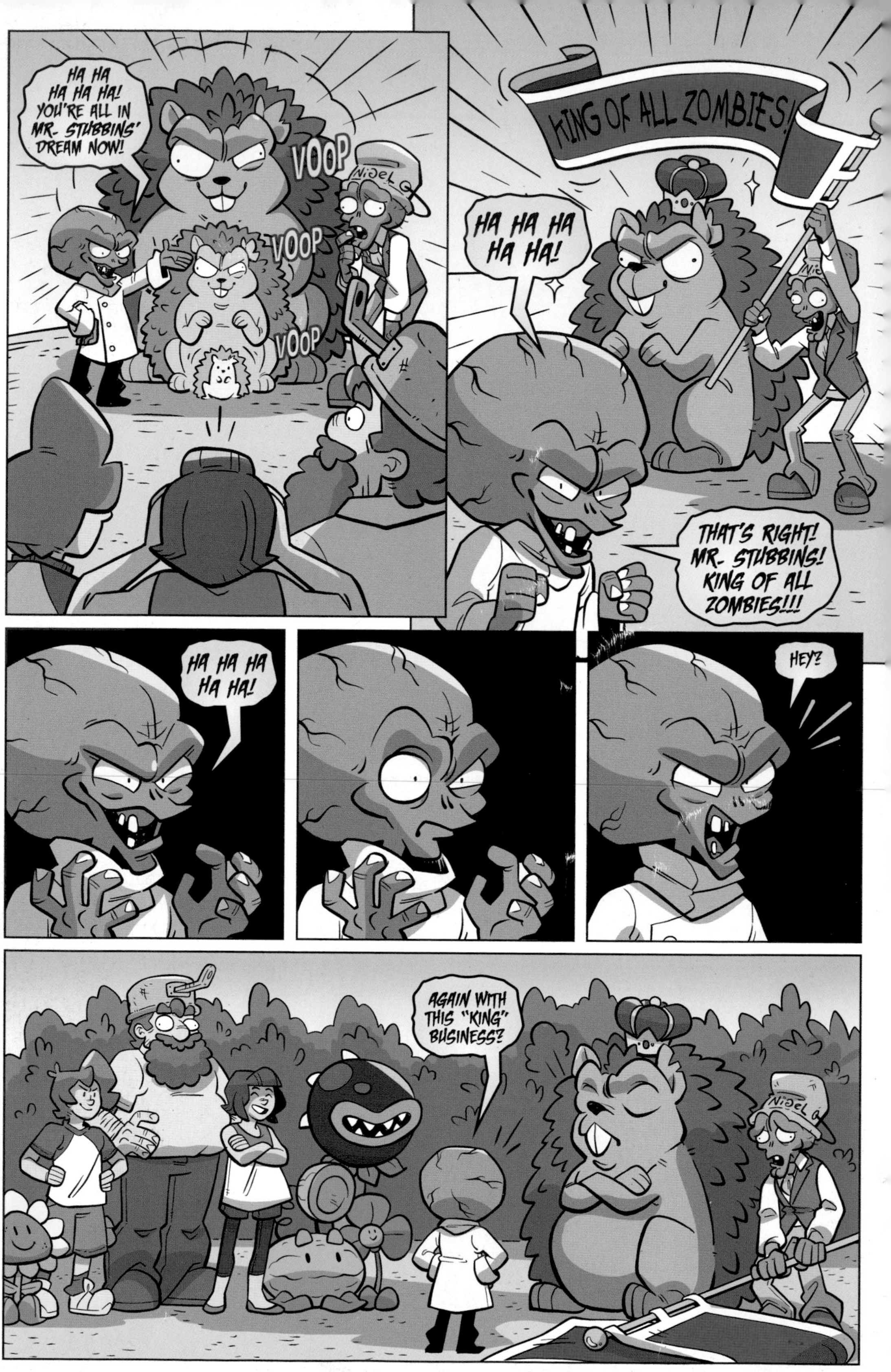
HA HA HA HA HA! YOU'RE ALL IN MR. STUBBINS' DREAM NOW!
VOOP
VOOP
VOOP
NIGEL
KING OF ALL ZOMBIES!
HA HA HA HA HA!
THAT'S RIGHT! MR. STUBBINS! KING OF ALL ZOMBIES!!!
HA HA HA HA HA!
HEY?
AGAIN WITH THIS "KING" BUSINESS?
NIGEL

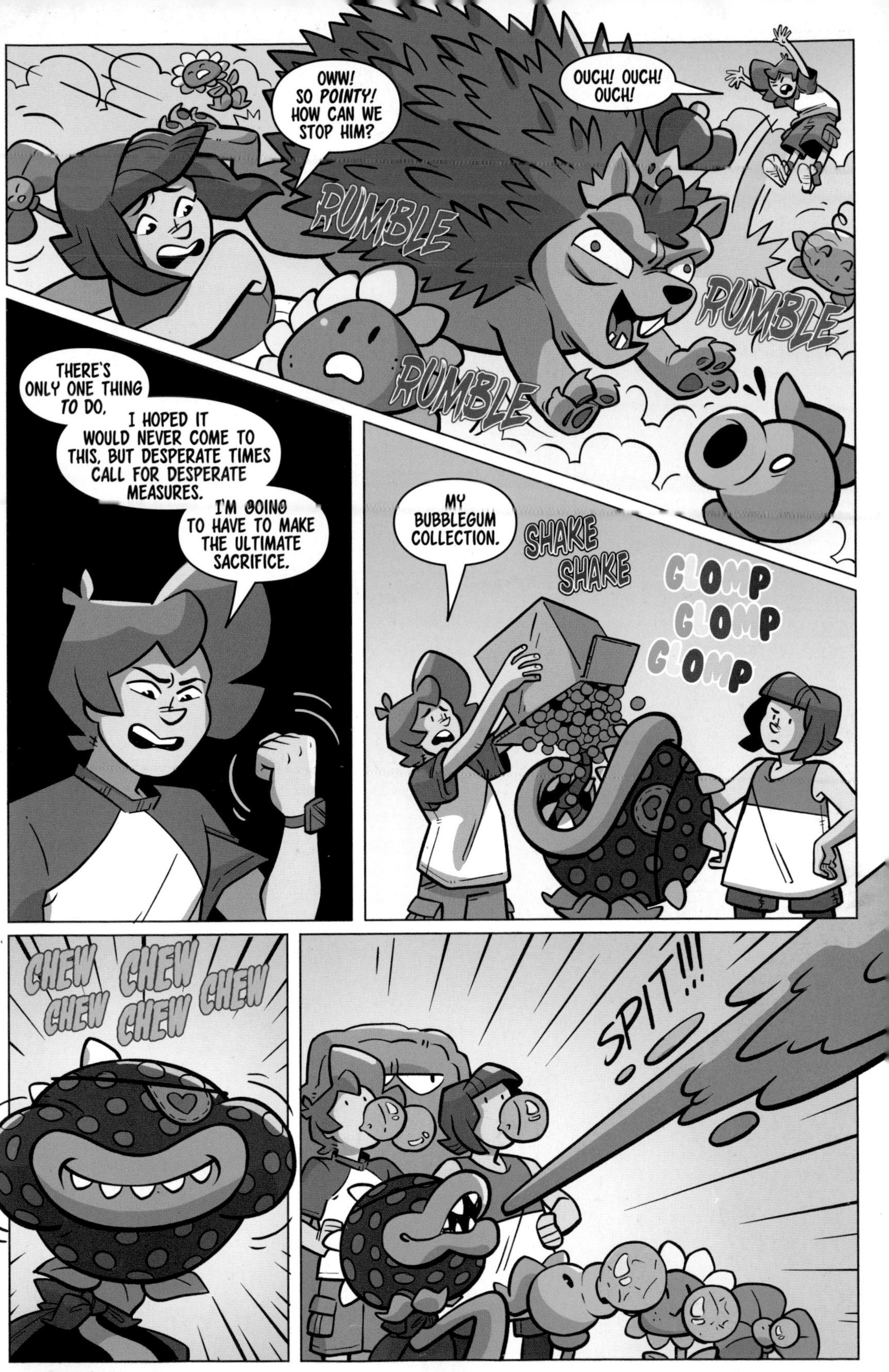
OWW! SO POINTY! HOW CAN WE STOP HIM?
OUCH! OUCH! OUCH!
RUMBLE
RUMBLE
RUMBLE
THERE'S ONLY ONE THING TO DO.
I HOPED IT WOULD NEVER COME TO THIS, BUT DESPERATE TIMES CALL FOR DESPERATE MEASURES.
I'M GOING TO HAVE TO MAKE THE ULTIMATE SACRIFICE.
MY BUBBLEGUM COLLECTION.
SHAKE SHAKE
GLOMP GLOMP GLOMP
CHEW CHEW CHEW CHEW CHEW
SPIT!!!

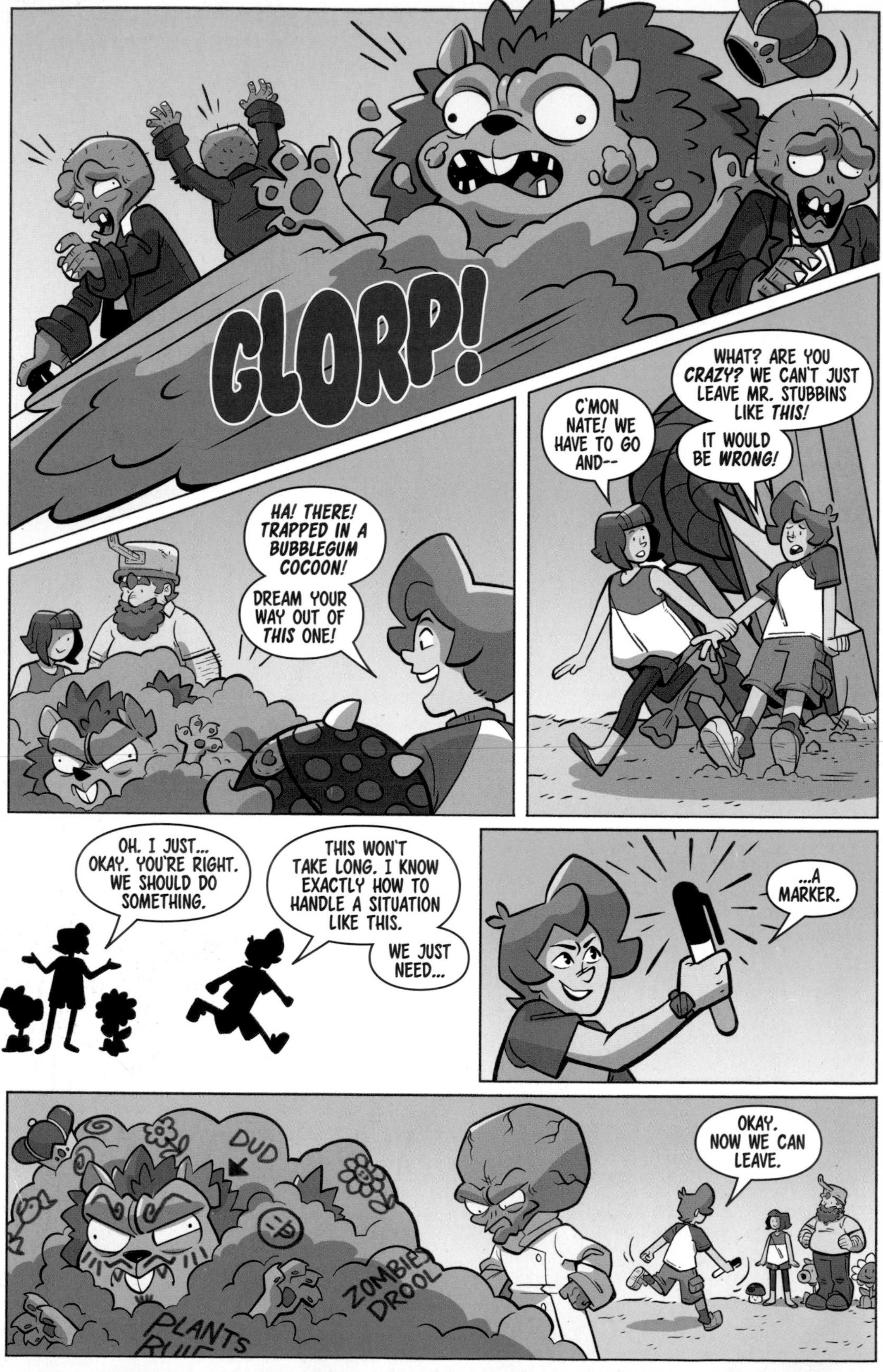
GLORP!
HA! THERE! TRAPPED IN A BUBBLEGUM COCOON!
DREAM YOUR WAY OUT OF THIS ONE!
C'MON NATE! WE HAVE TO GO AND--
WHAT? ARE YOU CRAZY? WE CAN'T JUST LEAVE MR. STUBBINS LIKE THIS!
IT WOULD BE WRONG!
OH. I JUST... OKAY. YOU'RE RIGHT. WE SHOULD DO SOMETHING.
THIS WON'T TAKE LONG. I KNOW EXACTLY HOW TO HANDLE A SITUATION LIKE THIS.
WE JUST NEED...
...A MARKER.
DUD
ZOMBIES DROOL
PLANTS RULE
OKAY. NOW WE CAN LEAVE.

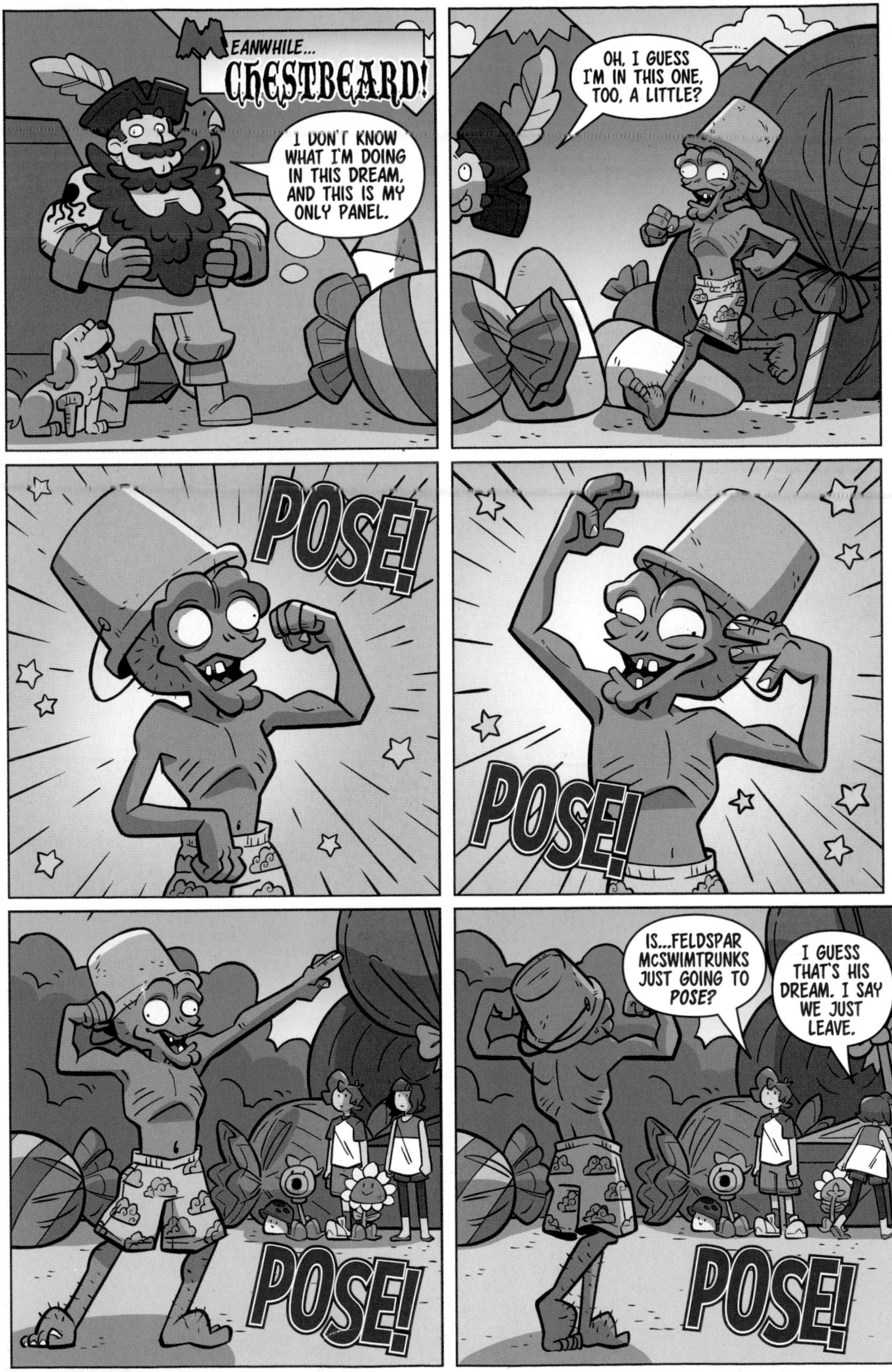
MEANWHILE...
CHESTBEARD!
I DON'T KNOW WHAT I'M DOING IN THIS DREAM, AND THIS IS MY ONLY PANEL.
OH, I GUESS I'M IN THIS ONE, TOO, A LITTLE?
POSE!
POSE!
POSE!
IS...FELDSPAR MCSWIMTRUNKS JUST GOING TO POSE?
I GUESS THAT'S HIS DREAM. I SAY WE JUST LEAVE.
POSE!

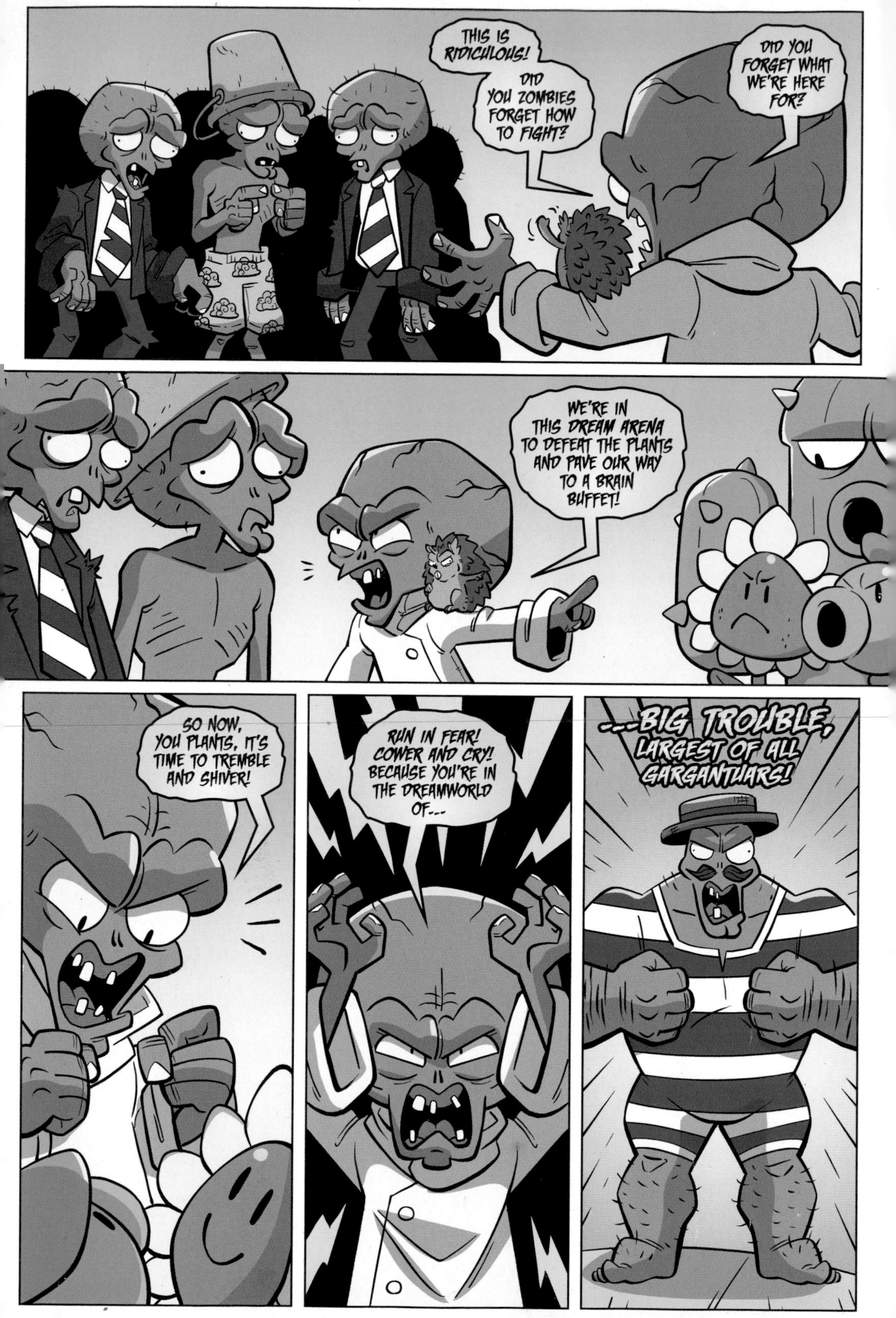

THIS IS RIDICULOUS!
DID YOU ZOMBIES FORGET HOW TO FIGHT?
DID YOU FORGET WHAT WE'RE HERE FOR?
WE'RE IN THIS DREAM ARENA TO DEFEAT THE PLANTS AND PAVE OUR WAY TO A BRAIN BUFFET!
SO NOW, YOU PLANTS, IT'S TIME TO TREMBLE AND SHIVER!
RUN IN FEAR! COWER AND CRY! BECAUSE YOU'RE IN THE DREAMWORLD OF...
...BIG TROUBLE, LARGEST OF ALL GARGANTUARS!

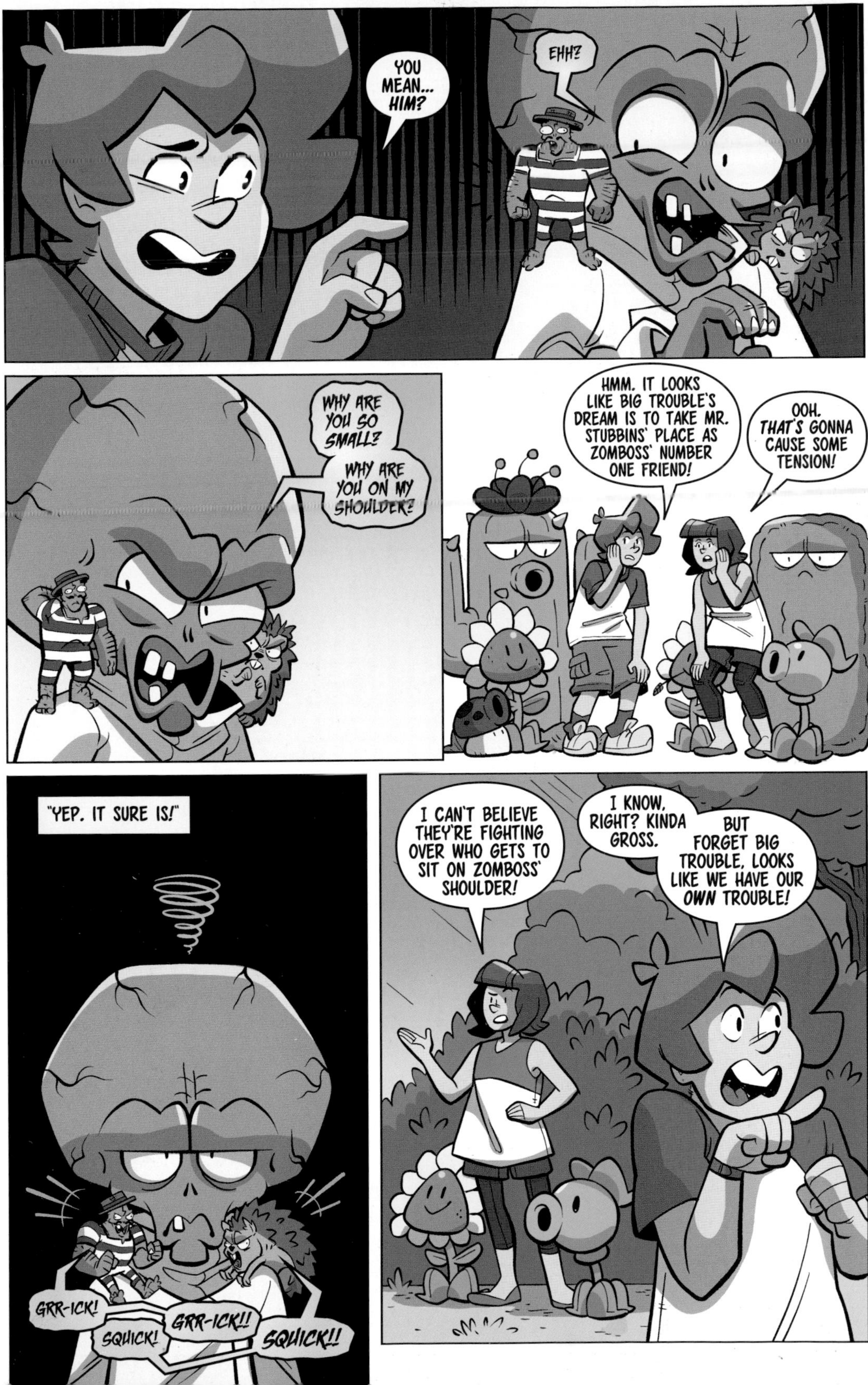
YOU MEAN... HIM?
EHH?
WHY ARE YOU SO SMALL?
WHY ARE YOU ON MY SHOULDER?
HMM. IT LOOKS LIKE BIG TROUBLE'S DREAM IS TO TAKE MR. STUBBINS' PLACE AS ZOMBOSS' NUMBER ONE FRIEND!
OOH. THAT'S GONNA CAUSE SOME TENSION!
"YEP. IT SURE IS!"
GRR-ICK!
SQUICK!
GRR-ICK!!
SQUICK!!
I CAN'T BELIEVE THEY'RE FIGHTING OVER WHO GETS TO SIT ON ZOMBOSS' SHOULDER!
I KNOW, RIGHT? KINDA GROSS.
BUT FORGET BIG TROUBLE, LOOKS LIKE WE HAVE OUR OWN TROUBLE!

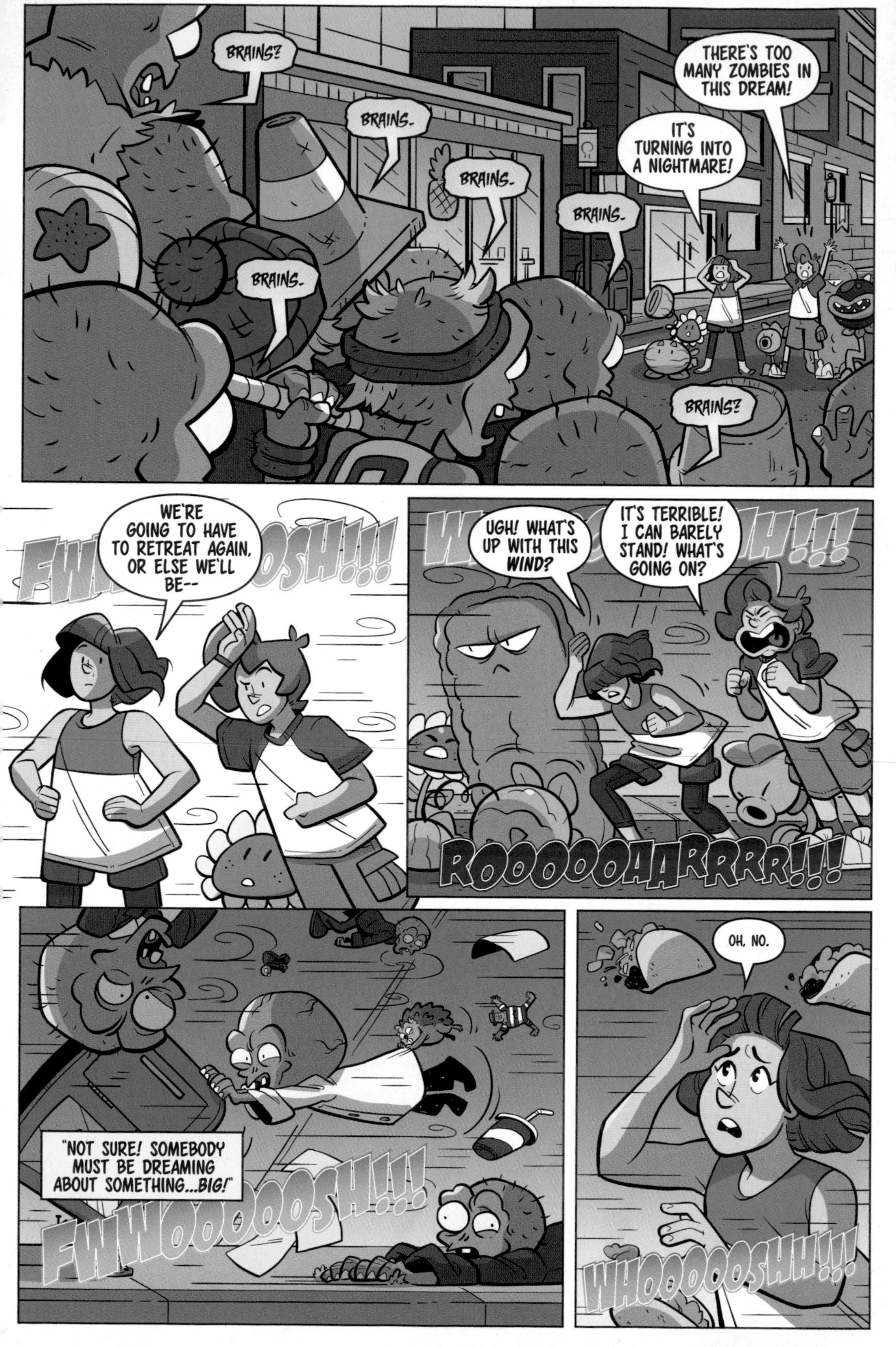
BRAINS?
BRAINS.
BRAINS.
BRAINS.
BRAINS.
THERE'S TOO MANY ZOMBIES IN THIS DREAM!
IT'S TURNING INTO A NIGHTMARE!
BRAINS?
WE'RE GOING TO HAVE TO RETREAT AGAIN, OR ELSE WE'LL BE--
UGH! WHAT'S UP WITH THIS WIND?
IT'S TERRIBLE! I CAN BARELY STAND! WHAT'S GOING ON?
ROOOOOOAARRRR!!!
"NOT SURE! SOMEBODY MUST BE DREAMING ABOUT SOMETHING...BIG!"
FWWOOOOOSH!!!
OH, NO.
WHOOOOOSHH!!!

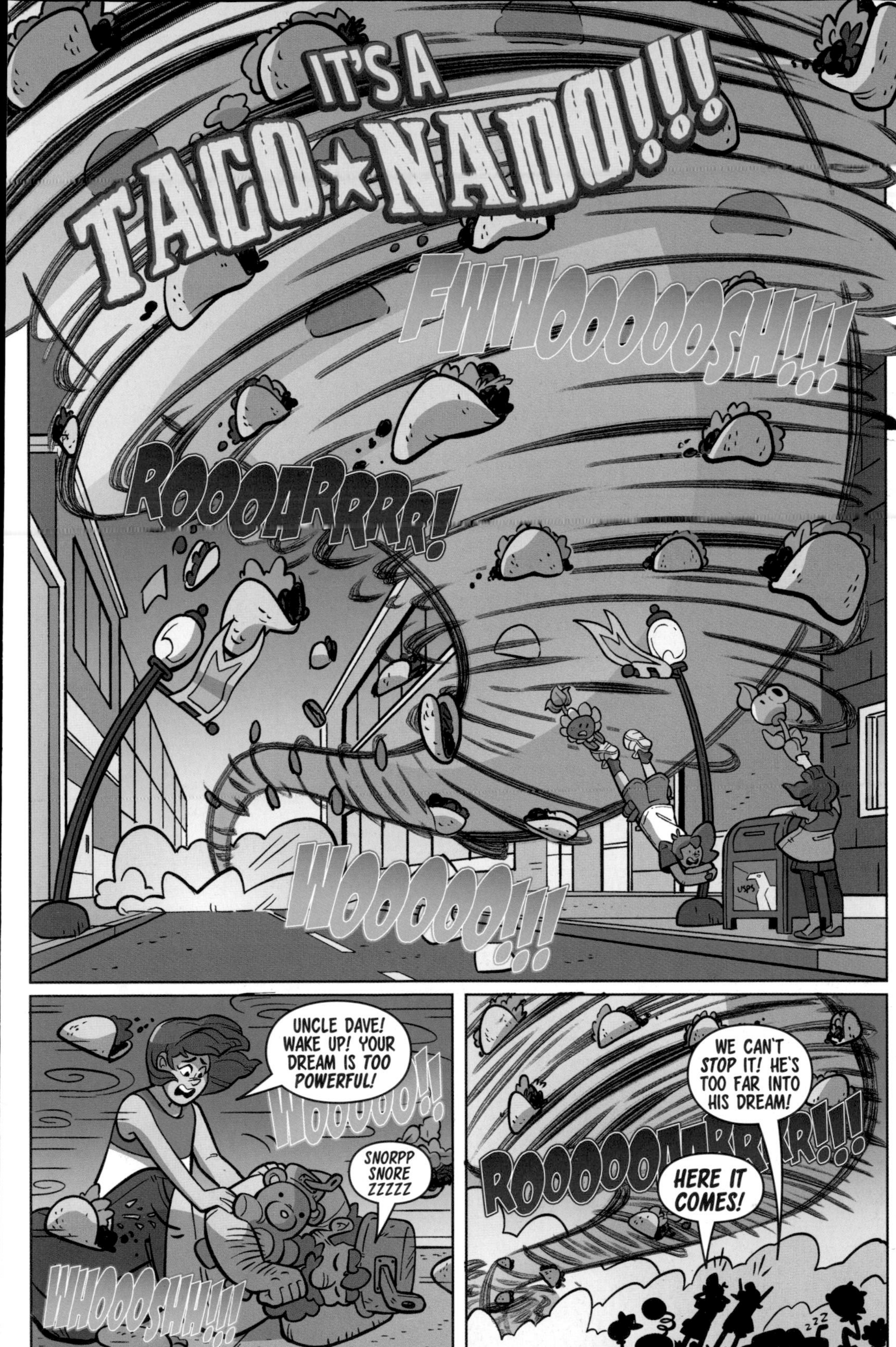
IT'S A TACO★NADO!!!
FWWOOOOOOSH!!!
ROOOARRRR!
WOOOOO!!!
UNCLE DAVE! WAKE UP! YOUR DREAM IS TOO POWERFUL!
WOOOOO!!
SNORPP SNORE ZZZZZ
WHOOOSHH!!!
WE CAN'T STOP IT! HE'S TOO FAR INTO HIS DREAM!
ROOOOOOARRRR!!!
HERE IT COMES!

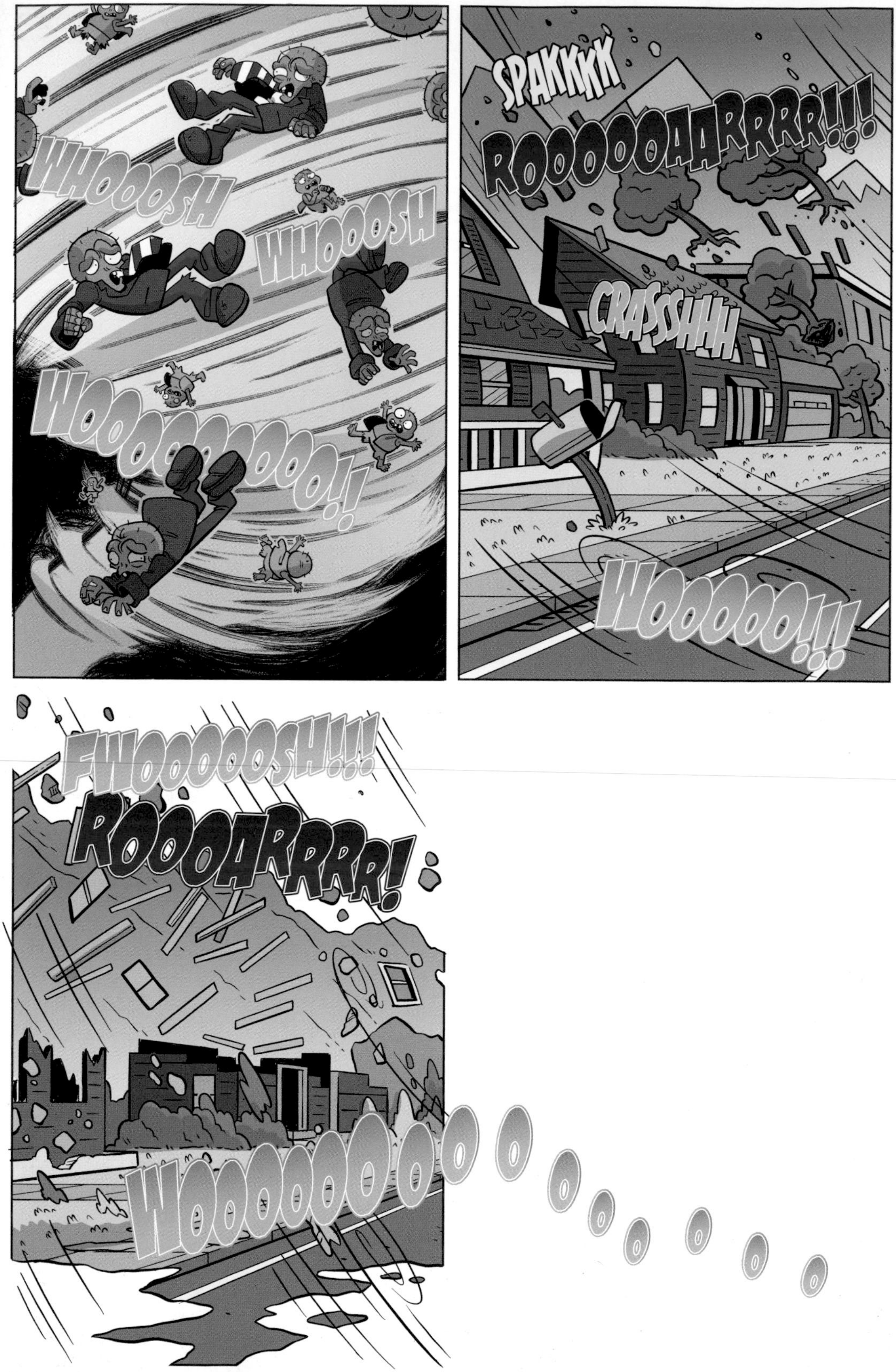
WHOOOSH
WHOOOSH
WOOOOOOOOOO!!
SPAKKKK
ROOOOOOAARRRR!!!
CRASSHHH
WOOOOO!!!
FWOOOOOOSH!!!
ROOOARRRR!
WOOOOOOO O O O O O O O O O O

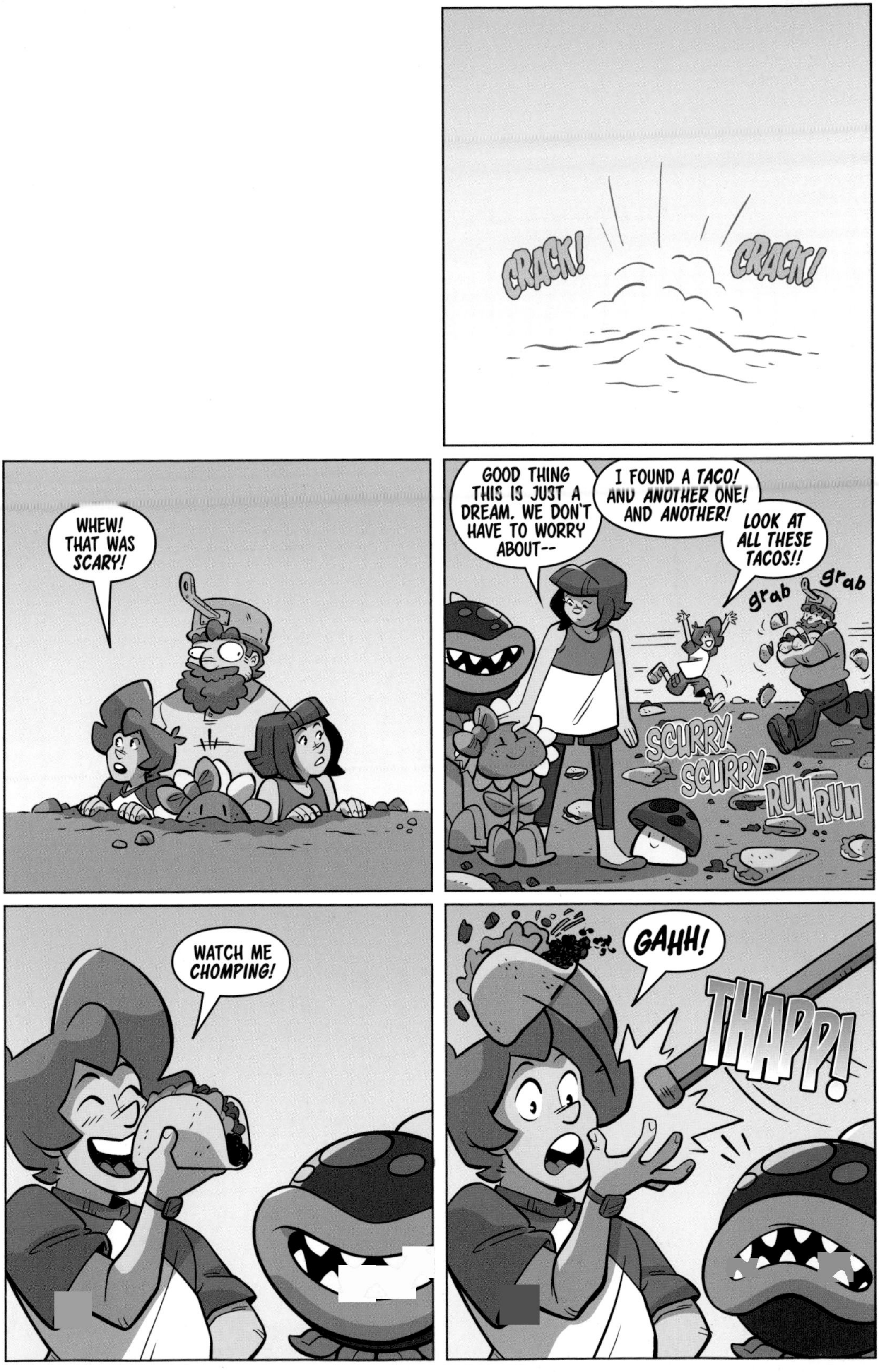
CRACK!
CRACK!
WHEW! THAT WAS SCARY!
GOOD THING THIS IS JUST A DREAM. WE DON'T HAVE TO WORRY ABOUT--
I FOUND A TACO! AND ANOTHER ONE! AND ANOTHER!
LOOK AT ALL THESE TACOS!!
grab
grab
SCURRY
SCURRY
RUN RUN
WATCH ME CHOMPING!
GAHH!
THAPP!

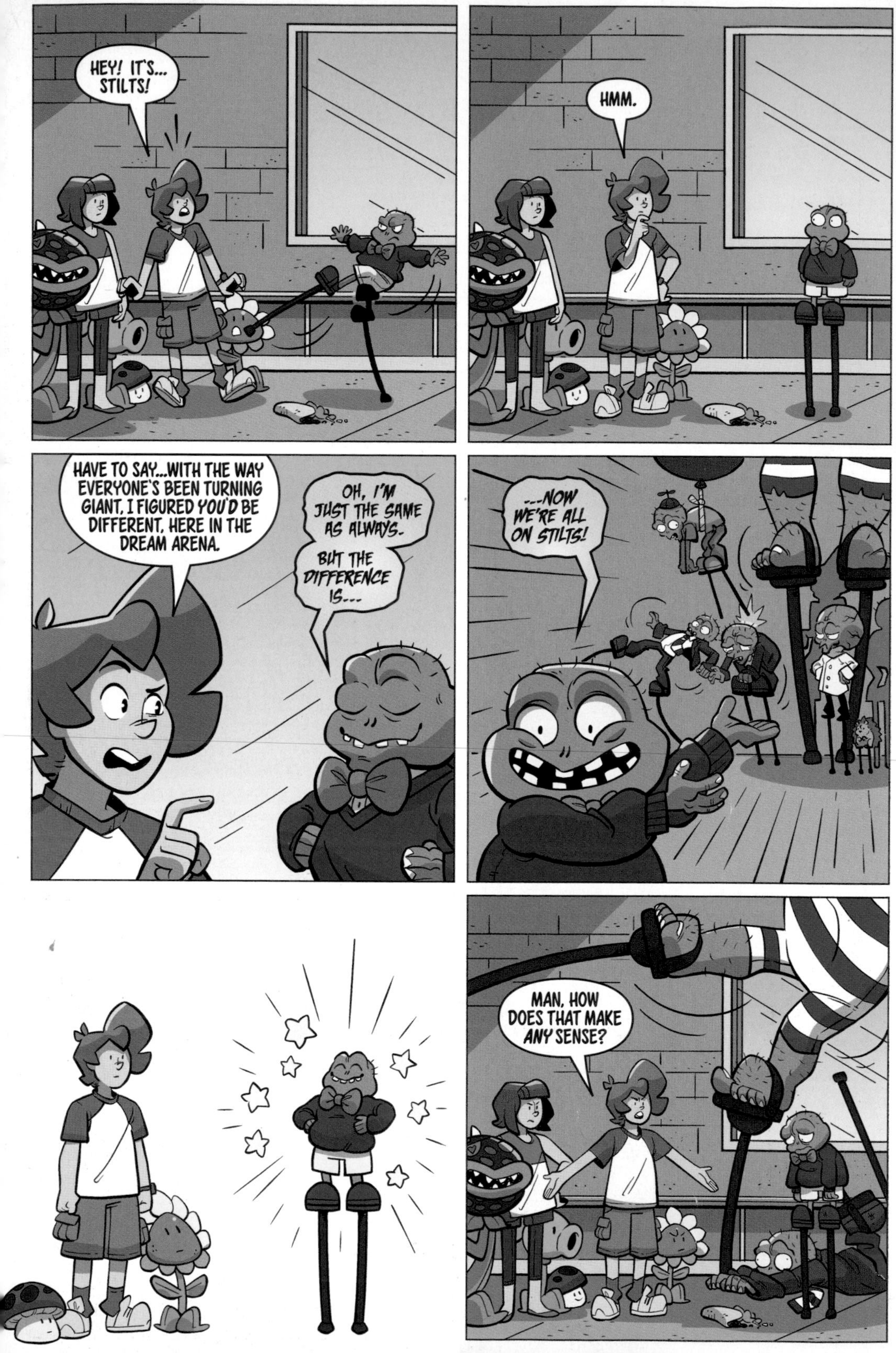
HEY! IT'S... STILTS!
HMM.
HAVE TO SAY...WITH THE WAY EVERYONE'S BEEN TURNING GIANT, I FIGURED YOU'D BE DIFFERENT, HERE IN THE DREAM ARENA.
OH, I'M JUST THE SAME AS ALWAYS.
BUT THE DIFFERENCE IS...
...NOW WE'RE ALL ON STILTS!
MAN, HOW DOES THAT MAKE ANY SENSE?

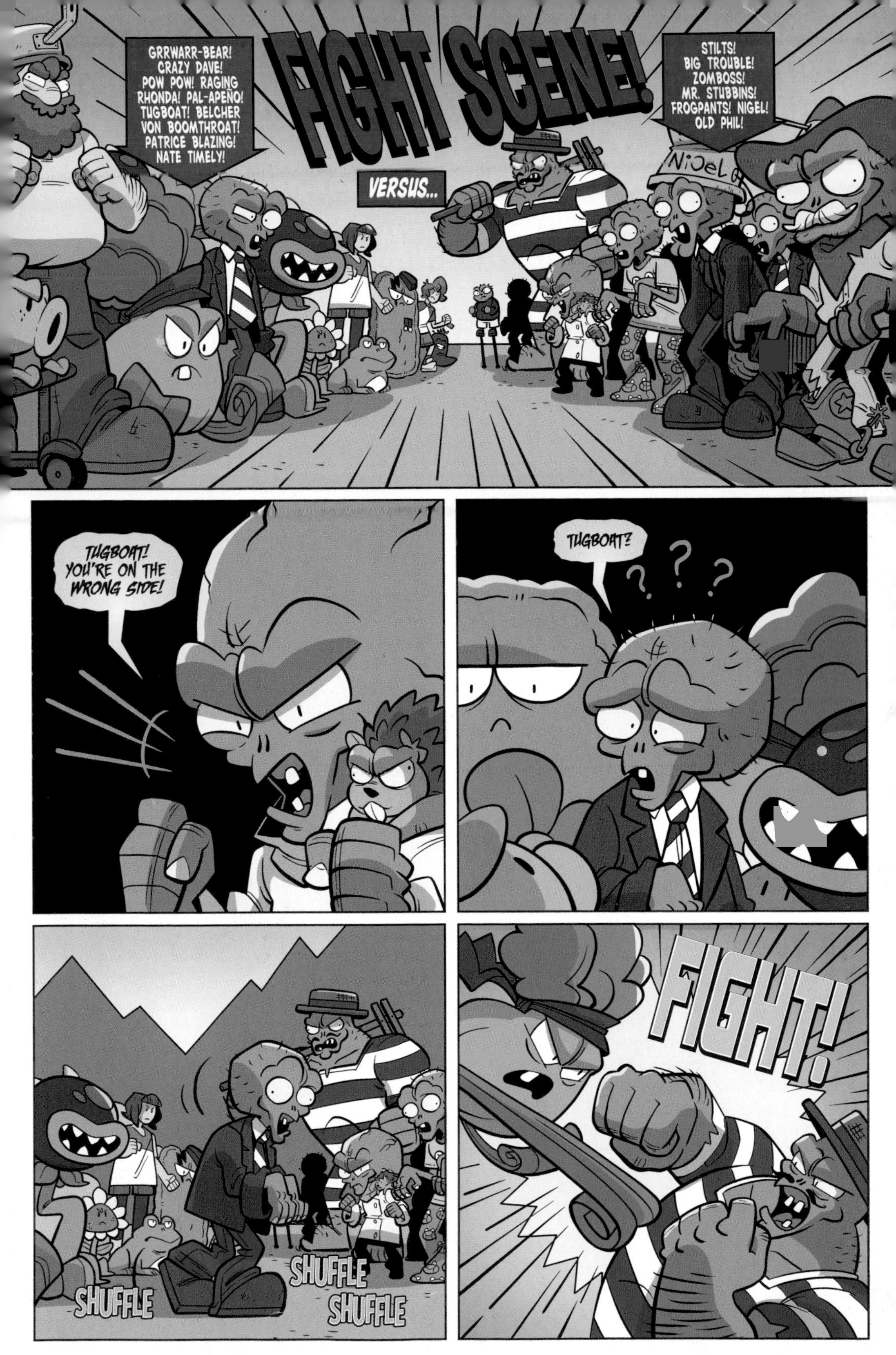
FIGHT SCENE!
GRRWARR-BEAR! CRAZY DAVE! POW POW! RAGING RHONDA! PAL-APEÑO! TUGBOAT! BELCHER VON BOOMTHROAT! PATRICE BLAZING! NATE TIMELY!
VERSUS...
STILTS! BIG TROUBLE! ZOMBOSS! MR. STUBBINS! FROGPANTS! NIGEL! OLD PHIL!
NIGEL
TUGBOAT! YOU'RE ON THE WRONG SIDE!
TUGBOAT?
? ? ?
SHUFFLE
SHUFFLE
SHUFFLE
FIGHT!

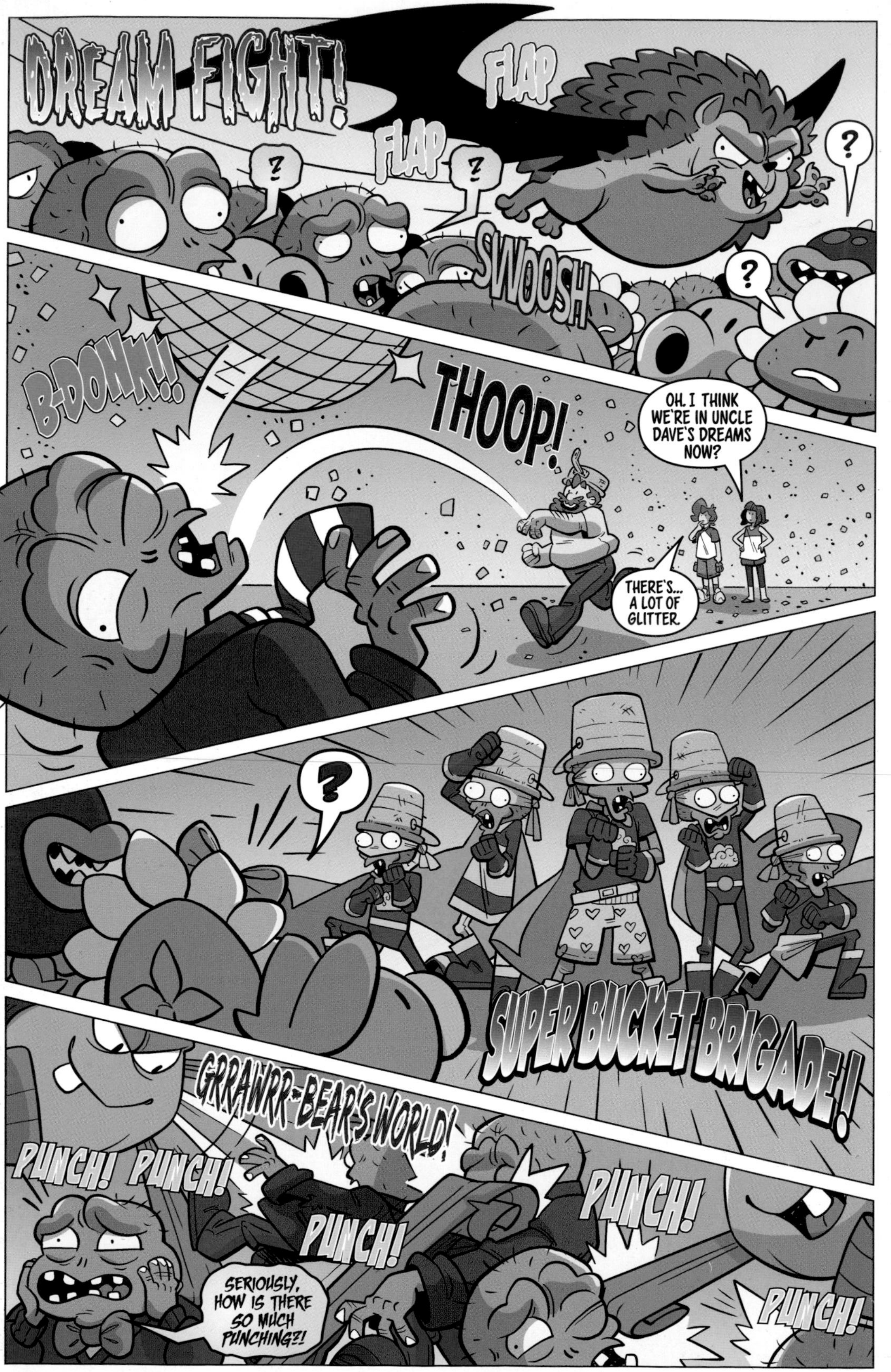
DREAM FIGHT!
FLAP
FLAP
?
?
?
SWOOSH
?
B-DONK!!
THOOP!
OH, I THINK WE'RE IN UNCLE DAVE'S DREAMS NOW?
THERE'S... A LOT OF GLITTER.
?
SUPER BUCKET BRIGADE!
GRRAWRR-BEAR'S WORLD!
PUNCH! PUNCH!
PUNCH!
PUNCH!
SERIOUSLY, HOW IS THERE SO MUCH PUNCHING?!
PUNCH!

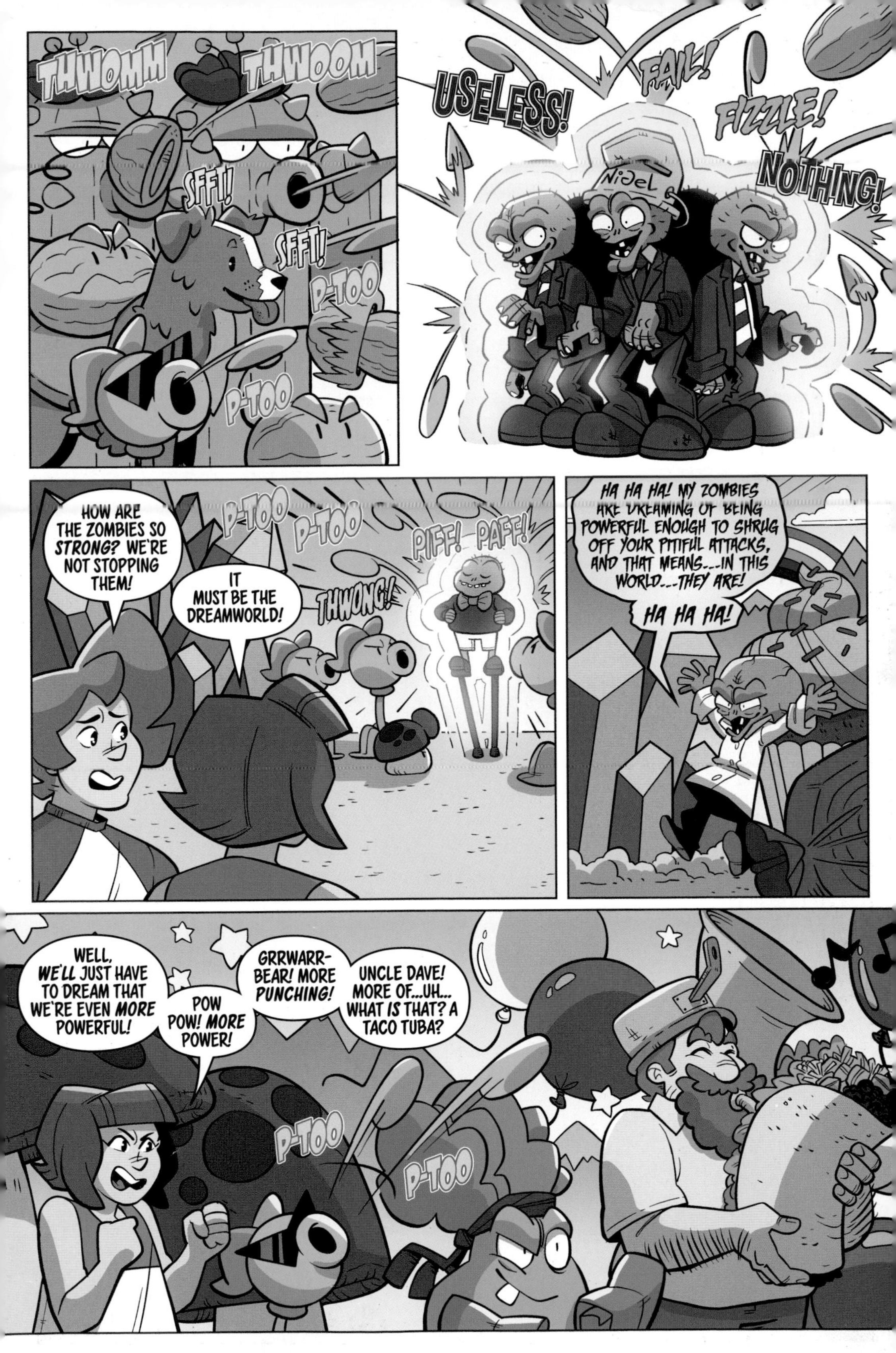
THWOMM
THWOOM
SFFT!
SFFT!
P-TOO
P-TOO
USELESS!
FAIL!
FIZZLE!
NOTHING!
NiGeL
HOW ARE THE ZOMBIES SO STRONG? WE'RE NOT STOPPING THEM!
IT MUST BE THE DREAMWORLD!
P-TOO
P-TOO
PIFF! PAFF!
THWONG!
HA HA HA! MY ZOMBIES ARE DREAMING OF BEING POWERFUL ENOUGH TO SHRUG OFF YOUR PITIFUL ATTACKS, AND THAT MEANS...IN THIS WORLD...THEY ARE!
HA HA HA!
WELL, WE'LL JUST HAVE TO DREAM THAT WE'RE EVEN MORE POWERFUL!
POW POW! MORE POWER!
GRRWARR-BEAR! MORE PUNCHING!
UNCLE DAVE! MORE OF...UH... WHAT IS THAT? A TACO TUBA?
P-TOO
P-TOO

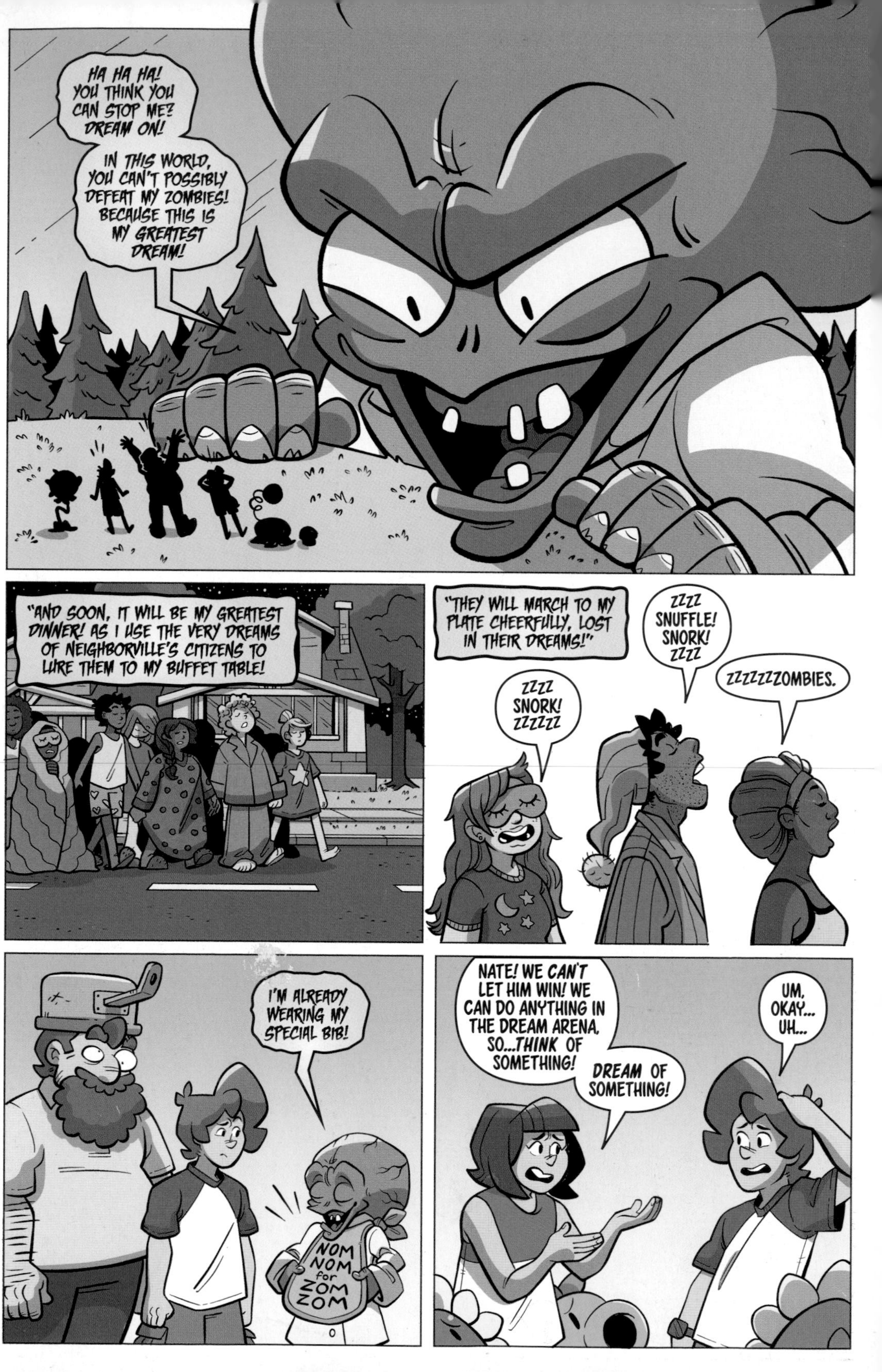
HA HA HA! YOU THINK YOU CAN STOP ME? DREAM ON!
IN THIS WORLD, YOU CAN'T POSSIBLY DEFEAT MY ZOMBIES! BECAUSE THIS IS MY GREATEST DREAM!
"AND SOON, IT WILL BE MY GREATEST DINNER! AS I USE THE VERY DREAMS OF NEIGHBORVILLE'S CITIZENS TO LURE THEM TO MY BUFFET TABLE!
"THEY WILL MARCH TO MY PLATE CHEERFULLY, LOST IN THEIR DREAMS!"
ZZZZ SNUFFLE! SNORK! ZZZZ
ZZZZ SNORK! ZZZZZZ
ZZZZZZZOMBIES.
I'M ALREADY WEARING MY SPECIAL BIB!
NOM NOM for ZOM ZOM
NATE! WE CAN'T LET HIM WIN! WE CAN DO ANYTHING IN THE DREAM ARENA, SO...THINK OF SOMETHING!
DREAM OF SOMETHING!
UM, OKAY... UH...

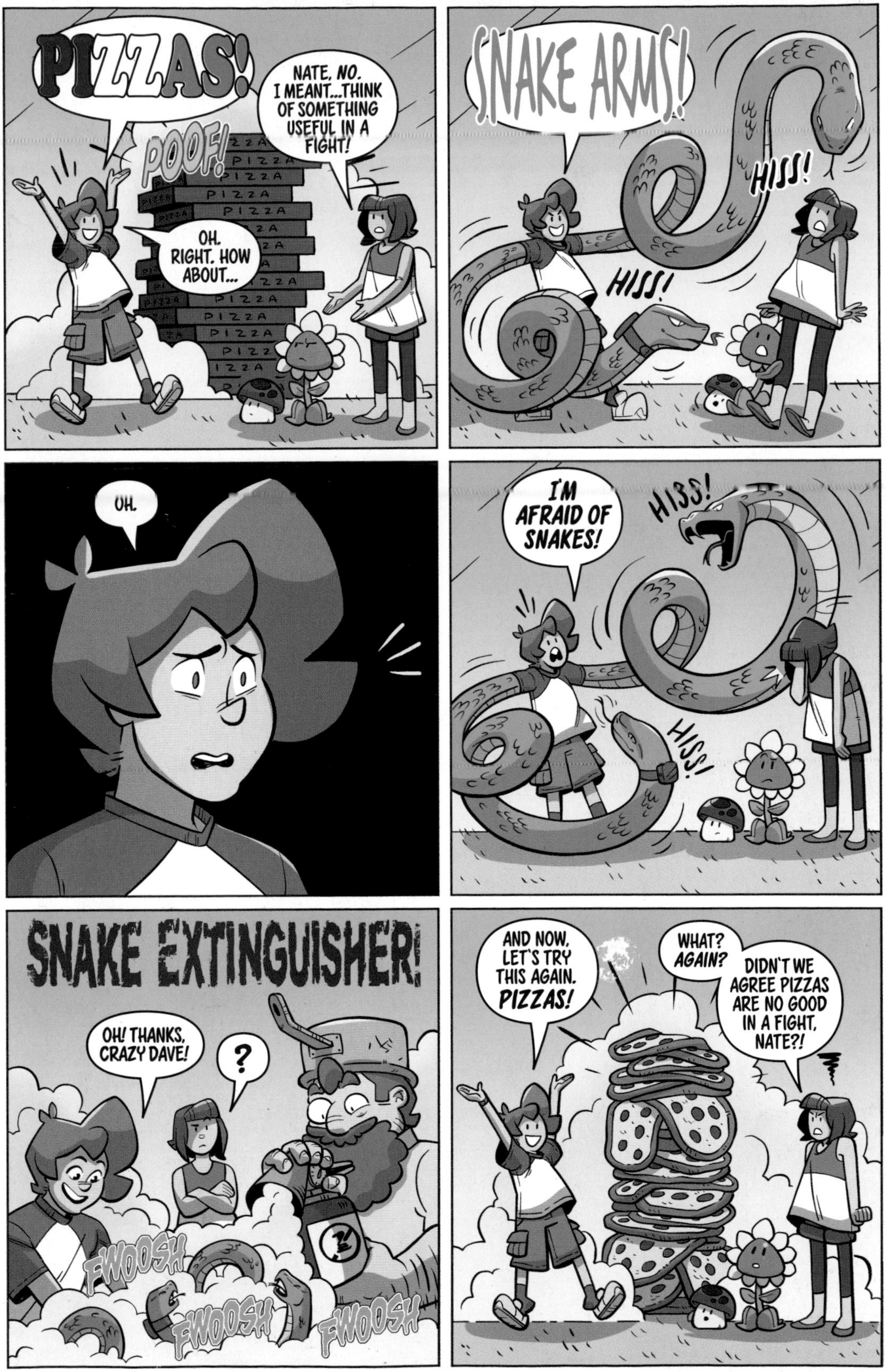
PIZZAS!
NATE, NO. I MEANT...THINK OF SOMETHING USEFUL IN A FIGHT!
POOF!
OH. RIGHT. HOW ABOUT...
SNAKE ARMS!
HISS!
HISS!
OH.
I'M AFRAID OF SNAKES!
HISS!
HISS!
SNAKE EXTINGUISHER!
OH! THANKS, CRAZY DAVE!
?
FWOOSH
FWOOSH
FWOOSH
AND NOW, LET'S TRY THIS AGAIN. PIZZAS!
WHAT? AGAIN?
DIDN'T WE AGREE PIZZAS ARE NO GOOD IN A FIGHT, NATE?!

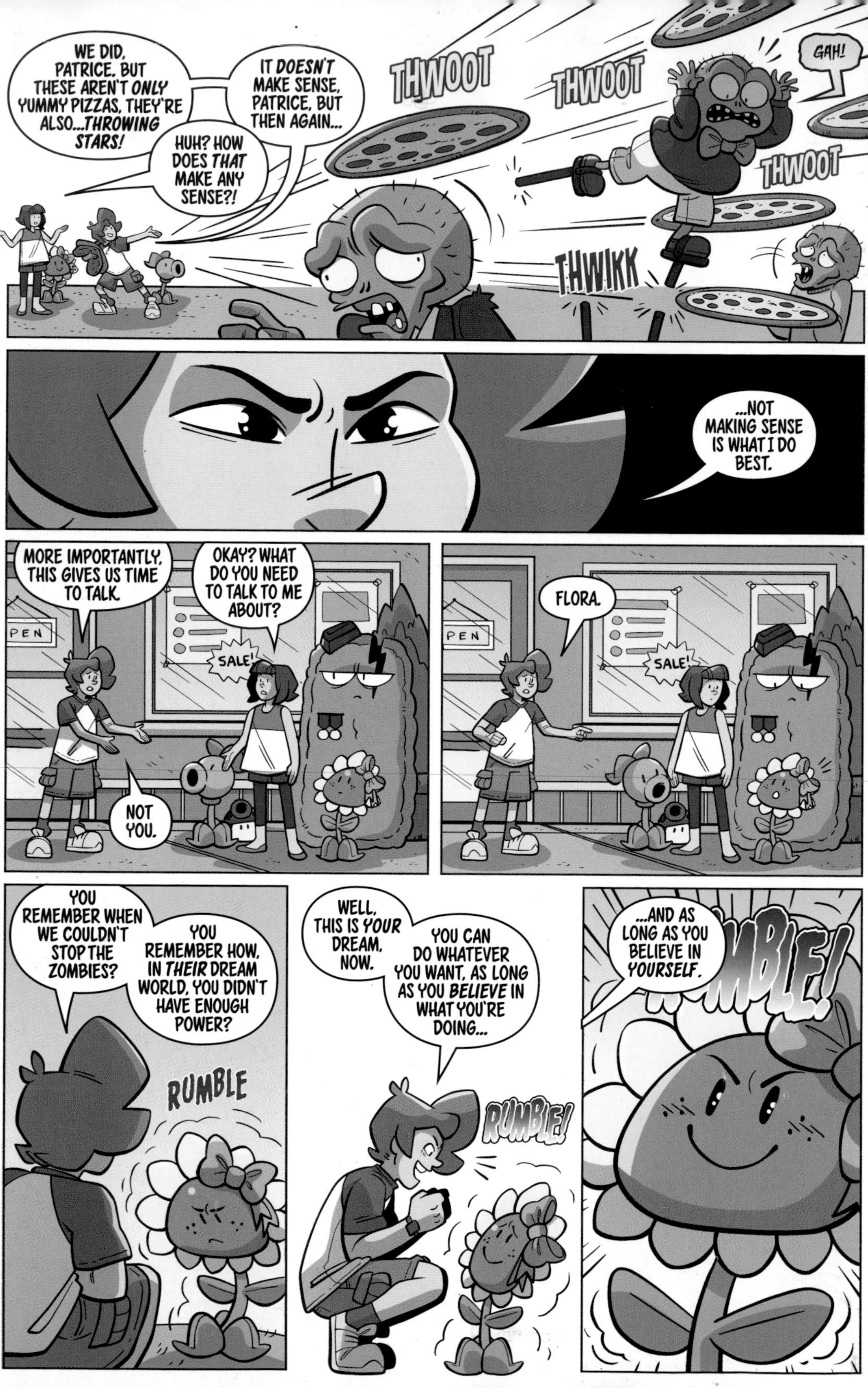
WE DID, PATRICE. BUT THESE AREN'T ONLY YUMMY PIZZAS, THEY'RE ALSO...THROWING STARS!
HUH? HOW DOES THAT MAKE ANY SENSE?!
IT DOESN'T MAKE SENSE, PATRICE, BUT THEN AGAIN...
THWOOT
THWOOT
GAH!
THWOOT
THWIKK
...NOT MAKING SENSE IS WHAT I DO BEST.
MORE IMPORTANTLY, THIS GIVES US TIME TO TALK.
OKAY? WHAT DO YOU NEED TO TALK TO ME ABOUT?
PEN
SALE!
NOT YOU.
FLORA.
PEN
SALE!
YOU REMEMBER WHEN WE COULDN'T STOP THE ZOMBIES?
YOU REMEMBER HOW, IN THEIR DREAM WORLD, YOU DIDN'T HAVE ENOUGH POWER?
RUMBLE
WELL, THIS IS YOUR DREAM, NOW.
YOU CAN DO WHATEVER YOU WANT, AS LONG AS YOU BELIEVE IN WHAT YOU'RE DOING...
RUMBLE!
...AND AS LONG AS YOU BELIEVE IN YOURSELF.

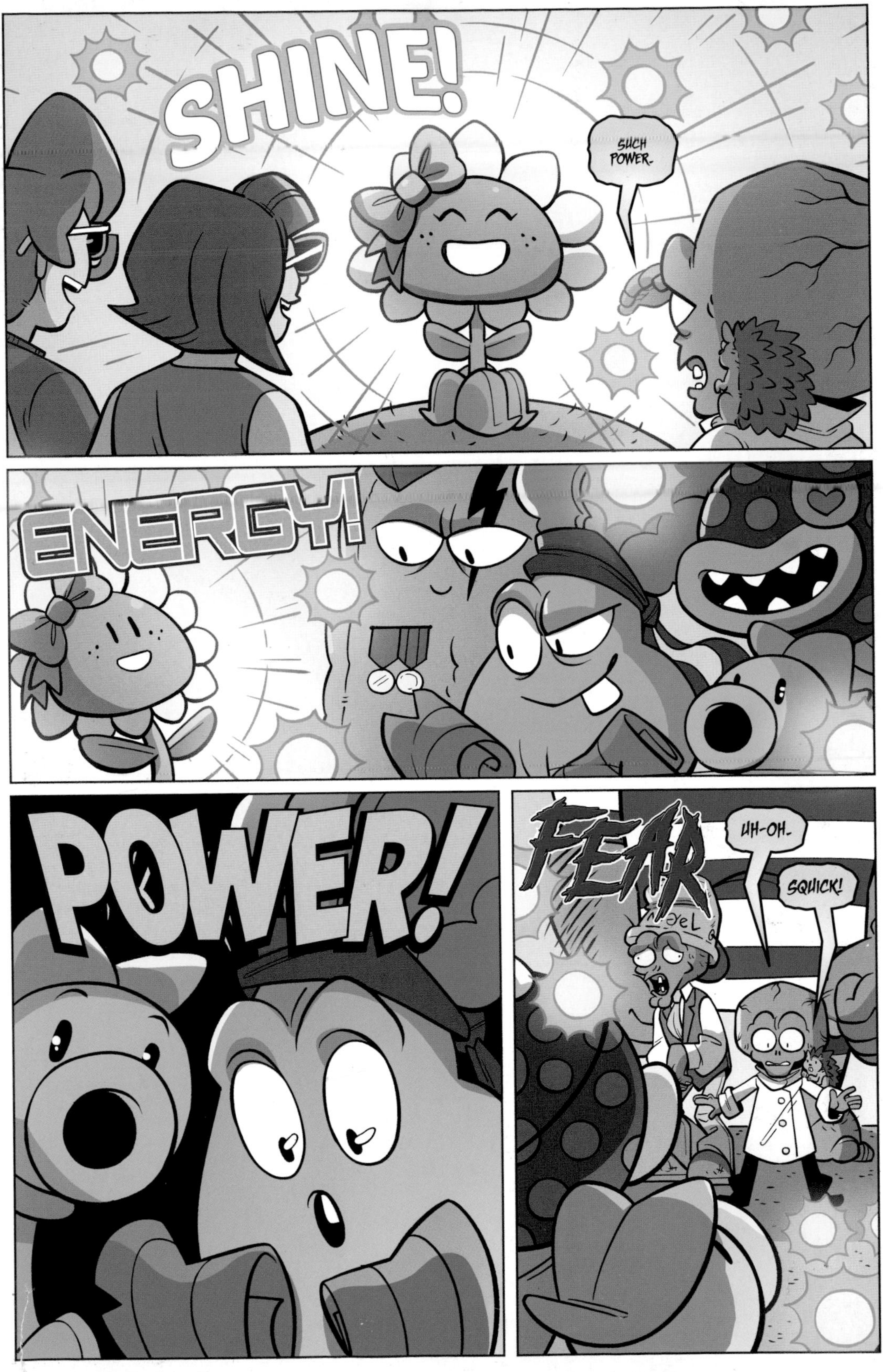

SHINE!
SUCH POWER...
ENERGY!
POWER!
FEAR
UH-OH...
SQUICK!

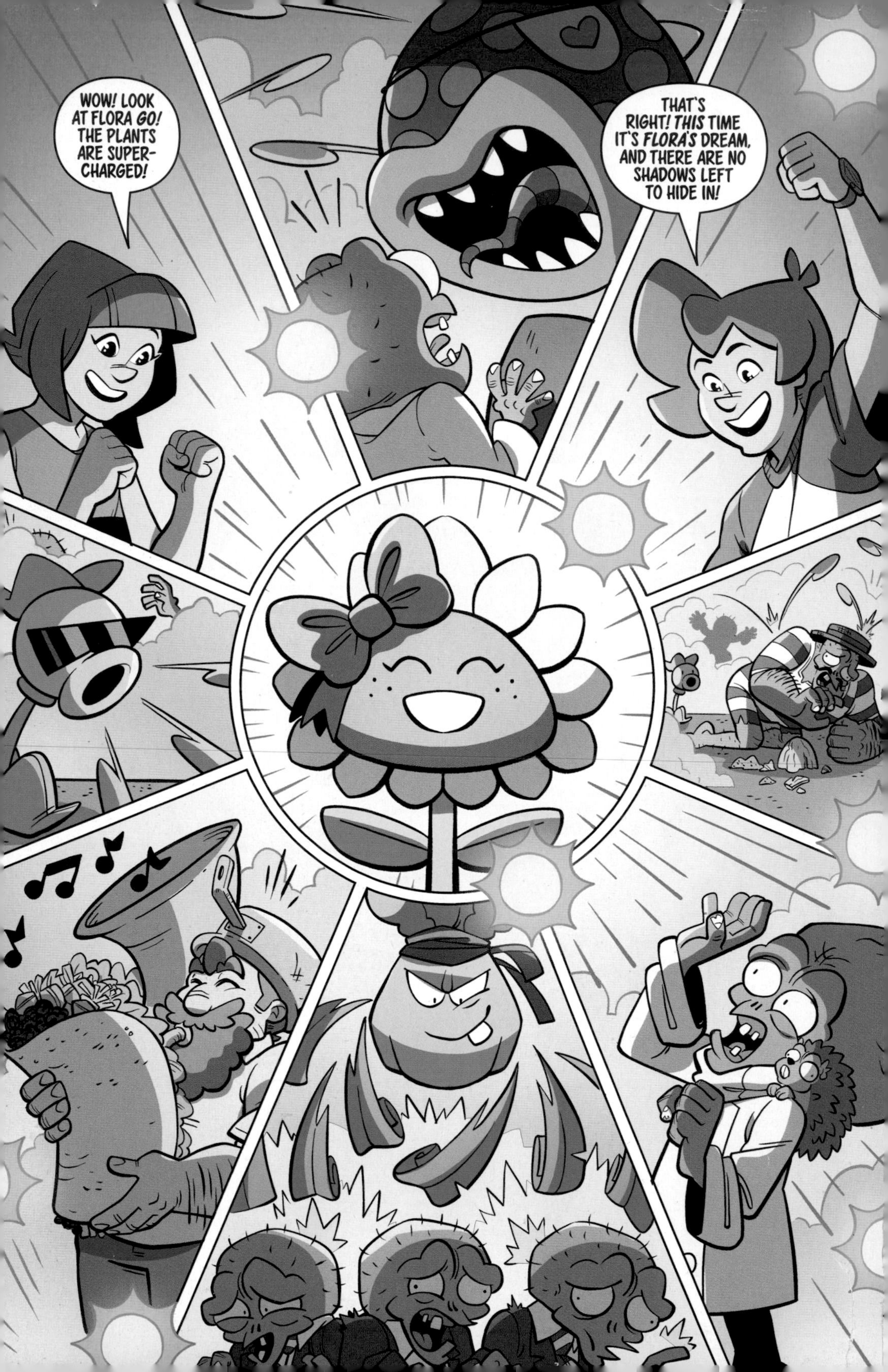
WOW! LOOK AT FLORA GO! THE PLANTS ARE SUPER-CHARGED!
THAT'S RIGHT! THIS TIME IT'S FLORA'S DREAM, AND THERE ARE NO SHADOWS LEFT TO HIDE IN!

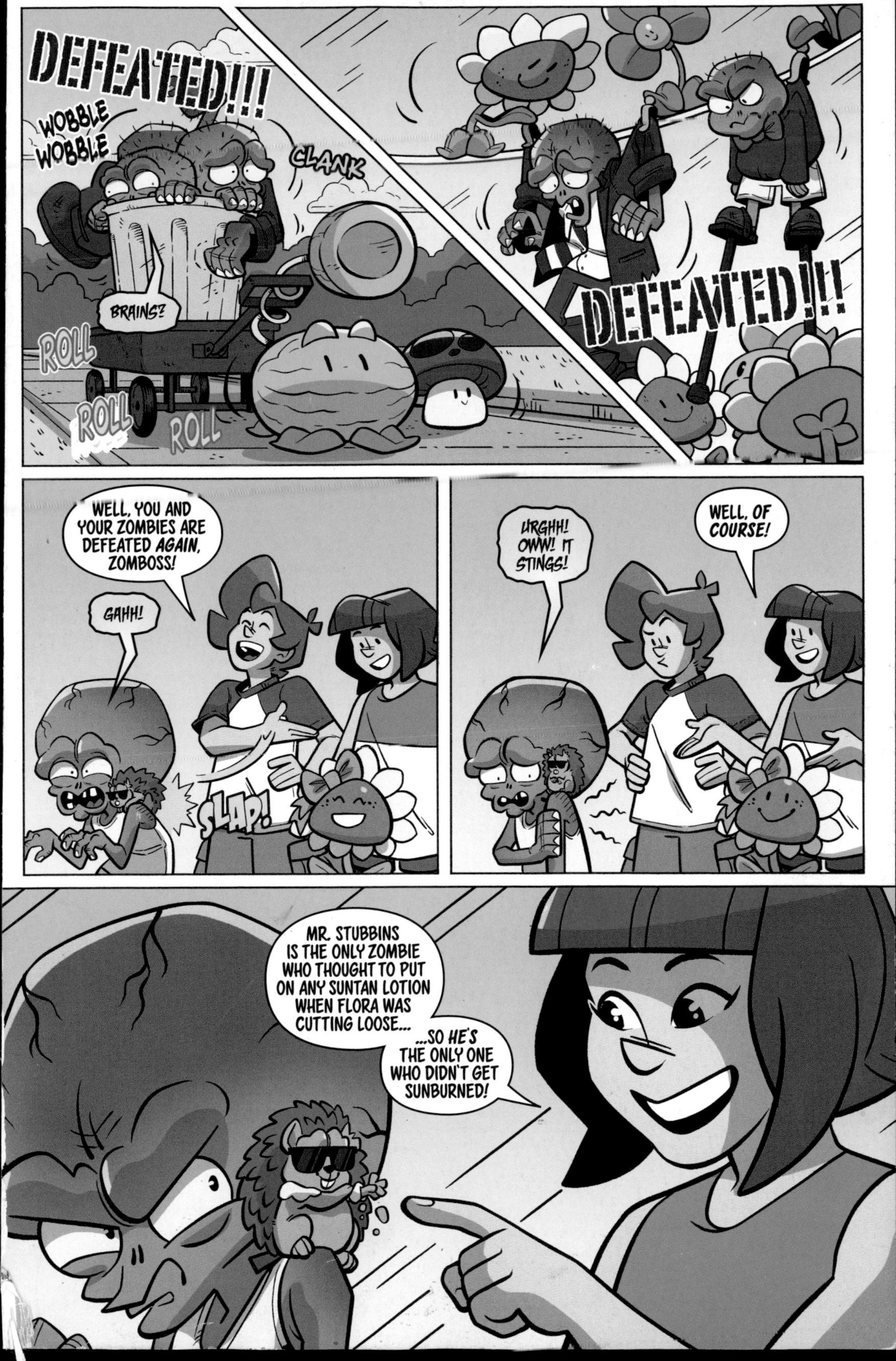

DEFEATED!!!
WOBBLE WOBBLE
CLANK
BRAINS?
ROLL
ROLL
ROLL
DEFEATED!!!
WELL, YOU AND YOUR ZOMBIES ARE DEFEATED AGAIN, ZOMBOSS!
GAHH!
SLAP!
URGHH! OWW! IT STINGS!
WELL, OF COURSE!
MR. STUBBINS IS THE ONLY ZOMBIE WHO THOUGHT TO PUT ON ANY SUNTAN LOTION WHEN FLORA WAS CUTTING LOOSE...
...SO HE'S THE ONLY ONE WHO DIDN'T GET SUNBURNED!

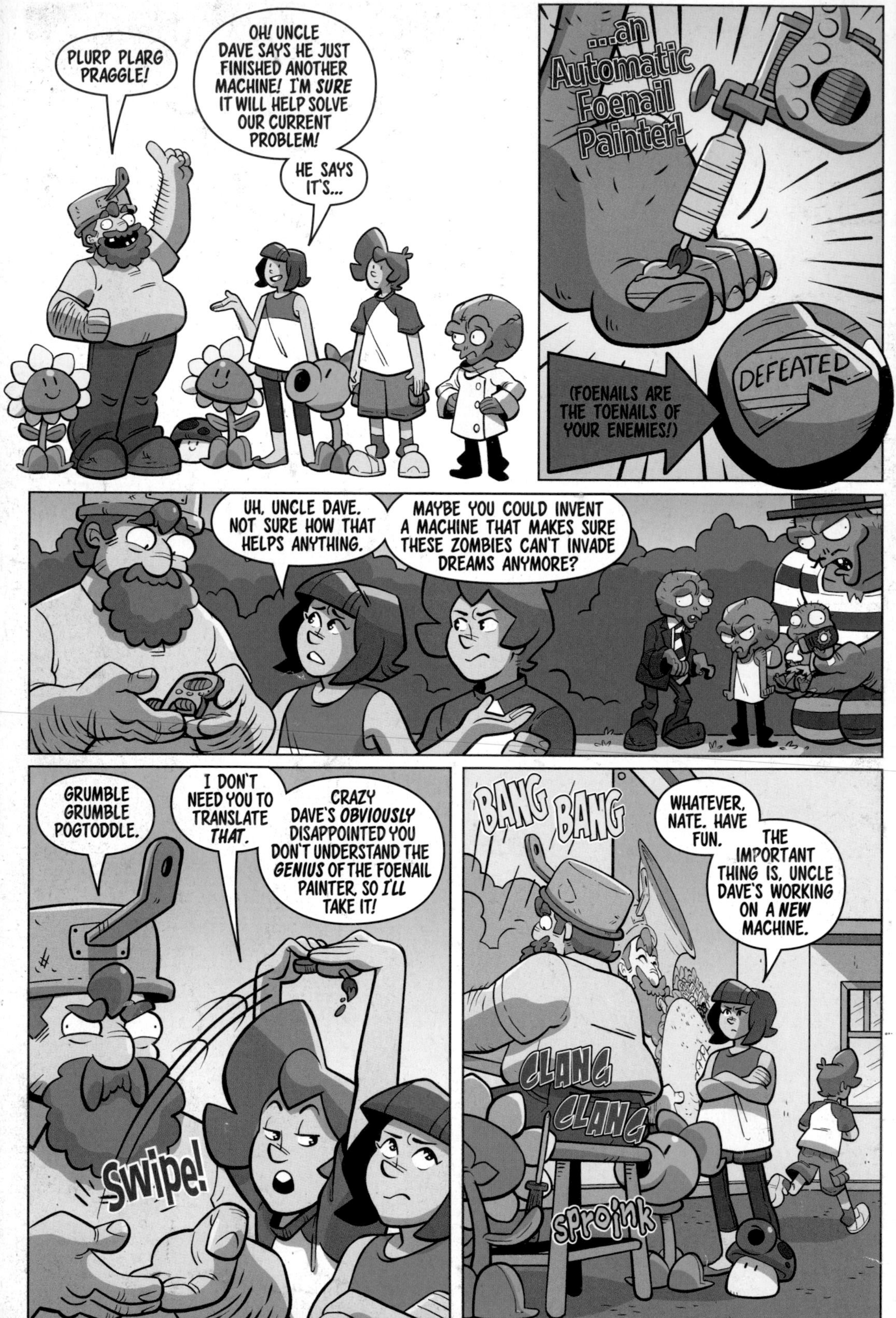
PLURP PLARG PRAGGLE!
OH! UNCLE DAVE SAYS HE JUST FINISHED ANOTHER MACHINE! I'M *SURE* IT WILL HELP SOLVE OUR CURRENT PROBLEM!
HE SAYS IT'S...
...an Automatic Foenail Painter!
(FOENAILS ARE THE TOENAILS OF YOUR ENEMIES!)
DEFEATED
UH, UNCLE DAVE. NOT SURE HOW THAT HELPS ANYTHING.
MAYBE YOU COULD INVENT A MACHINE THAT MAKES SURE THESE ZOMBIES CAN'T INVADE DREAMS ANYMORE?
GRUMBLE GRUMBLE POGTODDLE.
I DON'T NEED YOU TO TRANSLATE *THAT*.
CRAZY DAVE'S *OBVIOUSLY* DISAPPOINTED YOU DON'T UNDERSTAND THE *GENIUS* OF THE FOENAIL PAINTER, SO *I'LL* TAKE IT!
SWIPE!
BANG BANG
WHATEVER, NATE. HAVE FUN.
THE IMPORTANT THING IS, UNCLE DAVE'S WORKING ON A *NEW* MACHINE.
CLANG
CLANG
SPROINK

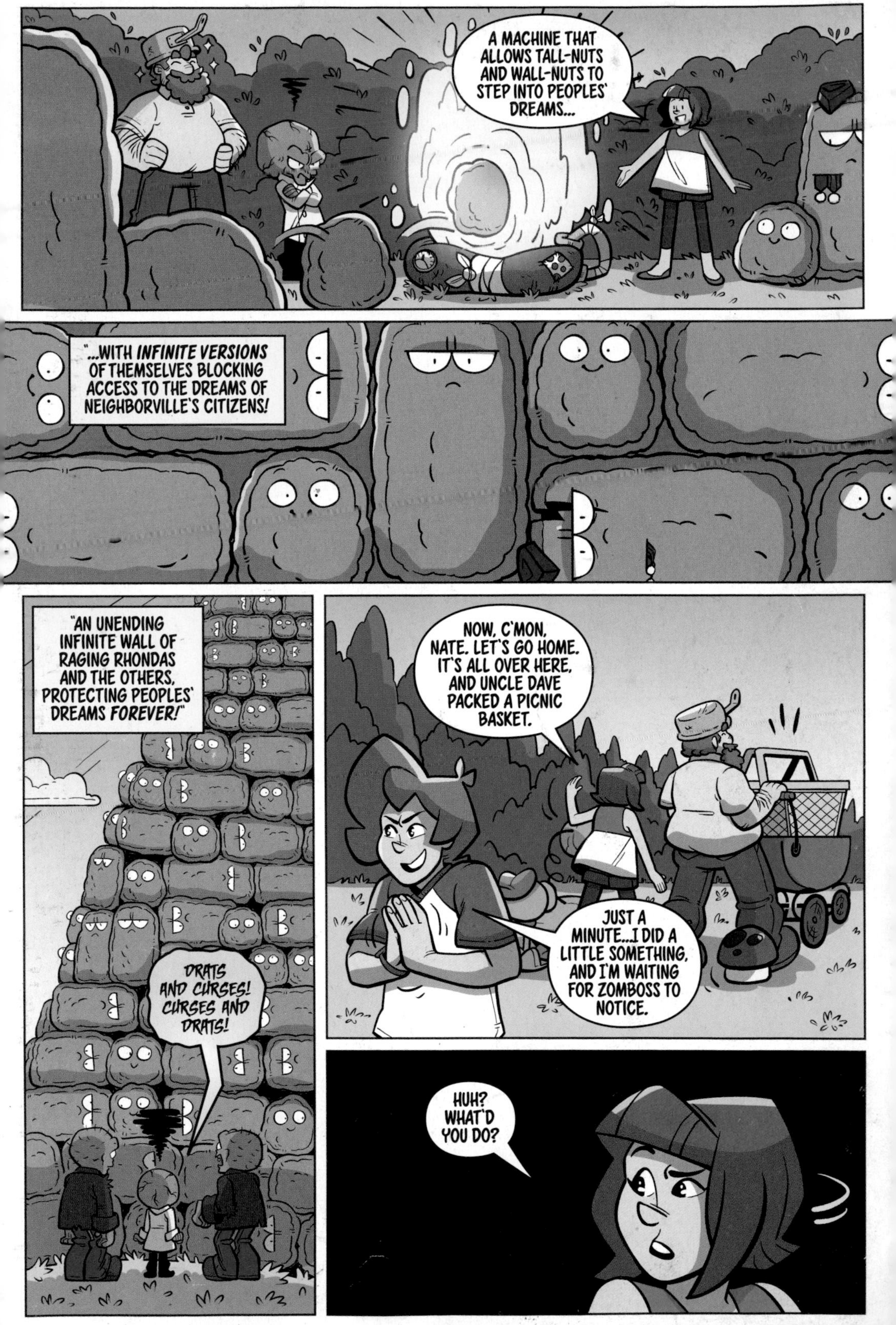

A MACHINE THAT ALLOWS TALL-NUTS AND WALL-NUTS TO STEP INTO PEOPLES' DREAMS...
"...WITH *INFINITE VERSIONS* OF THEMSELVES BLOCKING ACCESS TO THE DREAMS OF NEIGHBORVILLE'S CITIZENS!
"AN UNENDING INFINITE WALL OF RAGING RHONDAS AND THE OTHERS, PROTECTING PEOPLES' DREAMS *FOREVER!*"
DRATS AND CURSES! CURSES AND DRATS!
NOW, C'MON, NATE. LET'S GO HOME. IT'S ALL OVER HERE, AND UNCLE DAVE PACKED A PICNIC BASKET.
JUST A MINUTE...I DID A LITTLE SOMETHING, AND I'M WAITING FOR ZOMBOSS TO NOTICE.
HUH? WHAT'D YOU DO?

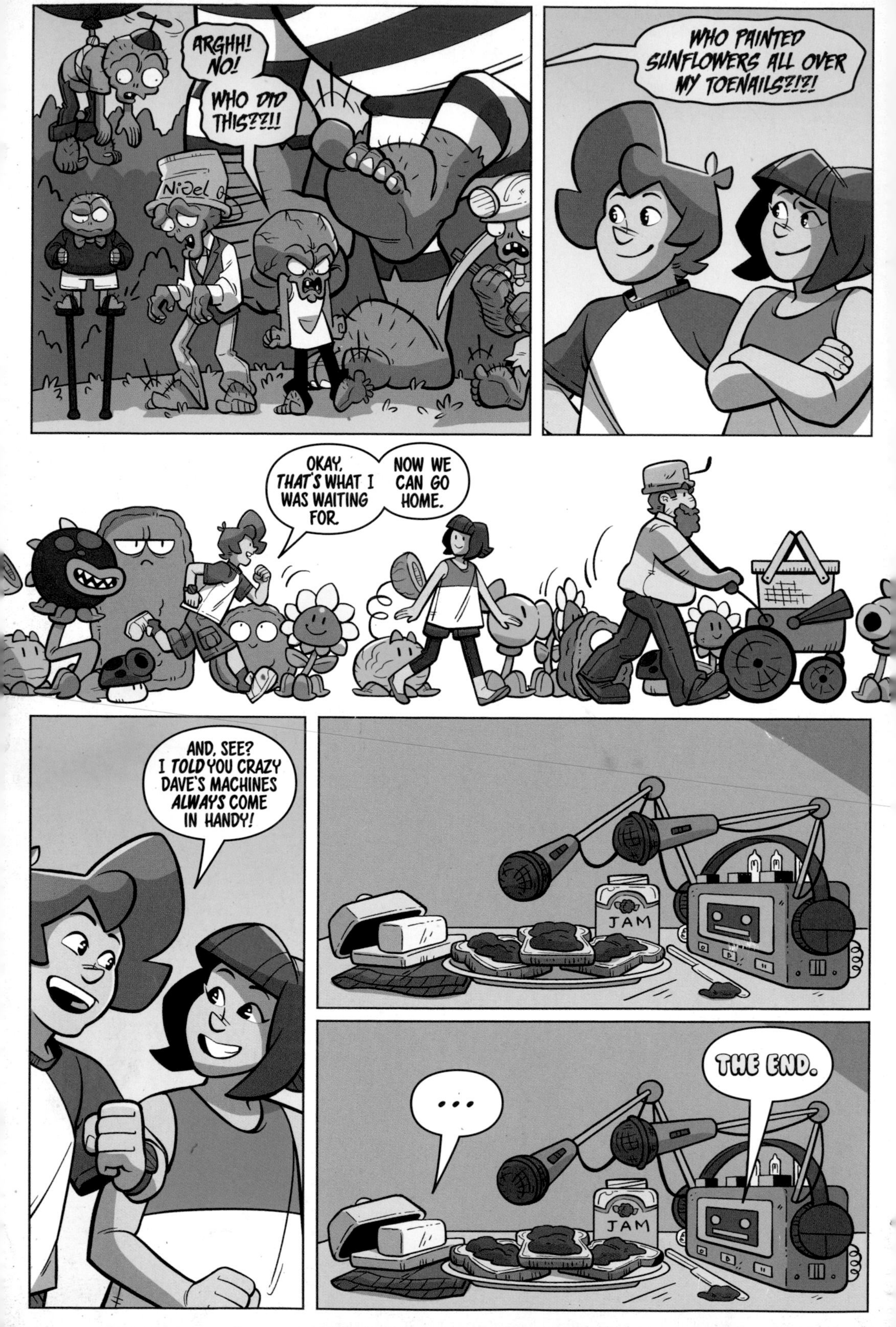
ARGHH! NO!
WHO DID THIS??!!
NiGel
WHO PAINTED SUNFLOWERS ALL OVER MY TOENAILS?!?!
OKAY, THAT'S WHAT I WAS WAITING FOR.
NOW WE CAN GO HOME.
AND, SEE? I TOLD YOU CRAZY DAVE'S MACHINES ALWAYS COME IN HANDY!
JAM
...
THE END.
JAM

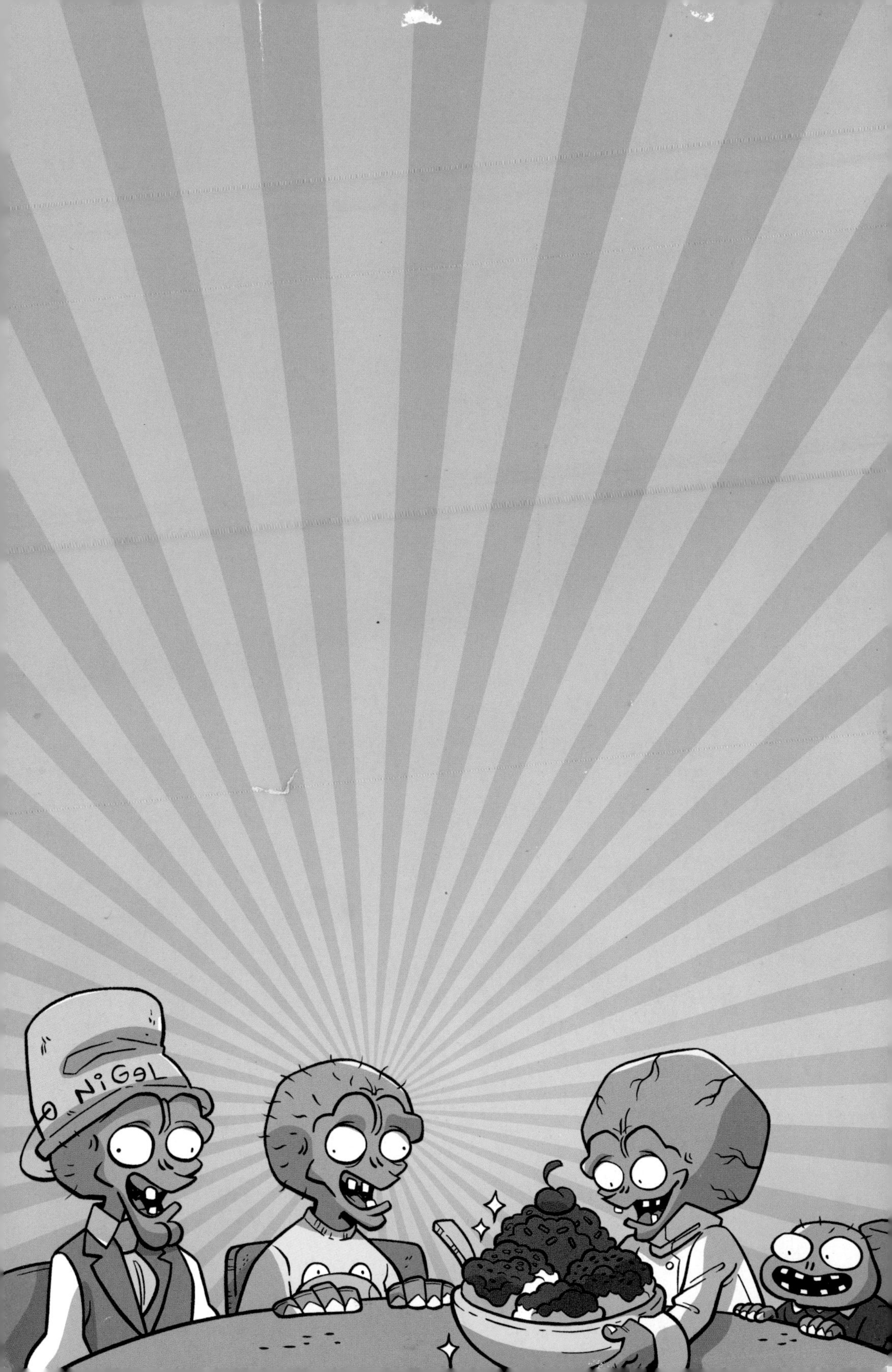
NiGeL

PLANTS VS. ZOMBIES: DREAM A LITTLE SCHEME

COVER PENCILS BY CHRISTIANNE GILLENARDO-GOUDREAU

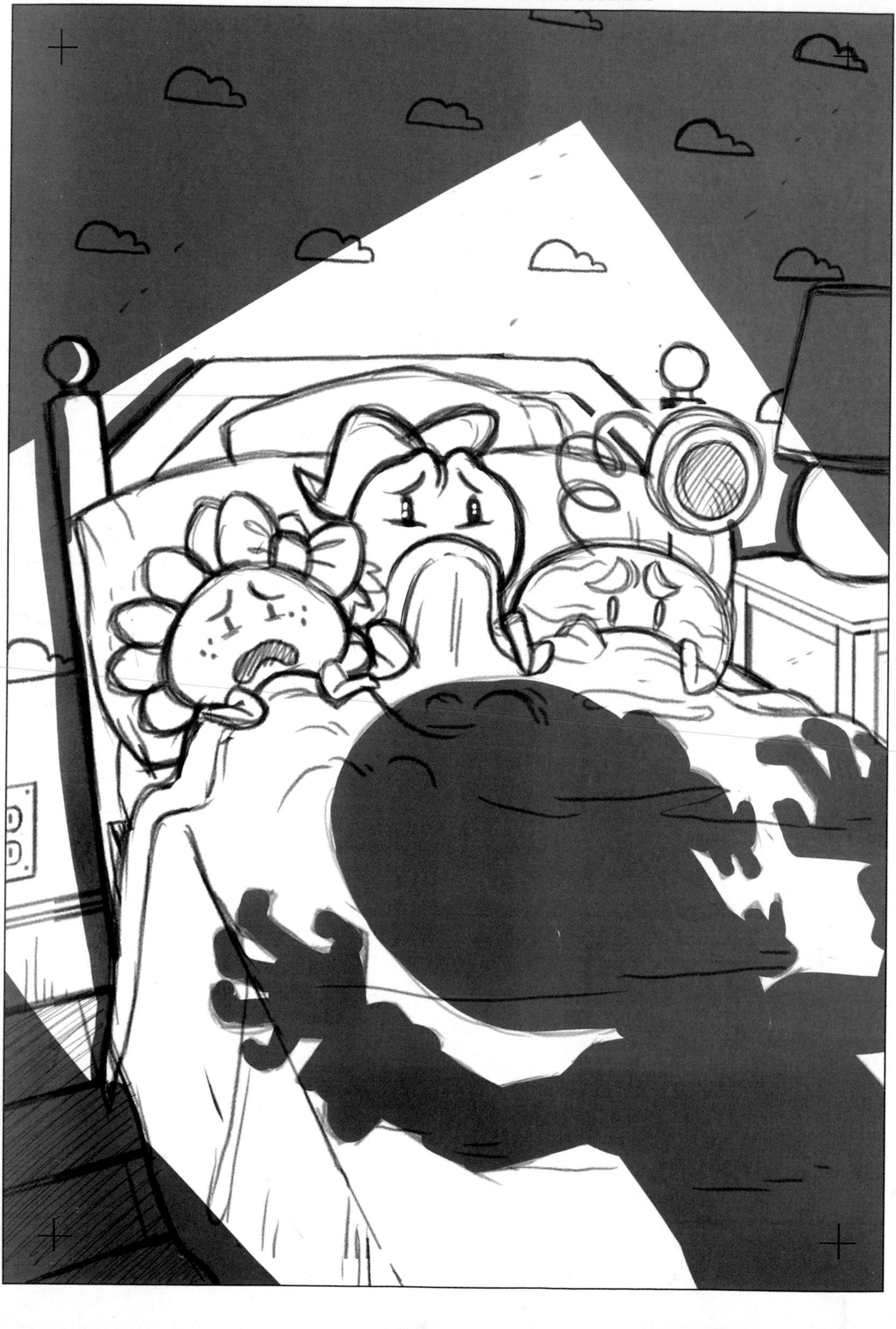

PLANTS VS. ZOMBIES: DREAM A LITTLE SCHEME
COVER INKS BY CHRISTIANNE GILLENARDO-GOUDREAU

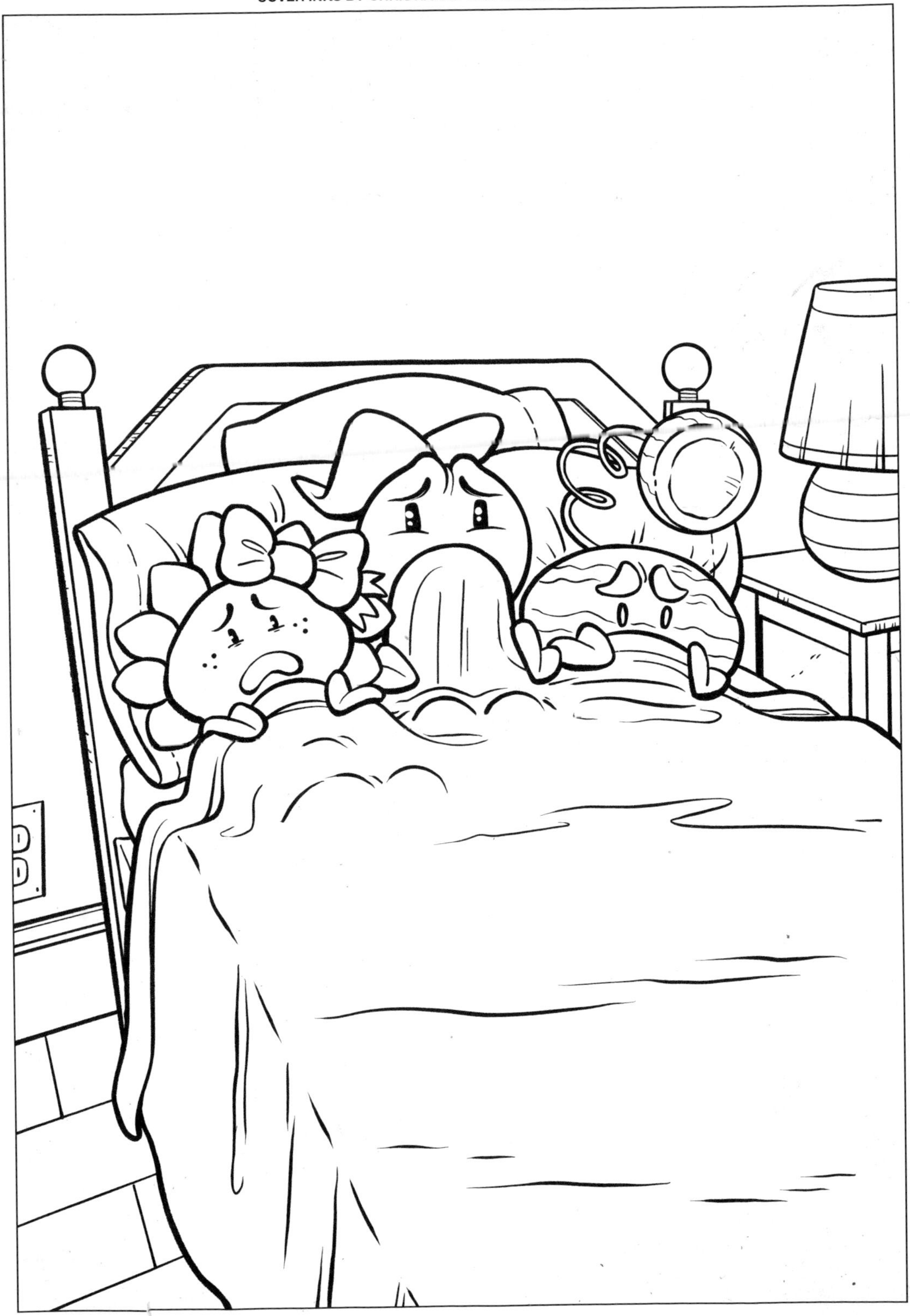

DREAM A LITTLE SCHEME PENCIL ART GALLERY!
ALL PAGES BY ARTIST CHRISTIANNE GILLENARDO-GOUDREAU

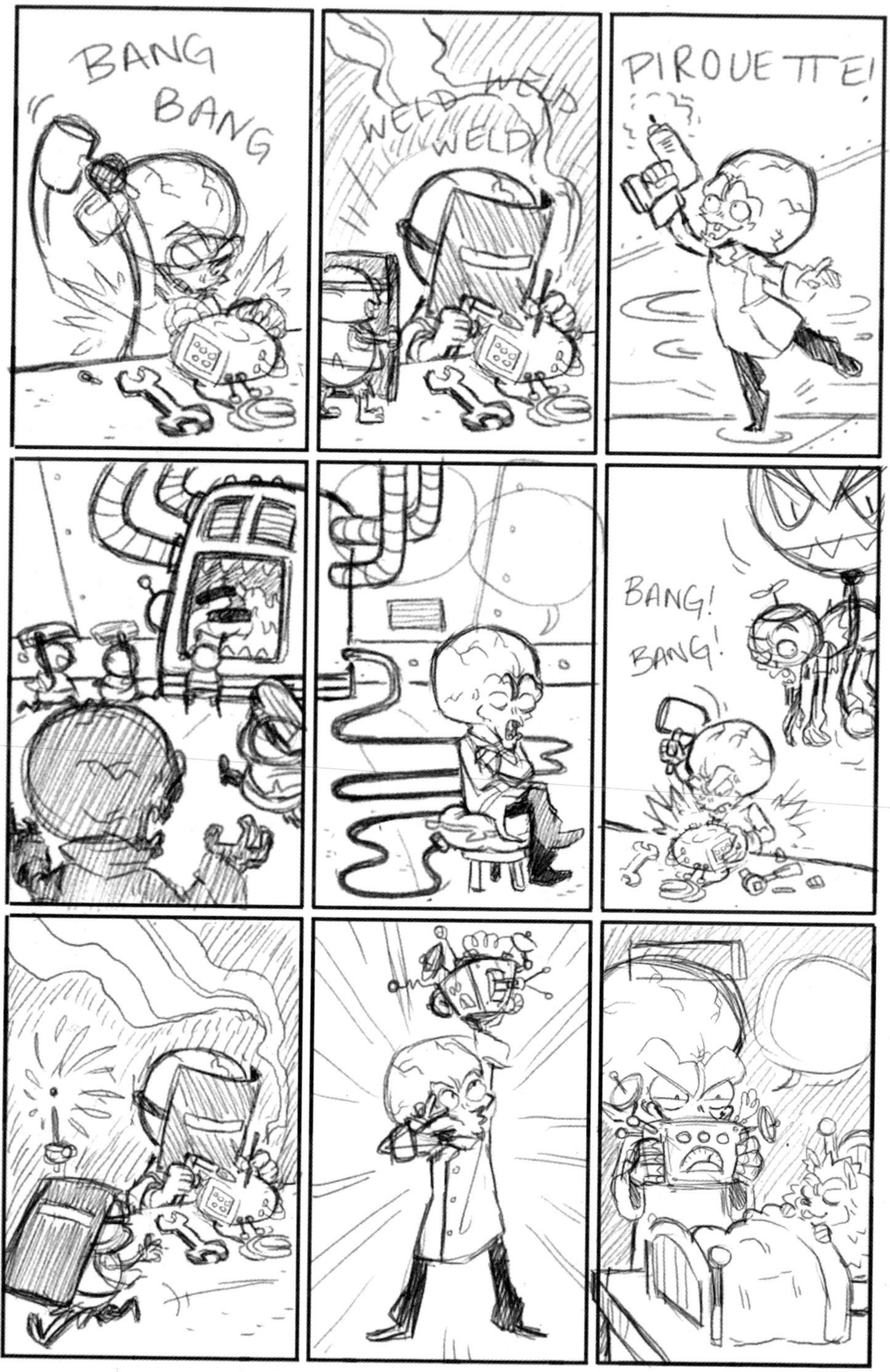
BANG
BANG
WELD WELD
WELD
PIROUETTE!
BANG!
BANG!

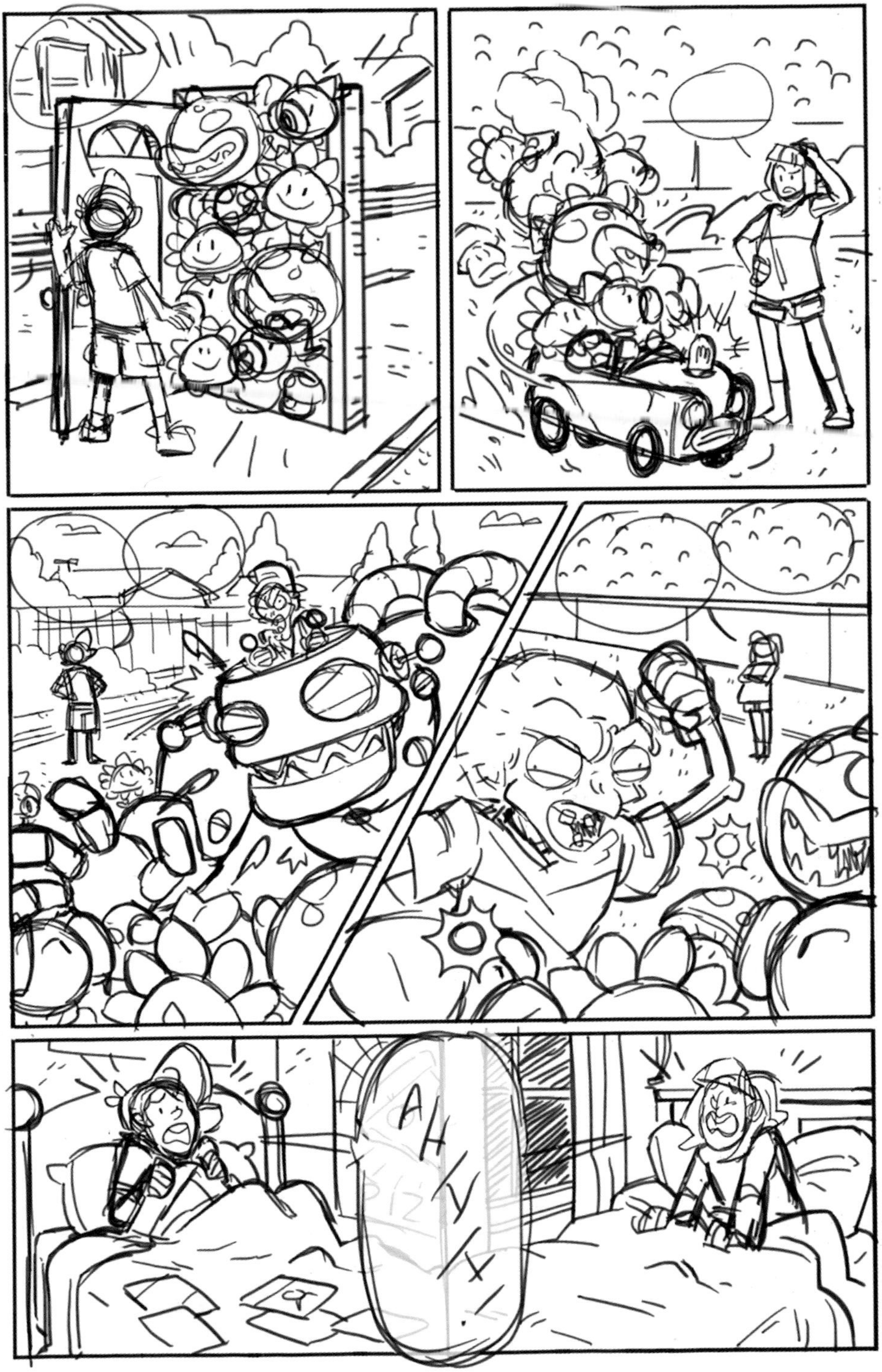
AH

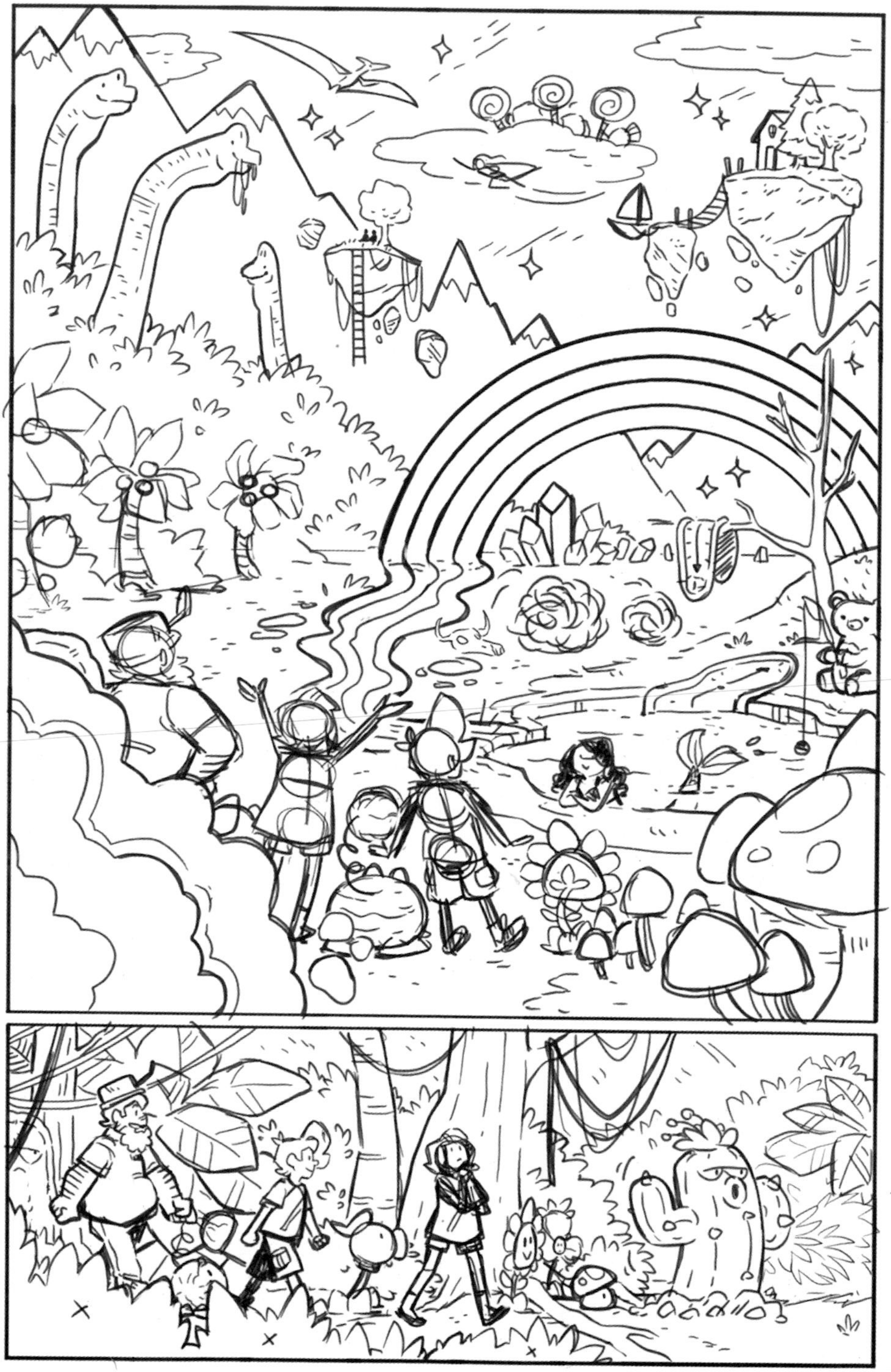

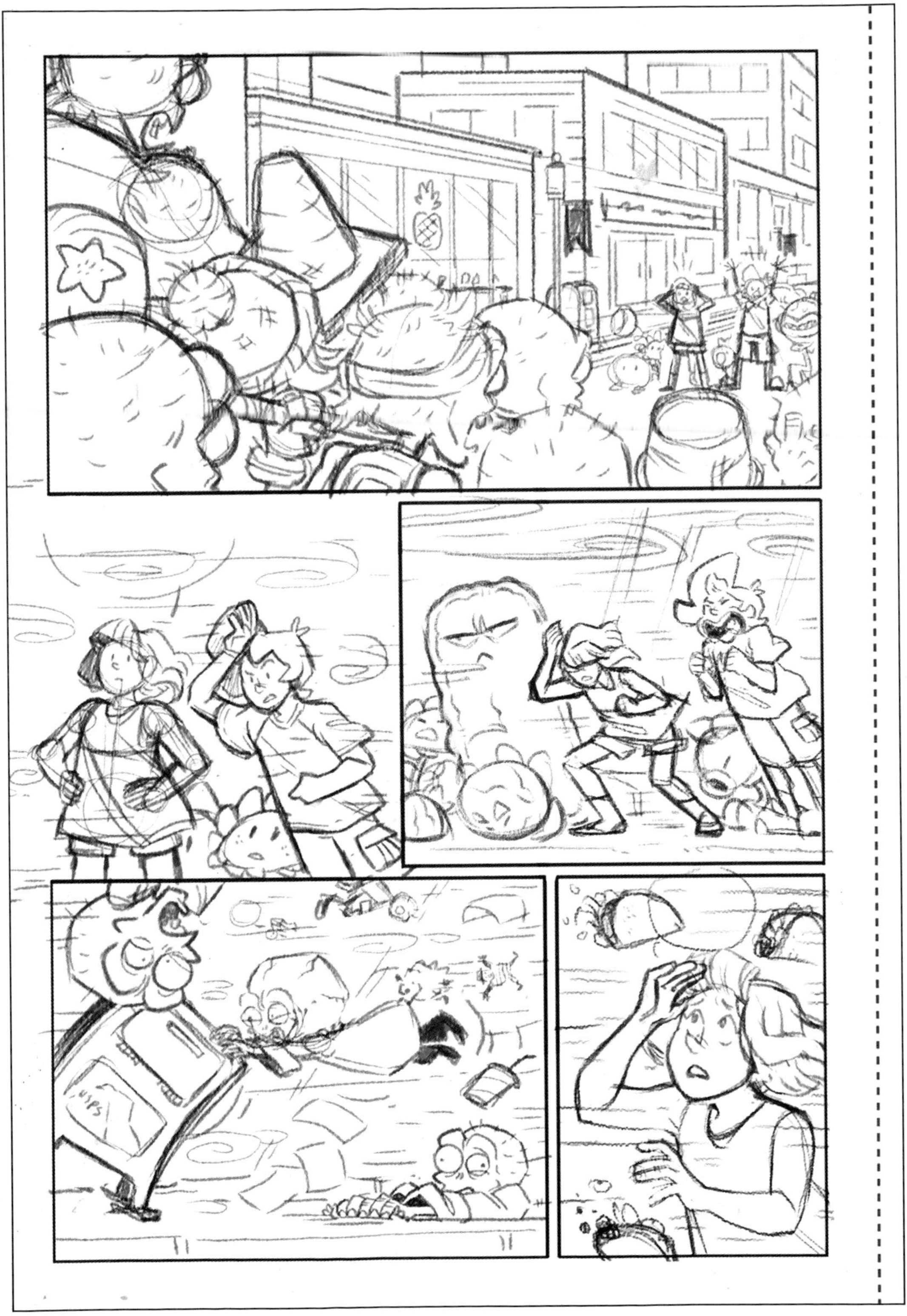
USPS

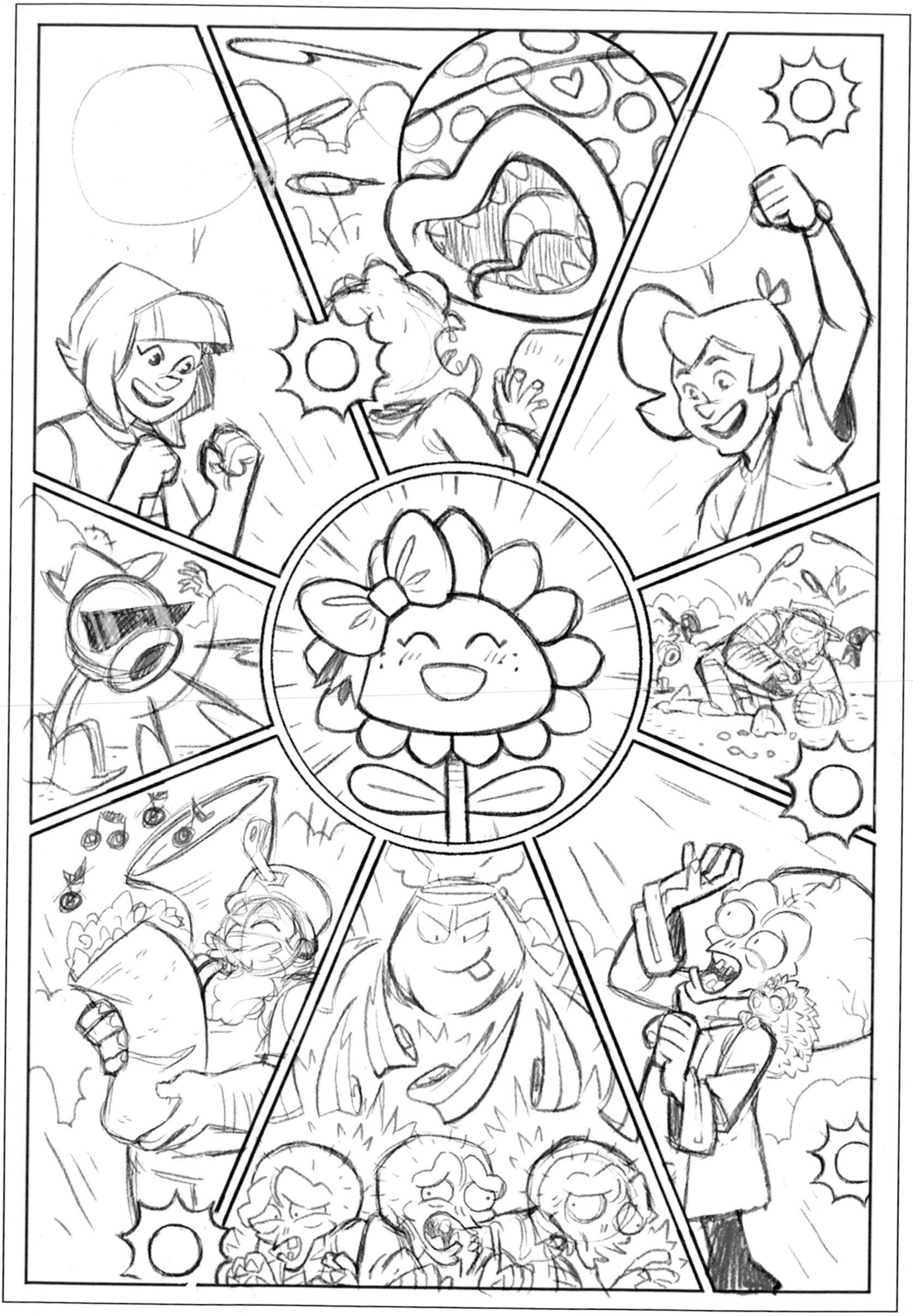

CREATOR BIOS

PAUL TOBIN is a 12th level writer and a 15th level cookie eater. He begins each morning in the manner we all do, by battling those zombies that have strayed too close to his pillow fort. Between writing all the *Plants vs. Zombies* comics and taking four naps a day, he's also found time to write the *Genius Factor* series of novels, the ape-filled *Banana Sunday* graphic novel, the award-winning *Bandette* series, the *Wrassle Castle* and *Earth Boy* graphic novels, and many other works. He has ridden a giant turtle and an elephant on purpose, and a tornado by accident.

Paul Tobin

Christianne
Gillenardo-Goudreau

CHRISTIANNE GILLENARDO-GOUDREAU is a comic artist and illustrator from Portland, Oregon. Her work has been featured in various anthologies and comics, including *Beyond: A Queer Sci-Fi And Fantasy Anthology*, *Plants vs. Zombies: Rumble at Lake Gumbo*, *Plants vs. Zombies: Better Homes and Guardens*, *Plants vs. Zombies: Multi-ball-istic*, *Harrow County*, and *Dept. H*. She is currently the interior artist for the series *I am Hexed*, by Kirsten Thompson. She lives with her wife, Donna, and their dumb cats, Hot Dog and Pancake.

HEATHER BRECKEL went to the Columbus College of Art and Design for animation. She decided animation wasn't for her, so she switched to comics. She's been working as a colorist for nearly ten years and has worked for nearly every major comics publisher out there. When she's not burning the midnight oil in a deadline crunch, she's either dying a bunch in videogames or telling her cats to stop running around at two in the morning.

Heather Breckel

Steve Dutro

STEVE DUTRO is a pinball fan and an Eisner Award-nominated comic book letterer from Redding, California, who can also drive a tractor. He graduated from the Kubert School and has been lettering comics since the days when foil-embossed covers were cool, working for Dark Horse (*The Fifth Beatle*, *I Am a Hero*, *StarCraft*, *Star Wars*, *Witcher*), Viz, Marvel, and DC Comics. He has submitted a request to the Department of Homeland Security that in the event of a zombie apocalypse he be put in charge of all digital freeway signs so citizens can be alerted to avoid nearby brain-eatings and the like. He finds the *Plants vs. Zombies* game to be a real stress-fest, but highly recommends the *Plants vs. Zombies* table on *Pinball FX2* for game-room hipsters.

ALSO AVAILABLE FROM DARK HORSE!

THE HIT VIDEO GAME CONTINUES ITS COMIC BOOK INVASION!

THE ART OF PLANTS VS. ZOMBIES
Part zombie memoir, part celebration of zombie triumphs, and part anti-plant screed, *The Art of Plants vs. Zombies* is a treasure trove of never-before-seen concept art, character sketches, and surprises from PopCap's popular *Plants vs. Zombies* games!
ISBN 978-1-61655-331-9 | $10.99

PLANTS VS. ZOMBIES: LAWNMAGEDDON
Crazy Dave—the babbling-yet-brilliant inventor and top-notch neighborhood defender—helps young adventurer Nate fend off a zombie invasion that threatens to overrun the peaceful town of Neighborville in *Plants vs. Zombies: Lawnmageddon*! Their only hope is a brave army of chomping, squashing, and pea-shooting plants! A wacky adventure for zombie zappers young and old!
ISBN 978-1-61655-192-6 | $10.99

PLANTS VS. ZOMBIES: TIMEPOCALYPSE
Dr. Zomboss attacks throughout different timelines, keeping Crazy Dave, Patrice, Nate, and their powerful plant army busy!
ISBN 978-1-61655-621-1 | $10.99

PLANTS VS. ZOMBIES: BULLY FOR YOU
Patrice and Nate are ready to investigate a strange college campus to keep the streets safe from zombies!
ISBN 978-1-61655-889-5 | $10.99

PLANTS VS. ZOMBIES: GARDEN WARFARE
Based on the hit video game series, these graphic novels tie in with the events in *Plants vs. Zombies: Garden Warfare 1* and *2* and *Plants vs. Zombies: Battle for Neighborville*!
VOLUME 1 ISBN 978-1-61655-946-5 | $10.99
VOLUME 2 ISBN 978-1-50670-548-4 | $10.99
VOLUME 3 ISBN 978-1-50670-837-9 | $10.99

PLANTS VS. ZOMBIES: GROWN SWEET HOME
With newfound knowledge of humanity, Dr. Zomboss strikes at the heart of Neighborville . . . sparking a series of plant-versus-zombie brawls!
ISBN 978-1-61655-971-7 | $10.99

PLANTS VS. ZOMBIES: PETAL TO THE METAL
Crazy Dave takes on the tough *Don't Blink* video game—and challenges Dr. Zomboss to a race to determine the future of Neighborville!
ISBN 978-1-61655-999-1 | $10.99

PLANTS VS. ZOMBIES: BOOM BOOM MUSHROOM
The gang discover Zomboss' secret plan for swallowing the city of Neighborville whole! A rare mushroom must be found in order to save the humans aboveground!
ISBN 978-1-50670-037-3 | $10.99

PLANTS VS. ZOMBIES: BATTLE EXTRAVAGONZO
Zomboss is back, hoping to buy the same factory that Crazy Dave is eyeing! Will Crazy Dave and his intelligent plants beat Zomboss and his zombie army to the punch?
ISBN 978-1-50670-189-9 | $10.99

PLANTS VS. ZOMBIES: LAWN OF DOOM
With Zomboss filling everyone's yards with traps and special soldiers, will he and his zombie army turn Halloween into their zanier Lawn of Doom celebration?!
ISBN 978-1-50670-204-9 | $10.99

PLANTS VS. ZOMBIES: THE GREATEST SHOW UNEARTHED
Dr. Zomboss believes that all humans hold a secret desire to run away and join the circus, so he aims to use his "Big Z's Adequately Amazing Flytrap Circus" to lure Neighborville's citizens to their doom!
ISBN 978-1-50670-298-8 | $10.99

PLANTS VS. ZOMBIES: RUMBLE AT LAKE GUMBO
The battle for clean water begins! Nate, Patrice, and Crazy Dave spot trouble and grab all the Tangle Kelp and Party Crabs they can to quell another zombie attack!
ISBN 978-1-50670-497-5 | $10.99

PLANTS VS. ZOMBIES: WAR AND PEAS
When Dr. Zomboss and Crazy Dave find themselves members of the same book club, a literary war is inevitable! The position of leader of the book club opens up and Zomboss and Crazy Dave compete for the top spot in a scholarly scuffle for the ages!
ISBN 978-1-50670-677-1 | $10.99

PLANTS VS. ZOMBIES: DINO-MIGHT
Dr. Zomboss sets his sights on destroying the yards in town and rendering the plants homeless—and his plans include dogs, cats, rabbits, hammock sloths, and, somehow, dinosaurs . . . !
ISBN 978-1-50670-838-6 | $10.99

PLANTS VS. ZOMBIES: SNOW THANKS
Dr. Zomboss invents a Cold Crystal capable of freezing Neighborville, burying the town in snow and ice! It's up to the humans and the fieriest plants to save Neighborville—with the help of pirates!
ISBN 978-1-50670-839-3 | $10.99

PLANTS VS. ZOMBIES: A LITTLE PROBLEM
Will an invasion of teeny-tiny miniature zombies mean the party for Crazy Dave's two-hundred-year-old pants gets canceled?
ISBN 978-1-50670-840-9 | $10.99

PLANTS VS. ZOMBIES: BETTER HOMES AND GUARDENS
Nate and Patrice try thwarting zombie attacks by putting defending "Guardens" plants *inside* homes as well as in yards! But as soon as Dr. Zomboss finds out, he's determined to circumvent this plan with an epically evil one of his own . . .
ISBN 978-1-50671-305-2 | $10.99

PLANTS VS. ZOMBIES: THE GARDEN PATH
You get to decide the fate of Neighborville in this new *Plants vs. Zombies* choose-your-own-adventure with multiple endings!
ISBN 978-1-50671-306-9 | $10.99

PLANTS VS. ZOMBIES: MULTI-BALL-ISTIC
Dr. Zomboss turns the entirety of Neighborville into a giant, fully functional pinball machine! Nate, Patrice, and their plant posse must find a way to halt this uniquely horrifying zombie invasion. Will the battle go full-tilt zombies?!
ISBN 978-1-50671-307-6 | $10.99

PLANTS VS. ZOMBIES: CONSTRUCTIONARY TALES
A behind-the-scenes look at the secret schemes and craziest contraptions concocted by Zomboss, as he proudly leads around a film crew from the Zombie Broadcasting Network!
ISBN 978-1-50672-091-3 | $10.99

PLANTS VS. ZOMBIES: DREAM A LITTLE SCHEME
Dr. Zomboss invents a machine that allows him to enter the dreams of Neighborville's citizens!
ISBN 978-1-50672-092-0 | $10.99

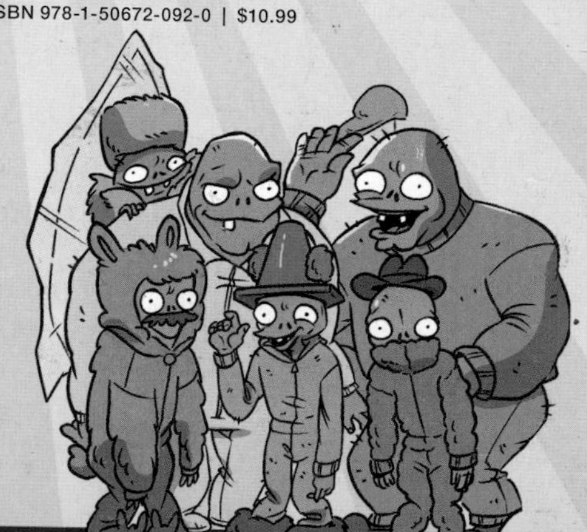

AVAILABLE AT YOUR LOCAL COMICS SHOP OR BOOKSTORE
To find a comics shop in your area, visit comicshoplocator.com. For more information or to order direct, visit **DarkHorse.com**

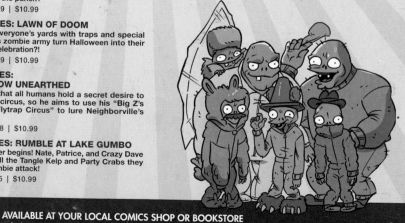

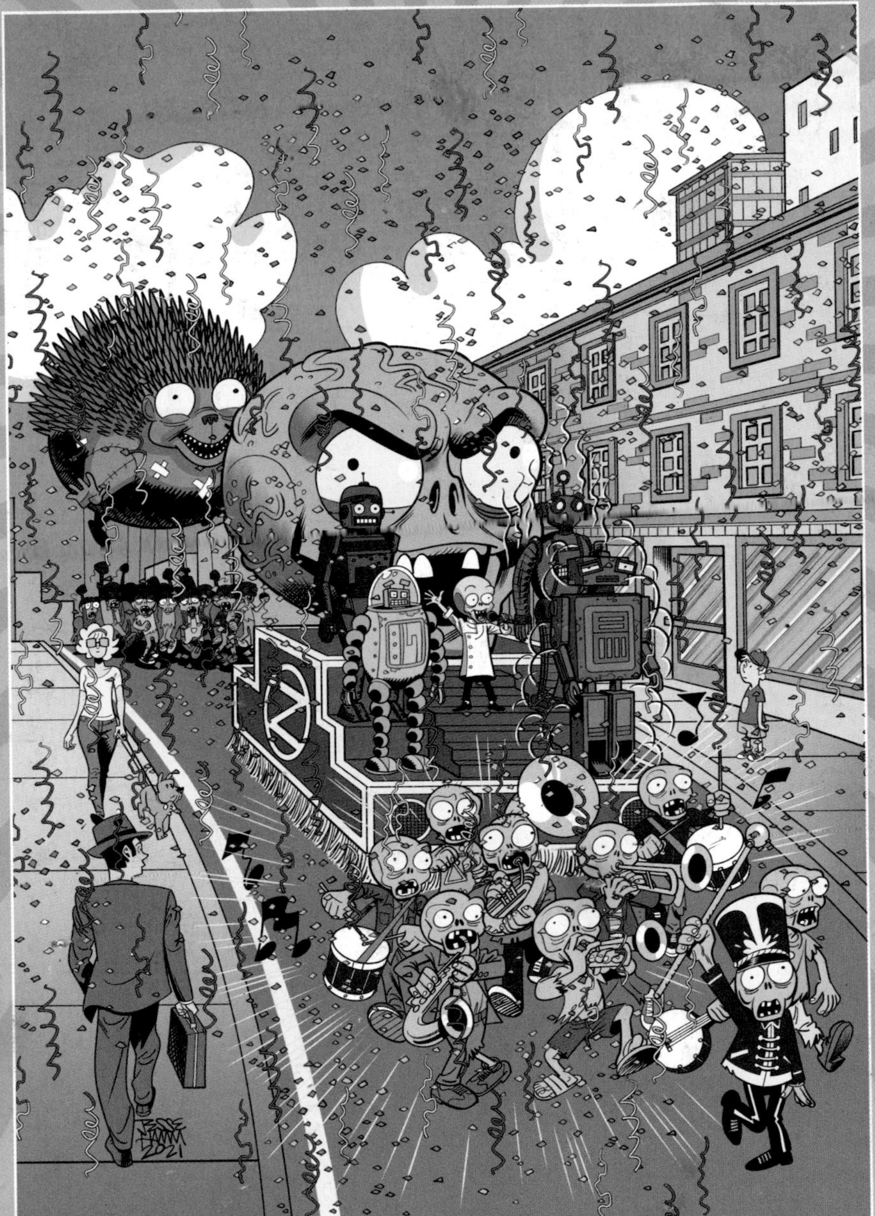
JESSE HAMM 2021

Our next volume—*Plants vs. Zombies: The Unpredictables*! After having countless dreams, schemes, capers, and heists easily thwarted by the plant team, Dr. Zomboss needs a win. With Crazy Dave and his powerful plant posse always one step ahead, Zomboss realizes the only way to achieve victory is by being *even one more* step ahead than that! So he builds his latest invention: four brain bots called the Unpredictables! With the bots' ability to predict their enemies' every move, Patrice, Nate, and Crazy Dave will have to pull out all the stops to protect Neighborville!

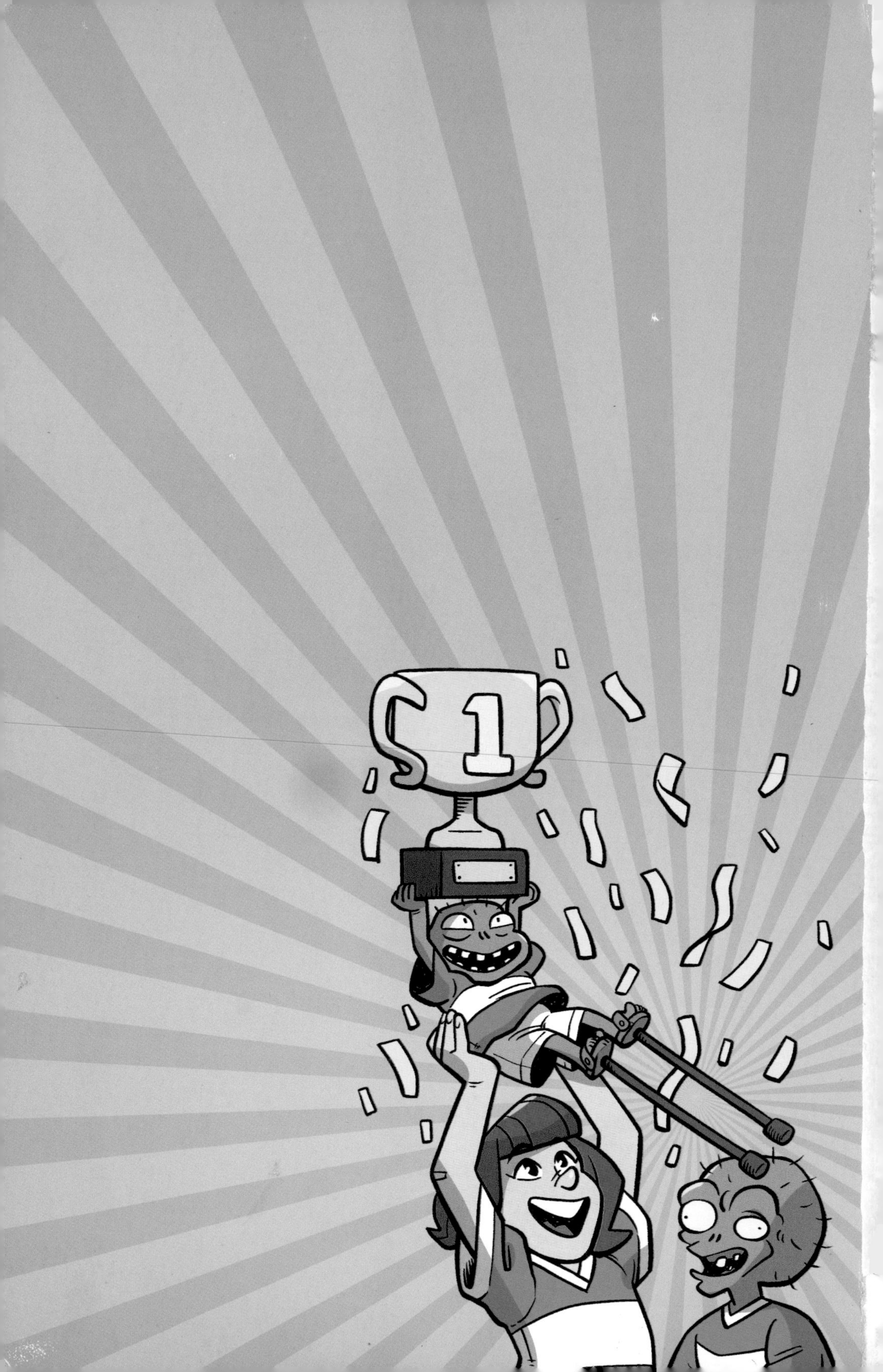

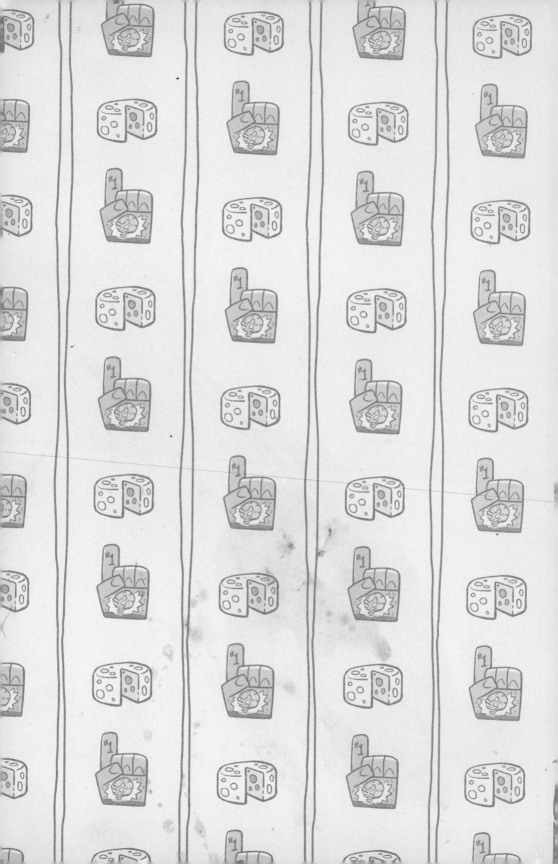